EQUAL TIME

David Keith

DAVID G. KEITH

Good Egg Press

Library of Congress Catalog Number: 2017963459

ISBN: 978-0-9863706-4-9 (print)
ISBN: 978-0-9863706-5-6 (ebook)

Equal Time is a work of fiction. Names, characters, places, and incidents are the products of the author's imagination or are used fictitiously. Any resemblance to actual events, locales, or persons, living or dead, is entirely coincidental.

Cover Design by OMG Media
Interior Design by Lorie DeWorken, MIND*the*MARGINS, LLC

Published in the United States by Good Egg Press
www.goodeggpress.com

To law enforcement officers everywhere
who protect and serve the public each and every day.

You are appreciated and supported
by the vast majority of Americans!

ACKNOWLEDGMENTS

I have so many people to thank for helping me write my third novel, *Equal Time*. First and foremost my beautiful wife and best friend, Giselle, who read each section as I wrote it, offering me feedback. Additionally, my three kids, Jessica, Michael, and Alyssa, would often listen patiently to me as I ran ideas for plot lines by them. Their help was invaluable.

As always, I thank Dara Murphy for keeping me on track with the mechanics of the story. Dara reviewed every word I wrote and corrected grammar and punctuation. Knowing she was there to back me up enabled me to write what I was feeling and not worry too much about the technical stuff. She is one of the brightest people I know and is a wonderful mom to eighteen-month-old Turner.

My friends at OMG Media in Monterey, California were once again a huge help to me. They are a wonderful resource for writers—keeping the story on track and assisting with all that's involved with putting together the finished product.

One of the byproducts of writing these stories is the discovery of the many book clubs that have read my novels. Being invited to participate in a fun evening of discussion of how I wrote the book has been a blast! And having an intimate gathering of people offering feedback has been hugely beneficial to me. I'm flattered by their interest and their support.

I also want to thank the Oxnard Police Department retirees who belong to the Fuzz that Wuzz group. Their support means a great deal to me. I hope to catch the next reunion!

I also appreciate the support of Kevin Bernzott of Bernzott Capital Advisors. He has generously provided me the opportunity to share my novels with his many friends and business associates.

CHAPTER 1

Mia Serrano grabbed a magazine from the coffee table and took a seat in the waiting room. She was a little early for her appointment, hoping she could get in and out in time to make it to a lunch date with her husband. She was in her seventh month and Mick had accompanied her to nearly all her previous checkups, but today he had a meeting with the county commissioners and as sheriff he was obligated to be there. He told her he'd make it up to her with a nice lunch out.

She looked around the waiting room and saw only one other person. A good omen for making her noon date with her husband, she thought.

"Ms. Serrano, the doctor will see you now."

Mia struggled to get to her feet, still not accustomed to the rather large belly on her small frame. She righted herself, gained her balance, and followed the nurse through the door. They stopped at the scale where the nurse asked Mia to slip out of her shoes.

"Hop on—let's see how you're doing."

Mia stepped onto the scale and watched the number pop up on the display.

The nurse glanced down at Mia's chart. "You're doing great—you've gained twenty-two pounds so far. Right where you want to be."

"I'm really trying to be good about what I eat."

"That's great, for the baby as well as for you. If you can keep your total weight gain around twenty-five to thirty pounds then you'll be back to your old weight soon after the baby is born."

"That's the plan."

The nurse led Mia to the examination room where she took her blood pressure and other vital signs. Soon Mia was alone with her thoughts, waiting on the doctor.

Kendra Gillespie stared at her phone. God, when was he going to leave her alone, she wondered. She scrolled through the other texts she had received—nine already today and it wasn't even lunchtime. She was growing concerned by the sudden aggressiveness of the messages; the guy was starting to act kind of scary. She had gone out just once with him, and that wasn't really even a date. A dozen or so of her friends had gone to the movies and Alex was just part of the group. It was obvious from the beginning that he was interested. No big deal, she'd thought, lots of guys came on to her. He grabbed the seat next to her when the group went for pizza afterward and they talked a little bit, but she had talked to everyone that night. She did absolutely nothing to lead him on; she was sure of that. Some guys just had a harder time getting the message, and it was becoming clear to Kendra that Alex was one of those guys.

Leave me alone, I'm not interested, she texted back. It was a bit harsh but if that's what it took to cool his jets, so be it. Hopefully that would do the trick, she thought, sneaking her phone back into her purse and turning her attention back to the ever-boring Mr. Kiplinger, her trigonometry teacher.

"Hey, Mia—nice to see you again. How are you feeling?"

Dr. Ed Stile was a tall, lanky man in his early fifties. He had been an OBGYN for more than twenty years and had a thriving practice in Castle Springs. He specialized in women having babies later in life, and given that Mia was forty-one, she and Mick felt he was the right doctor to handle the pregnancy.

"I'm doing pretty well. A little tired, but I guess that's to be expected."

"Any trouble sleeping?"

"A little bit, and it's getting harder to get comfortable lying in bed. I'm shifting around a lot and don't seem to be able to find the right position."

"That's a very common complaint. Remind me and I'll give you some literature that'll give you some tips on ways to get a better night's sleep."

"That sounds good, thanks."

"So, you're thirty-two weeks along. Any thoughts about when you want to start your maternity leave from work?"

"I'd really like to work as long as possible, then take at least three months off after the baby is born. That's the plan, anyway."

"You're on light duty, correct?"

"Yes, I'm practically tied to a desk. My husband insists on it," she added with a chuckle.

"Good thing you're an investigator. If you were assigned to uniform patrol duties you'd be off already."

"That's true. I've got a regular caseload to work in major crimes, but I can do ninety percent of that no matter what condition I'm in."

"We'll do an ultrasound and get a nice photo of the baby so you can show Mick what he missed out on today."

∽

Feeling a vibration in his pocket, Alex Washington pulled out his cell phone. The penalty was after school detention if he got caught texting in class, but all the kids did it and Alex was no exception. He sneaked a peek at the phone hidden in his lap.

Leave me alone, I'm not interested

He fixated on the message for a few moments, then calmly slipped the phone back into his pocket. That fucking bitch, he thought. Another girl at school who wasn't interested in him.

He thought Kendra was different; they had talked while having pizza after a movie a few nights earlier. She seemed cool but now she was shutting him down, just like every other girl he had tried to get to know since arriving at Woodrow Wilson High. This school was supposed to be different, but it wasn't. The kids here were just as stuck up as the other three high schools he had previously attended. His shrink was wrong; this "new start" was proving to be just as shitty as the other places.

He stared at the whiteboard at the front of the classroom. He tried to relax and take deep breaths like the psychologist had instructed him to do whenever he was feeling stressed. But it brought no relief and within seconds he felt the familiar pain starting in his forehead then radiating toward his temples. A slow rage began building within him and he knew he needed to get his meds. He raised his hand and interrupted his Spanish teacher, asking if he could go to the bathroom. Rie Jacobs knew his history—all the teachers did. If Alex Washington needed some time, she wasn't going to tell him no. The kid was scary.

"Of course, Alex."

⁂

"You can clearly make out the head and the rest of the body. Now, you and Mick don't want to know the sex, correct?"

Mia was mesmerized by what she saw on the monitor.

"No, we want to be surprised. Although it is tempting . . . "

Dr. Stile laughed. "Well, I won't tell if you won't!"

Mia thought for a moment, enticed by the doctor's offer, but then she thought better of it.

"No, I'm good. We're doing it the old fashioned way—being surprised."

"Okay, no problem. It's great to see you and Mick so excited about this baby."

Dr. Stile moved the transducer across Mia's belly to show different angles of the baby. Mia couldn't stop staring at the monitor. There was a little human being in her belly. Simply amazing.

CHAPTER 2

Alex Washington cut across the quad and headed for the student parking lot. He had remembered that his meds weren't in his locker; he had left them in his car. He climbed into the front seat and opened the glove box, looking for his pills. The pain in his head had worsened, making it hard to focus. He sat in his car looking at the open glove box, contemplating what he should do. He wasn't going back to Spanish class; the lunch bell would be ringing in just a few minutes. He thought about Kendra and the text she had sent him. What did he have to do to get a girl's attention? Why did they all reject him? His heart began to beat rapidly as he reached into the glove box and grabbed the Glock 9 mm pistol. He stuck it into his waistband, covered it with his shirt, and headed to the lunch area.

"Do you want to make your next appointment now?"

Mia was back at the reception desk and was in a hurry to meet Mick for lunch.

"No, I don't have my calendar with me. Let me give me you a call when I get back to work and we'll set it up."

"That'll work, Mia. Talk to you soon."

Mia turned and walked out of the medical arts building toward her car parked in an adjacent lot. It was nearly noon and she had just enough time to make the short drive to BG's Cafe, a favorite lunch spot in Castle Springs. As she approached the lot she could hear the commotion of the two thousand students at the school directly across the street. Looking over at the campus of Woodrow Wilson High school, she thought back on her own teaching career some twenty years earlier. Her time as a teacher at Columbine High School had ended abruptly the day of the massacre; she never set foot back on the campus after witnessing firsthand what happened that awful day. Soon after she had started her career with the Rocklin County Sheriff's Department.

She saw the kids moving about as they started their lunch break. As she reached her car she began fishing her keys from her purse. They were never at the top, she thought; somehow the damn things always worked their way to the bottom. Finally she put her hand on the keys and unlocked the door. At that moment she heard a change in the cacophony coming from the campus. There was almost a collective gasp, followed by high-pitched screaming. She instantly knew there was something very wrong. She wasn't sure if her instincts were coming from her days as a teacher or her years in law enforcement, but she knew that things weren't right.

She jammed her keys back in her purse and ran toward the campus, found an open gate, and hurried toward the commotion. It seemed that whatever was happening was taking place in the quad. She could see students running from that area, some taking cover and others just running as fast as possible to get away. Judging from the terror on the faces of the students she passed she knew that whatever was happening was serious. Mia was surprised at how quickly she was able to move, even at seven months pregnant. She wasn't carrying her police radio, so she grabbed her cell and dialed 9-1-1. She identified herself to the dispatcher and gave a quick description of she was seeing.

"I need units responding code three to the campus of Woodrow Wilson High School. I'm on scene and there's pandemonium among the students near the quad."

"Wait for backup; ETA is four minutes."

"I can't wait for backup. Stay on the line with me."

Mia approached the quad, feeling like a salmon swimming upstream against the onslaught of students.

She stopped one young girl and asked what was happening.

"There's a guy with a gun and he's got a girl. He has a gun to her head," she replied, sobbing.

"Is it a student? Can you describe him?"

The girl didn't respond and took off running.

Mia spoke into her cell. "Station one, I have an eyewitness reporting there is someone on campus with a gun and he's taken a hostage. The witness says it's in the quad. Please let responding units know. I'm nearing the location."

"Mia, hold back. Wait till backup arrives. Their ETA is two minutes."

Mia could hear the sirens in the distance. As she proceeded toward the quad, she was consumed with visions of what she witnessed that day at Columbine. There was no way she was going to let that happen again. She reached into her purse and pulled out her department-issued Beretta.

As she approached the quad she saw a young African-American male, maybe sixteen or seventeen, holding a young girl in a headlock. He held her tight to his body with a gun pressed to her head. Her face was contorted with fear and tears streamed down her cheeks.

Mia looked for a place to shelter. She saw a collection of trash bins thirty yards to the left of where the kid had the girl in the headlock. She ducked behind the bins for cover and readied her firearm. Mia could hear the sirens getting closer to the campus, as could the young man; the sirens were clearly increasing his anxiety. Mia whispered into her cell phone, telling the dispatcher to have the approaching deputies kill their sirens. It clearly wasn't helping the situation.

"Don't anybody move or I'll blow her head off!" he yelled to the students walking through the quad. The students froze and stared in disbelief at the scene unfolding before them. The young man hadn't noticed Mia take her position behind the trash bins but several others in the area did. They started to whisper to each other and point at her, giving away her location.

The young man looked Mia's way and studied the situation. He could see only the trash bins, but suspected that someone was hiding there.

"Stand up! I need to see you!" he screamed, temporarily moving the gun from the girl's head and waving it in Mia's direction.

Mia didn't move. The other deputies had to be on campus by now, she thought. She would try to wait him out.

"Stand up and show yourself or she's dead! I swear to God, I'll kill her!" he yelled, shoving the gun against the girl's right temple.

Mia sneaked a quick glance around the trash bins to get an idea of where exactly the kid was standing. She pulled her head back, hoping he hadn't seen her. It didn't work.

"I saw you. Stand up, now!"

Mia didn't move. Her backup had to be close. Just wait him out, she thought.

The angry young man began walking toward the trash bins, dragging his young female victim with him. Mia looked around and saw those in the quad reacting to whatever the gunman was doing, but she didn't want to risk another peek. But after a few seconds she felt she had no choice, so she poked her head around the bins. The gunman was now less than twenty feet from her location, still with the young girl in his grasp. She knew she couldn't wait; she'd have to make her move. Mia wasn't going to let another child die on a high school campus. She had witnessed enough bloodshed.

"All right, I'm going to stand up slowly," she said in a loud, confident voice.

Washington stopped in his tracks, unsure if the voice belonged to a teacher or a staff member. He certainly had no idea it was a sheriff deputy in her seventh month of pregnancy.

Mia slowly raised her head above the trash bins.

"Why are you hiding?" he asked angrily.

"I didn't know what was going on. I was just walking by and saw you with the girl. It was a gut reaction, I guess," Mia responded, her heart beating a mile a minute.

"No one cares," he replied. "No one cares about me or what I'm going through!"

Mia saw this as an opening, a chance to start a dialogue with the young man. As she looked at him she could peripherally see three deputies surreptitiously taking positions in different areas of the quad. Each had his weapon drawn, aimed directly at the young man. Not yet, she thought, give him a chance.

"What's your name?"

"Who cares? You don't care, Kendra doesn't care, no one fucking cares about me!"

"I care about you. Tell me your name. My name's Mia."

The gunman looked at Mia but didn't respond.

"Tell me your name. I want to help you."

The young man shifted his weight from one foot to another, careful to keep his grip on Kendra and the gun fixed on her head.

"Alex."

Progress, Mia thought. Just keep him talking and maybe she could get him to put the gun down.

"What grade are you in, Alex?"

"I'm a senior, just like Kendra here. She leads guys on and then yanks their fucking chain. I got no use for girls like Kendra."

He gave Kendra a little tug and moved the barrel of the gun to her throat.

"Maybe you should have given me a chance," he added, hissing at Kendra.

A terrified Kendra responded, "I'm sorry. Please let me go. Please!"

"Let her go, Alex. We can work this out."

"It's too late for me. I might as well finish the job," he replied, moving the gun back to Kendra's temple.

"Oh my God, oh my God, please help me!" Kendra whimpered, looking at Mia.

Mia could see the three deputies inching closer to the trio, getting into position to end the standoff. She knew she needed to keep Alex talking.

"Alex, listen to me. You need to put down the gun and then we can talk about all this. But I need you to put the gun down. Can we do that?"

Mia could see a little change coming over the young man. He seemed to be listening to her and considering what she was saying. It was a definite move in the right direction. A glimmer of hope. She pressed forward.

"Let's do it now, Alex. Put down the gun and walked toward me. No one is going to hurt you."

Nothing.

Mia wanted to show the young man she was serious and knew a good way to do this was to take the first move. Her heart was pounding as she fought off the demons of Columbine. Flashbacks kept flooding into her consciousness.

"Alex, I'm going to stand up. I won't do anything you don't want me to do. Is it okay if I stand up and show myself?"

Alex seemed to relax a bit and took a deep breath. "Yeah, but don't try anything funny."

"You have my word, Alex. I won't hurt you. I just want this to be over with so we can talk and maybe get you some help. So, is it okay if I come out?"

Alex looked at Mia and said, "Okay."

Mia slowly stood and looked directly at Alex. She held her Beretta in her right hand and made sure it was obscured by one of the trash bins. Alex still had a death grip on Kendra and the poor thing was beyond terrified. Mia saw that the three deputies were now closer than they were a minute earlier, moving into position to overpower him, or worse. Mia didn't want that to happen; she knew was making progress. She needed to convey this to the deputies without Alex noticing. The last thing she wanted was for Alex to see the deputies closing in on him.

Suddenly, a noise from above distracted Alex. He looked up and saw a news helicopter hovering above.

"Get that fucking helicopter outta here!" he screamed.

Mia was suddenly back at Columbine, the sky filled with news choppers. She shook the image from her mind and tried to focus. Her hand holding the Beretta, still obscured by the trash bin, was shaking.

"Alex, listen to me. The best way to get rid of that helicopter is for you to put the gun down, let go of Kendra, and walk over to me. Then we'll get out of here and talk and those helicopters will leave."

"I don't know what to do," he replied, tears rolling down his cheeks.

"You know what's right, Alex. You're a good person. Let Kendra go, put the gun down, and walk to me. Come on, you can do it. Please, Alex . . . "

Mia sensed that if he was going to cooperate, it would be now. It was the moment of truth.

"Come on Alex, put the gun down and walk over to me."

As Alex was considering Mia's words, one of the deputies shifted his position and Alex caught the movement out of the corner of his eye. He wheeled in the direction of the deputy to see what was happening. Mia, feeling a surge of fear at Alex's movement, instantly fired off three 7 rounds from her Beretta. Kendra screamed and ran away as Alex crumpled to the ground.

Horror stricken, Mia grabbed her cell, reporting to the dispatcher what had happened. She ran to Alex and dropped to her knees to offer first aid to the young man.

"Don't say anything, Mia," advised one of the deputies, looking around at the people who had quickly closed in on the scene.

"Oh my God, is he going to be all right?" she asked, recognizing the deputy as someone she had worked patrol with years earlier.

The deputy surveyed Alex's wounds. They both saw it at the same time—a round had entered the back of Alex's head a few inches above his neck. There was no exit wound.

The deputy checked for a pulse. He found one, but it was faint. He put his head to the young man's chest and found he wasn't breathing. The deputy began administering CPR as Mia and the other two deputies watched. Mia removed her sweater and wrapped it around the Alex's head, trying her best to stop the bleeding.

Mia knelt down on the grass, grabbed Alex's hand, and held it tight. "Hold on Alex, we've got help coming. Just hold on."

A siren wailed in the distance as Mia watched the deputy pump rhythmically on Alex's chest. The crowd, now numbering a few hundred, inched closer, causing one of the other deputies to stand and order everyone back. He ran to his patrol car to get some yellow caution tape.

The deputy continued with CPR. Alex was unconscious, but that didn't stop Mia from trying to comfort him, stroking his hand and talking to him. An ambulance pulled into the quad and the crowd parted to allow room. The paramedic did a quick assessment of the situation and took over CPR from the deputy.

Mia released the Alex's hand and stood. For nearly two decades she had experienced nightmares about what she witnessed at Columbine, but felt she had come to grips with it and was managing her life. Or at least she thought she had it under control. But now she was standing over a high school student fighting for his life. And she had caused it.

She looked up and saw Mick running across the quad toward her. The tears began to flow.

CHAPTER 3

B ack at headquarters in Castle Springs, Rocklin County Sheriff's Spokesman Mark Archer carefully monitored the situation playing out at Woodrow Wilson High School. He stared at the television in his office, tuned to Channel Eight, which had turned its regularly scheduled noon news broadcast into a live play by play of the events unfolding at the school. Channel Eight's news chopper hovered in place nearly fifteen hundred feet above the scene, sending back remarkable images for the world to see. With the incredible zoom capabilities of modern cameras, the chopper could almost show a freckle on someone's nose.

That camera had been fixed for more than thirty minutes on the school's quad and had shown the shooting occurring live. As soon as they realized what was happening the news director in the studio's control room cut away from the shot, and news anchor Angela Bell immediately offered an apology to all those watching. Truth be told, the brass at Channel Eight were quite pleased that their video had caught the shooting. They knew the footage would go viral and millions would see the young man being shot by a pregnant woman. And Channel Eight News in Denver would be credited with the clip.

Archer had been the RCSO spokesman for nearly twenty years and had handled all kinds of cases, from the sensational to the mundane. Not surprisingly he was getting a flood of phone calls from the media about the shooting. He told each reporter that he didn't have anything for them quite yet, and that he was about to go to the campus where he could gather the facts of the case. He informed them he would be available for interviews at the campus, something that reporters loved. He grabbed his coat and headed to his car.

As he made the short drive to the campus he went over the facts of the case in his head. As he had watched the event unfold on campus, Mark had been in constant contact with the watch commander on duty, receiving a play-by-play assessment as things transpired. He knew that Mia Serrano was the deputy involved in the shooting, which really puzzled him. She was an investigator, not a patrol deputy—what could possibly have put her on that campus, squaring off with an armed student holding another student hostage? It made no sense, and it was the first thing he would need to figure out when he arrived. The media had not caught onto the identity of the shooter but were widely reporting that it was a pregnant woman on campus who had shot the student. They certainly weren't aware that the pregnant woman was an RCSO deputy and the wife of Sheriff Mick McCallister. Once that information got out, Mark knew this story would grow exponentially. Despite his excellent media instincts, there was no way Mark Archer could ever fathom what a big story this was about to become.

∽

"My God Mia, are you okay?"

Mia didn't respond, she just collapsed into her husband's arm and sobbed.

Mick held her tightly and looked around, surveying the situation.

The paramedics were loading the young man into the back of the ambulance. A good sign, he thought; at least they were transporting him. The crowd around the scene had grown to several hundred, with reporters standing around the perimeter, interviewing anyone willing to share what they had seen. Three news choppers were hovering above. The three deputies present when the shooting occurred had been separated from each other and were waiting to be interviewed by investigators.

Mick had asked the watch commander to call District Attorney Dave Baxter and let him know what had transpired. In officer-involved shootings, or OIS, it was customary to run simultaneous investigations—one handled by the RCSO and the other by the DA's office. In highly controversial or difficult cases an outside agency could be called in to coordinate the investigation in lieu of the agency involved in the OIS. This was done to assure the public that a fair and objective investigation would be conducted.

One of the reporters standing around the perimeter was Denise Elliott, reporter for Channel Two in Denver. Elliott, keeping a careful eye on what was unfolding around her, turned to her videographer and asked, "Why is the sheriff hugging the pregnant woman that shot the kid?"

"Beats the hell out of me," was the response.

"Get some video of that, Sean."

The young videographer swung the camera around to capture footage of Mick and Mia standing in the quad. It certainly appeared to be more than a sheriff comforting someone after a shooting. This was clearly personal.

Denise Elliott grabbed her cell phone and googled the sheriff.

"The sheriff is married to one of his deputies. Here, take a look."

Elliott handed him the phone and Sean studied the Wikipedia entry, which was complete with photos.

"Wow, that's her!"

"Yep, and it looks like she's the shooter."

"Oh man, now we've got a story!"

❧

Mark Archer arrived at the high school and did his best to navigate the bedlam. There were people everywhere and traffic was jammed up. Word of the shooting had spread quickly and hundreds of concerned parents were arriving at the school to pick up their children. Archer flashed his ID to the cadets directing traffic and they waved him under the yellow caution tape and onto the campus. He parked near the cafeteria and made his way to the quad where he saw the sheriff with Mia and several other members of the RCSO. He approached the group.

"Mia, I'm so sorry. How are you doing?"

Mia looked at Mark and replied, "I can't believe this happened. I was trying to help him, I swear."

"I know, Mia. But sometimes, despite our best intentions, things just go to shit."

"I'm guessing you're getting a ton of calls on this from the media?" asked the sheriff.

"Yeah, pretty much. I plan to do a live press conference here as soon as I can gather the information I need. I'd like you to be part of that, sheriff."

"Of course. I'm always available to the media when we have an officer-involved shooting. It's not going to be any different this time. Just let me know when and where you want me."

Mick nodded at his boss. "I'm thinking of doing it about an hour from now, and I'll probably use the gym so there's electricity and plenty of room. Who's the on-scene commander?"

"Lumas."

"I'll call you when I'm ready for the press conference. We should huddle before we do it."

Archer left Mick and Mia and took a walk around the quad. He stopped and spoke with several RCSO personnel to get their perspective on things, and even chatted a little with bystanders standing behind the yellow tape. He had handled the media on hundreds of cases and had a routine he liked to follow. Get a feel for the scene, talk with several different people, and then formulate in his mind how he'd present the case to the reporters. He knew from experience what would interest the media and he would find things they could report on—different and interesting angles. He had learned over the years that doing his job was really more of an art than a science. No two cases were alike and he always looked to find the best way to tell the particular story.

He was, of course, deeply concerned that Mia was the deputy involved in the shooting. It wouldn't be long before that information leaked out, so it would be his suggestion to the sheriff that they tell that part of the story right up front. Normally they would take a day or two before releasing the name of the officer or officers involved, giving them some time to come to grips with what had happened and allow them time to tell their friends and families, and get counseling. But in this case they needed to be above reproach—they couldn't give any cause for belief that the department was trying to hide the fact that the sheriff's wife was the one who fired the shots.

He located Commander Lumas in the middle of the quad. As the incident commander, Lumas was charged with managing the scene.

"So, give me the rundown."

"Mark, it's a hot mess."

"I don't doubt it."

"It's all preliminary at this point, but I've talked to enough folks to get a lay of the land," responded Lumas.

"Okay, give me what you've got so far."

"At approximately 11:40 this morning, seventeen-year-old Alex Washington, a student here at the school, asked his teacher if he could use the restroom. She granted him permission and off he went. A few minutes later the bell rang for lunch and the students filed out of their classrooms. But instead of going to the bathroom, Washington somehow procured a gun, a Glock nine millimeter, and found Kendra Gillespie, another student, having lunch here in the quad."

"Okay, go on."

"Apparently, Washington had a thing for Gillespie but his interest in her wasn't reciprocated. He texted her several times this morning—we have both their cell phones—and she got fed up and told him to go pound sand. That must have been what set him off because the next thing we know he's got a gun to her head and there's widespread panic."

Archer shook his head. "So what happened next?"

"The kids scattered and several called nine-one-one from their cell phones. Our communications center lit up like a Christmas tree from what I've been told. We send everybody and their mother code three, but the nearest unit is still a few minutes away. Then we get a call from Mia Serrano saying she's already on campus, that she's on foot and approaching the scene. Not sure how that happened or why she was on campus. The dispatcher tells her to hold off and wait for backup. But Mia says she's going in anyway."

Mark instantly thought about Mia's experience at Columbine. That had to explain her motivation for continuing without backup. He didn't say anything about it to Lumas, but Mark was already putting his press statements together in his head. Mia was a hero; she saved that girl's life. That fact needed to be hit and hit hard, he thought.

"So, go on . . . "

"Mia is able to get pretty close to where the guy has the girl and she takes cover behind those trash cans," he replied, pointing to the bins. "Meanwhile, backup arrives and they take positions around the quad. All this goes unnoticed by Washington. At first he didn't know about Mia behind the bins, but some kids start pointing at her and Washington catches on. He yells for her to come out and she does, probably figuring she had no choice at that point and she starts a dialogue with him. At first the kid didn't want to talk, but Mia was able to get him to open up a little bit make some progress, at least that's what several eyewitnesses told us."

That sounded like Mia, he thought. It was the high school teacher coming out in her.

"So why did things go south?"

"So Mia was making some headway with the kid and actually offered to stand up from behind the bins, kind of a peace offering. I bet she figured if she did that, maybe he'd give her something in return, like putting down the gun."

"Pretty gutsy on her part. It didn't work?"

"He didn't put down the gun, but his demeanor seemed to soften a bit. But that's when the news chopper showed up and the kid got antsy."

Archer flinched. While he had no control over what the media did or did not do, many at RCSO blamed him for anything that appeared in the paper or on the news. He could see some blame coming his way for "allowing" the news chopper to screw things up. Oh well, he thought. He'd deal with it.

"The deputies that had taken their positions around the quad didn't know why the kid was suddenly acting all hinky and one of them shifted a bit in his position to get ready to take the shot or do whatever was necessary. Unfortunately, the kid caught the movement peripherally and started to wheel around to see what was going on."

"And Mia saw the kid's sudden movement and had a split-second decision to make?"

"Yep, fired three quick rounds, hitting the kid twice. The girl was unharmed."

"Shit. And no one else was injured, correct?"

"That's right. Just Washington."

Neither spoke for a few seconds.

"Anything new on his condition?" Mark asked.

"No, but the initial assessment by paramedics was that it was pretty bad. The kid was unconscious and barely had a pulse. But who knows, they get him to Springs Memorial and maybe they're able to bring him back."

Mark knew that there was a huge difference between a deputy shooting someone and having that person survive versus the person dying. If the kid lived the whole thing would likely go away after a day or two. The county would write him a large check and the media would move onto the next sensational story. If the kid died, then all bets were off. He hated to think like that, but it was part of his job. And the fact that the kid was African-American added a whole new layer of issues.

"Do you know why Mia was out here?"

"We got just the basics from her—we knew it would be best if we isolated her and let investigators do their thing. But she did tell deputies she was at a medical appointment across the street. She was walking to her car afterwards and heard the commotion. Her instincts told her something was amiss so she hightailed it over here to see what was happening."

"Sounds like Mia."

"As she was running toward the quad she called it in on her cell and asked for backup. By then we had already been flooded with calls from kids. She asked a kid who was running away what was going on and the student told her there was a student with a gun holding another kid hostage."

"But she didn't wait for backup?"

"Evidently not. She probably thought there wasn't enough time and that something might happen to the girl before backup got there. She said she thought she could talk to the kid and maybe get him to put the gun down."

"I'm not surprised. Before she was with the RCSO, Mia was a high school teacher. She probably thought she could talk the kid down."

"I didn't know that. It adds a little insight into her actions here today."

Archer looked at the commander and tried to read him. Did the commander feel Mia acted inappropriately in this case?

Mark offered, "I think Mia did what she thought was best under some very difficult circumstances. She didn't run from the situation;

she ran toward the trouble. Some deputies would have just turned the other way."

"Yeah, that's true. I guess it's easy to second guess."

"There will be plenty of second guessing in this case. There always is, but I'd hate to think that some of that thoughtless commentary comes from our own personnel."

Archer's message wasn't missed by the commander.

"No, I wasn't implying that Mia did anything wrong."

"Good, and I hope that the other members of this department feel the same way. This could get really rough, and we need to be united."

"Of course."

CHAPTER 4

⟋⟍

Mia sat alone in the front seat of a patrol car parked on the lawn in the quad while Mick stood outside the vehicle talking with deputies. Mick had offered some initial support to her when he arrived on scene, but both he and Mia knew that she couldn't discuss the case with him. Aside from some initial statements made to patrol deputies, Mia had remained isolated in the patrol unit.

As Mick was talking with his deputies he saw a large, black SUV pull up to the quad. He recognized the vehicle as the one that transported the DA around town. A minute later Dave Baxter emerged from the back and walked toward Mick.

"So sorry to hear about this, Mick. How's Mia doing?"

"About as well as expected. She's waiting to be taken to the RCSO. What's the ETA on your OIS team?"

"They should be here any minute; I guess I beat them here. So, what've you got?"

Mick filled in the DA on what he knew. The DA listened intently, nodding throughout the briefing.

"Anything on the kid's condition?"

"Not since he was transported. But it didn't look good. Took one to the head and another to the shoulder."

Baxter looked at Mick. "I understand the kid is African-American?"

"Yeah, and he had a seventeen-year-old girl in a headlock in front of a couple hundred kids. A Glock nine millimeter pressed to her temple. Mia saved her life."

"Yeah, from what you're saying, it sounds like it. What was Mia doing here? I thought she'd be on maternity leave."

"She's seven months along. She was planning to work another month then take the leave. She was at a doctor's appointment nearby and just happened to catch what was going down. She didn't hesitate to run onto the campus and help the girl."

"Well, it looks like her maternity leave will start a little early. We'll do our best to get the investigation done quickly, but you know these things take time."

Tell me something I don't know, thought Mick. Just then his cell phone went off.

"Sheriff McCallister, this is Sergeant Diana Walker. I'm over at Springs Memorial. I was just informed that Alex Washington died about five minutes ago."

Mick turned to Baxter. "The young man just passed away. I need to notify his family and give them the news."

"Are you sure you want to do that, Mick? Maybe you should have one of your major crimes guys tell them. It could get really ugly really fast."

"Nope, I'll do it. It's my duty as sheriff."

Baxter shrugged and Mick walked over to the patrol car. He wanted Mia to hear the news from him.

She looked at Mick as he approached the unit. He didn't have to tell her anything; she could see by the look on his face that Alex Washington was dead.

❧

As Archer surveyed the crime scene he scribbled down his thoughts and observations in his notebook. Once he had a good idea of what had happened, he walked over to Mick.

"We need to get something out before the media starts speculating. This isn't going to be pretty and we need to get ahead of it."

Mick nodded, obviously distracted.

Recognizing this, Mark reached over and lightly grabbed Mick's arm.

"Mia's going to be fine. But we need to come up with a strategy for how we're going to handle this. This isn't going to be your run-of-the-mill officer-involved shooting."

"There's no such thing, Mark. They're all difficult."

"I know that, but this one involves the sheriff's wife. We're always scrutinized no matter what we do, but there are going to be a million eyes on this one—everyone looking to make sure we don't give Mia any special treatment."

Mick looked at Mark and replied, "We're not going to be handling this investigation. I'm going to ask the Denver PD to step in so we avoid even a hint of impropriety. This has to be totally above board; we can't have it any other way."

"Are you sure you want to do that?"

"Yes. I'm sure the DA will have some heartburn over it, but it's my call."

"Okay, but we still need to do a press briefing here on campus. The place is crawling with reporters and they're not going to be very happy if we all just pack up and leave. They'll scream cover up once the word gets out that Mia is the deputy involved. I've already been approached by half a dozen reporters asking what happened."

"He died, Mark," Mick replied, looking off into the distance.

"I know . . . I heard."

Mark continued, "But remember—Mia saved the girl's life. You and Mia can't forget that."

"Yeah, but that doesn't make this any easier. A young man is dead and my wife is going to take the blame. As the sheriff, it's ultimately my responsibility."

There wasn't much Mark could say in response to his boss, so he moved forward. "Let's go over the plans for the press conference. I've gathered the information we need to get out and have it here in my notes. We should find some place quiet to go over everything before we face reporters."

"Sure. What time do you want to do the press conference?"

"It's after one now, so I'm thinking maybe two o'clock. We can do it in the gym. I'll send the info to all our reporters via Twitter. Does that work for you?"

"Yeah, that's fine. It'll give me time to go tell the DA I'm going to have Denver PD take over."

"Okay, I'll go ahead and send out the tweet."

Mick walked back over to where the DA was standing in the quad. He was holding court with a small audience of law enforcement personnel. The guy was a blowhard and a politician to the core, but Baxter was the DA and Mick had to maintain a positive working relationship with him.

Baxter noticed Mick approach and turned his attention away from the group.

"Can I have a few minutes with you, Dave?"

"Sure."

The two walked to an area where they couldn't be overheard.

"Look, Dave, I wanted you to know before we do our press conference—I plan to bring in Denver PD to do the investigation. I just don't think—"

"What? Are you kidding me? Why bring them in? We can handle it, Mick. Bringing in an outside agency to do the investigation is just a really bad idea."

"I know we *can* do it, but I want to ensure that this investigation is completely independent and above board. There can be no perception that we're whitewashing this thing. Denver PD has some very capable people and I think having them come in is the prudent thing to do."

"But you give up control, Mick. And that's never good."

"This is my wife, Dave. People are always quick to jump on the cops anytime there's a shooting, but in this case the potential for that is magnified tenfold. I can't be accused of favoritism by having RCSO do the investigation. And your guys would come under the same scrutiny. Don't you see that?"

"Sure, there will be some difficult moments, but we can handle it. Giving up control by bringing in another agency puts us at a far greater risk. I don't like it, Mick. Not one bit."

"Well, it's my call and I think it's the best thing to do. I just wanted to give you a heads up before I tell reporters at the press conference we're going to do here shortly."

Baxter didn't respond, but turned and walked back to his SUV.

Mick grabbed his phone and glanced through his contact list. A minute later he was speaking to Chuck Hookstra, chief of the Denver PD.

"Hey, Mick. I've been watching the news. How you holding up down there?"

"The young man died a few minutes ago, so this is about to get even more difficult."

"Sorry to hear that, Mick. But from what I can gather your deputy saved that young girl's life. She's a hero."

"I'm not sure everyone will see it that way, Chuck. The kid is African-American and the deputy is white."

"That's not automatically a problem, Mick. People have a capability for understanding. I have faith."

"The deputy involved is my wife."

Chief Hookstra paused before answering.

"Well, that does add a wrinkle to things. Sorry to hear this, Mick."

"Mia and I got married about ten months ago. And there's another thing going on here—she's seven months pregnant."

"Oh, Jesus."

"Look, I need a favor. You and I go back all the way to the academy and I trust you. I don't think the RCSO should investigate this thing. I want to bring in an independent outside agency to do it so there's no room for accusations of bias. I think Denver PD is a good choice. How do you feel about your guys taking this on for us?"

Hookstra didn't respond immediately, turning over the various the implications in his mind.

"Sure, I think we can do that. Let me get my top guys together; I can have them down there in an hour. Does that work?"

"That would be great. Thanks so much. I'll let Dave Baxter know."

"Did you run this by him before asking me? I can't think he'll be too excited at the prospect."

"I did, and you're right—he wasn't too happy. But this is my agency and I want to bring you guys in. He accepted it."

That was probably an exaggeration, Mick thought, but it was done and he felt confident it was the right decision.

"Okay. Who should my guys check in with when they get down there?"

"Tim Lumas is the incident commander on scene. I'm going to assign Jack Keller from our investigative bureau to run things at our end. He's the best I've got, so if your guys can coordinate with Keller that should work. I'll let them both know what's going on. I really appreciate this, Chuck."

"No problem, Mick."

Mick certainly had his issues with Keller, having nearly fired him months earlier for serious ethical breaches in a homicide investigation. But he could overlook that for now—this OIS involved his wife.

Chief Hookstra hung up and looked out the window of his office. He considered the task before him and hoped he wasn't making a mistake by agreeing to get involved in the investigation. Mick was a friend and they had become close during their academy days more than twenty years earlier. If he could help Mick out, he should do it, he thought. Mick McCallister was a good man, but Hookstra couldn't help but wonder if part of the reason his friend called and asked for the help was the fact that he was African-American.

CHAPTER 5

〜

After the call to Chief Hookstra, Mick found Mark Archer so they could go over plans for the press conference. Mark had notified the media that the press conference would be held at two o'clock at the school. That gave the sheriff and him half an hour to get their notes together. They went over all the information that Mark had gathered and determined who would say what. He showed the sheriff the press release he had assembled, with hard copies available to the reporters, courtesy of the staff in the school office. Then they walked over to the gym, located a hundred yards or so from the quad.

As they approached they could see a large crowd gathered outside the entrance, along with a half dozen satellite news trucks parked in the adjoining lot. Reporters and their camera people were busy getting ready, with many planning to do live coverage from the gym. The live footage from the Channel Eight news chopper showing the shooting go down had made this a very large story. All the Colorado news agencies were covering it, as well as two of the national cable networks. Good video always heightened a story's arc, and video of a police shooting occurring on live TV never failed to capture the public's attention.

As Mark and the sheriff walked into the gym they saw Theresa O'Sullivan from the RCSO setting up a podium. Several news people were busy getting their microphones placed strategically on top of it.

Theresa helped out at press conferences and she saved Mark a lot of time and hassle with the preparation.

They also saw Dave Baxter talking with with several members of the RCSO. Off in the corner of the gym stood Bill Hammond, principal of Woodrow Wilson High School, and Felice Woodward, president of the Castle Springs school board. Both looked very anxious about being there. The others gathered there were mostly reporters, with a handful of interested Rocklin County residents rounding out the group.

"You ready to go, sheriff?" asked Archer.

"Yep, let's do it."

Mark walked to the podium and began to speak.

"Good afternoon, everybody. Thanks for being here. My name is Mark Archer, lieutenant with the Rocklin County Sheriff's Department. I'm here with Rocklin County Sheriff Mick McCallister. We have a press release for each of you. I only have it in hard copy, but I'd be happy to send you the information electronically once I get back to my office. I'll be giving an initial statement and then the sheriff would like to speak, and he will answer any questions you might have."

The group was quiet, waiting patiently for the information Mark was about to offer.

"At approximately eleven fifty this morning the Rocklin County nine-one-one center received multiple calls reporting a student on the campus of Woodrow Wilson High School holding another student hostage in the quad. The callers reported that the young man had a gun pressed against the head of his female hostage. Multiple units were immediately dispatched to the school. A few moments later our dispatch center received another call, this one from one of our deputies who happened to be in the area on her lunch break.

"This deputy, sensing a serious situation, had run onto the campus. She saw the young man holding his hostage at gunpoint. She took cover nearby and surveyed the scene. Fearing for the young girl's life, the deputy determined that time was of the essence and, at great personal risk, began a dialogue with the young man. She asked him to put the gun down and surrender. At first he didn't want to hear anything she had to say, but over the course of a few minutes he began to converse with the deputy.

"At around this time, other deputies arrived and took up positions around the quad. Seeing that the deputy seemed to be making headway with the young man, they stayed patient, hopeful that she could talk the young man into surrendering. At this point the deputy offered to come out from behind some trash receptacles she was taking cover behind. In exchange, she asked the young man to put the gun down. Just as this dialogue was taking place a news helicopter appeared above, presumably to get live video of the events unfolding below. The noise from the chopper agitated the young man, resulting in him making sudden and aggressive movements. Faced with a split-second decision and fearing for the young lady's life, the deputy fired her service weapon.

"The young man was hit twice and the hostage was quickly escorted to safety by deputies. I am glad to report that she was not physically harmed during the ordeal. Paramedics quickly arrived at the scene and were able to administer aid to the young man. They transported him to Castle Springs Memorial Hospital, where he died a short time later."

The crowd grew quiet. Archer continued.

"That's as much as I can share with you right now. There will be more information later as it becomes available. At this time I'd like to call up Sheriff McCallister."

Mick walked to the podium, looked out at the crowd, and began.

"Lieutenant Archer has given you a rundown of what occurred here today. I have a few other details I'd like to share. First off, because of the age of the young man and the female student he took hostage we won't be releasing their names. As far as questions about school security and other school-related issues, I'll defer those questions to the school district. Both Mr. Hammond and Ms. Woodward are available to you today."

Hammond and Woodward quickly folded their arms and looked away. This was new territory for them, and both were clearly uncomfortable in their roles.

The sheriff continued, "Now, as most of you know, it is customary not to release the name of the deputy in officer-involved shootings for at least a couple of days. We do this to allow them to catch their breath, if you will, so they have the opportunity to process what's happened, talk with their family and friends, and prepare for the onslaught of media coverage. They are also offered the services of a therapist so they can talk to someone on a professional level. I think this approach works well and for the most part, the media here have been understanding about it.

"However, in this case, I'm going to make an exception." Mick took another long look at the reporters gathered in the gym. They stared back, not sure what the sheriff was going to say next.

"The deputy involved in the incident today is Mia Serrano-McCallister. She's my wife."

There was a collective gasp.

"Further, because of the unusual nature of this situation, I've asked the Denver Police Department to take the lead on the investigation into the shooting. I talked with Chief Hookstra a short time ago and he has agreed to have his investigative team handle this case. The Denver PD has an exemplary record in investigating officer-involved shootings and I have every confidence that this investigation will be thorough, unbiased, and transparent. Deputy Serrano-McCallister will not receive any kind of special treatment."

A hand shot up from the back of the room.

"Yes, in the back," said Mick.

"Sheriff, Denise Elliott, Channel Two News in Denver. It appears that Deputy Serrano-McCallister is pregnant. Can you confirm that?"

Mick hesitated a second before responding. His first thought was that it was no one's business, but he quickly realized Mia's pregnancy wasn't a secret among RCSO personnel and at seven months, it wasn't something that could really be hidden. It was time for some transparency.

"Yes, that's true. She's seven months along."

Every reporter quickly began writing down what Mick had said. The story was getting juicier by the minute.

"She was not wearing a deputy's uniform—is she on maternity leave?" asked another reporter in the front row.

"No, she's not on maternity leave; her current assignment is in the investigations bureau so she wouldn't typically be wearing a uniform," Mick responded.

Now the hands began shooting up all at the same time. Mick patiently answered each question as best he could.

∽

While the press conference was underway in the school gym, Mia was transported to RCSO headquarters. She was brought into the interview room and offered something to drink. She asked for a bottle of water and was brought two. She took a long pull on one of them and tried to gather herself. She couldn't believe the young man was gone; the whole thing seemed so surreal. Three hours ago she was in her doctor's office, looking at the ultrasound of her baby.

She instinctively placed her hand on her stomach, thinking about the new life inside her. She could feel the baby moving. Tears started again as her thoughts returned to the family of Alex Washington. They would be getting the awful news of his death any minute. The paradox didn't escape her.

Her mind shifted back to her wedding day ten months earlier. Her relationship with Mick had its share of ups and downs, but ultimately the two found they couldn't be without each other. They married at a small church in Castle Springs with just forty family members and close friends. It was Mick's second marriage and Mia's first and they both agreed to keep the event simple but elegant. Mia's father, Chuck, had walked her down the aisle and Mark Archer had served as Mick's best man. Mia's closest friend, an old college roommate, had served as her maid of honor.

The reception was at Mick's home in the hills above Castle Springs. He had a large property and a wedding planner friend of Mia's had turned it into a beautiful venue for the party. It had been the happiest day of her life, and now, just ten months later, she was experiencing one of the worst days of her life.

The doors of the interview room swung open and RCSO Investigator Jack Keller walked in. He didn't say anything as he took a seat next to Mia. She looked up at him but didn't speak. She and Keller weren't on the best of terms.

"Mia, I know how you're feeling right now. I've been through this before and it's really shitty. But I need to tell you what's going to happen here."

Mia nodded at Jack and tried her best to maintain her composure. It wouldn't be easy but she was determined not to let her former partner see her crack.

"First off, do you want someone from the union present during the interview? You're also entitled to have legal counsel. You might want to think about getting an attorney from the legal defense fund. It's free—covered through our union dues."

Mia wasn't sure what to do. Her feeling prior to this moment had been that people who wanted representation, or those who wouldn't speak without their lawyer present, were hiding something. Now she wasn't so sure.

"I want to speak with my husband before I make that decision. Can I do that?"

"Sure, I don't see why not. Give me a minute and I'll see if I can find him." Keller stood up and walked out of the room, leaving Mia alone once again with her thoughts.

CHAPTER 6

After answering questions from reporters for nearly forty-five minutes, McCallister and Archer finally broke away and drove to the home of Alex Washington. The purpose of their visit wasn't to deliver the news of the young man's death; the family already knew what had happened. Mick wanted to visit personally with the family so he could express his condolences. It wouldn't be easy or pleasant and he knew there was a risk that things could blow up in his face, but he believed it was the right thing and he was determined to do it.

The family lived in one unit of a rundown triplex on the southern outskirts of Rocklin County. As Mick and Mark pulled up, they noticed quite a few cars parked on the street outside the house. There were people standing on the front lawn of the residence and crowded onto the front porch. They drove slowly by the home, looking for a place to park.

"Looks like Alex had a lot of family and friends," Mark said.

They parked the car in the first open spot they found, a block away, and walked toward the home.

As they approached the triplex, those gathered on the front lawn grew silent, looking at the two white men dressed in suits coming up the walkway.

A well-dressed man who appeared to be in his early forties stepped forward.

"Can I help you with something?"

"I'm Sheriff McCallister and this is Lieutenant Archer. We're here to pay our respects to Alex's family. Can you direct me?" responded Mick.

The man stared at Mick and Mark for several seconds and then replied.

"I'm not sure that's a good idea, sheriff. The family is devastated by what your deputy did to Alex today and this is probably not a good time."

"I understand. What's your name?" asked Mick, extending his hand to the man. The others in the yard were watching the exchange closely.

The man reluctantly shook Mick's hand. "Floyd Liston. I'm Alex's uncle. Alex is—or was—my kid sister's boy."

"I'm sorry for your loss, Mr. Liston. I truly am."

Liston stared at Mick. The sheriff knew the next words from Liston would be critical. Either he would be dismissed immediately or Liston would reconsider his request to meet with the family. The others on the lawn, which looked to number thirty or more, closed ranks and surrounded Mick and Mark. Archer, feeling a bit uncomfortable with how things were unfolding, felt his coat pocket for his Beretta. The move, though subtle, didn't go unnoticed by several in the crowd.

"What you gonna do, pig? Shoot us in cold blood, foo?"

Archer and McCallister turned and saw a young man, clearly posing for all present, pointing at them with a couple fingers extended from both hands. Both Mick and Mark recognized the gang signs of the 120th Street gang, prevalent in the southern part of Rocklin County.

Mick spoke in a quiet but firm voice, "We're just here to pay our respects. That's all."

"Well, maybe you best get the fuck outta here, cracker!"

Liston spoke up, "Jaquon, that's enough."

"These fuckers gotta go, man. Ain't no place for them here!" he screamed back.

"Shut up, Jaquon."

Liston turned to the sheriff, "He's upset. We're all upset. Jaquon is—was—Alex's cousin. I'll let Alex's mother know you came by to pay your respects."

McCallister and Archer took the not-so-subtle hint and left for the car.

Once they were out of earshot, Mark muttered to Mick, "Well, that went well."

❧

Upon Mick's return to the station he was told by Jack Keller that Mia wanted to speak to him. Mick knew he couldn't talk to his wife privately. He would certainly turn down the request from anyone else. And now, with it being his wife involved in the shooting, he knew he needed to be above reproach. But if he turned down her request, how could he convey that to her? He didn't want her to think he was abandoning her, his wife of ten months and the mother of his unborn child.

He realized he'd have to trust Keller to let her know he couldn't speak to her. That might be easier said than done, given that Mick and Keller hadn't spoken to each other in well over a year. Ever since Mick had tried to terminate Keller, things between them had been more than chilly.

"Please explain to her why I can't talk to her."

Keller nodded and headed back to the interview room.

CHAPTER 7

꧁꧂

"Sheriff, I wanted to let you know that a crowd is gathering at the campus of Wilson High. It seems peaceful at this point, but I've deployed a half dozen deputies just to make sure things stay that way."

The call was from Commander Jim Bailey at the watch commander's desk.

"Okay, thanks for letting me know, Jim. Monitor it closely and call in any resources you need. Hopefully it won't be necessary but I don't want to take any chances. And please keep me posted."

"Will do, sir."

"Does Archer know about this?"

"He's my next call, sir."

"Okay, good. Thanks for the heads up."

Mick sat at his desk contemplating the day's events. He felt very unsettled about things, not just because of Mia's involvement in the OIS, but about what had happened at Alex Washington's home. The gangbanger concerned him and he hoped the young kid wouldn't try to make a name for himself with the gang by using his cousin's death. The sound of his phone startled him. The caller ID showed it was Mark Archer calling.

Mick didn't waste any time.

"Hey, Mark, did Jim Bailey tell you about the crowd at Wilson High?"

"Yes, he did and I just turned on my TV. Channel Eight has its chopper up. They're covering it live."

"Jesus, haven't they already caused enough trouble today?" replied Mick.

Mark could certainly sense his boss's frustration. The media played a necessary role in a free society but they could be very problematic at times. It was a reality he lived with every day.

"Just doing their job, boss."

"Yeah, yeah . . . I know."

Mick reached for the remote control on his desk and turned on Channel Eight. The screen showed the campus of Wilson High and a group of fifty or so people gathered in the quad. Many were carrying signs, but because of the angle of the shot it was impossible to read what was written.

"Does Channel Eight have any reporters on the ground, Mark?"

"Not yet, but Angela mentioned on air that they have people en route."

Angela Bell was a popular Channel Eight anchorwoman who also was in a serious relationship with Mark Archer.

"Okay, I want to know what's written on those signs. I'm hoping they're in memoriam Alex Washington and not something negative directed at the RCSO."

"We should know pretty soon. Whoever they send to the scene will certainly have the folks carrying the signs in the shot."

There was a period of silence, then Mark spoke up, "Have you talked to Mia yet?"

"No, I want her to get through the interviews first. The Denver PD investigative team arrived a few hours ago, and the DA's office has their people here as well. I've asked Jack Keller to coordinate things."

"Well, Keller has been through enough of these kinds of things before. I think he's a good choice at our end."

"Yeah, I agree."

The sheriff bit his tongue and didn't express to Mark his true feelings about the veteran homicide investigator. But then again, Mark certainly knew the history between the two.

"Looks like the Channel Eight crew has arrived," Mark pointed out. The two men turned to watch the news coverage in their respective offices. On screen, Caroline Ellis, a pretty, young reporter, began to speak.

"Angela, I'm here in the quad at Woodrow Wilson High School in Castle Springs where an officer-involved shooting earlier today took the life of a seventeen-year-old student. That student, whose identity has not been released by authorities, was holding another student, a seventeen-year-old female, hostage at gunpoint. Rocklin County sheriff's deputies responded to the scene and were unable to convince the young man to drop his weapon. According to officials with the RCSO, the young man made some sudden movements and was shot by a deputy on scene. He was pronounced dead thirty minutes later at the hospital. The deputy who fired the fatal shots has been identified as Mia Serrano-McCallister, a name that is likely familiar to many of our viewers. Deputy Serrano was one of the investigators who put together the case against Scott Lennox, the man who was convicted two years ago for the murder of Castle Springs businessman George Lombard. It is also interesting to note that Deputy Serrano is the wife of the sheriff of Rocklin County, Mick McCallister. The sheriff was very forthcoming about that fact at a press conference earlier today, where he also confirmed that his wife is seven months pregnant. Now, as you can see over my shoulder, there is a large crowd gathered here at the quad."

The videographer panned the crowd, which now looked to number about one hundred. A handful of people carried signs which were visible in the shot.

"Damn it!" exclaimed Mick.

"Oh, God . . . " sighed Mark.

On screen were two people, each holding a sign. One sign read *Alex Washington would be alive if he was white* and the other said *RCSO - we're watching you....no coverup!*

Mick was furious. He also recognized one of the people—Jaquon.

"What bullshit."

Mark tried to calm him down.

"Look, an overwhelming percentage of Rocklin County residents are going to be totally supportive of us in this shooting. Mia is a hero— she saved that girl's life today."

"That may be true but if we let these assholes say this stuff then we could be heading for trouble. We can't let them take center stage and turn this into a race thing. Did you see who that was?"

Mark responded, "Yeah, it's Jaquon. Can't say I'm very surprised. He's just taking advantage of the situation to try to rip us a new one. We need to get out in front on this and make sure people focus on what really happened here. We need to check in with the girl who was held hostage today—talk with her family and see how she's doing. It would be great to have people hear her side of things. She has a compelling story to tell and the media would love to help her tell it."

"I'm not sure I'm comfortable with that, Mark. She's been through a traumatic event and who knows what her emotional state is right now."

"I'm not saying we throw her in front of a camera. I'm just saying we contact her family to see how she's doing. A personal visit from the sheriff to check on her would be a classy move. I'm guessing her family would be very appreciative. And I would go along with you and let them know their options as far as media goes. Tell them they don't have to speak to any reporters if they don't want to. Give them a little guidance in that area. It could be helpful to them."

"And if they're willing to talk to reporters?"

"Then I can make that happen in a very controlled environment. We don't want some big news conference—just a nice, quiet conversation with a reporter."

"Let me guess . . . Angela?"

Mark chuckled. "It doesn't have to be Angela. We could pick someone else."

"Yeah, but given your relationship with her, she would be your first choice."

"Well, I do trust her and I think she would do the interview within any parameters we and the family establish. I'm not sure I can trust other reporters not to ask anything that's out of bounds."

As the media relations person for RCSO, Mark knew something else was in play. It was sweeps week and each Denver station would be doing everything possible to boost viewership during this time. Future advertising rates for each station would be set based on ratings during these sweeps periods. Mark knew Angela would jump at the chance to do the interview with the Gillespies—it would be a ratings bonanza. The timing of all of this fit perfectly into his plans.

Mick continued, "Will the other reporters be pissed off if Angela gets an exclusive interview with the girl? I can see some reporters raising hell about it."

"It would be the family's decision, not ours. Besides, Angela has the number-one rated newscast in Denver. The Gillespies selecting her to do the interview would be a logical choice. Reporters don't have to know we orchestrated it a bit behind the scenes."

"If they find out, we'll definitely take some heat for it."

"I can handle the fallout from reporters if that happens, but the heat from this blowing up into a race thing is a much bigger problem if we don't get out in front of it."

Mick considered what Mark was telling him. Anything he could to do stem the tide of a potential racial war was something he was willing to try.

"Okay, let's pay a visit to the girl's family."

CHAPTER 8

Kendra Gillespie lived on the western side of Castle Springs in a neighborhood that was relatively new, built in the early 2000s during the booming construction buildout which took place across the country. It was a large, beautiful home with a perfectly landscaped front yard. There were several upscale late-model cars parked in the driveway and on the street in front of the home. Mick and Mark found a place to park on the street a few doors down.

They rang the bell and soon saw the silhouette of a person through the stained glass in the front door. The door swung open and there stood a woman, very attractive, in her late thirties.

"Can I help you?"

"Yes, I'm Sheriff Mick McCallister and this is Lieutenant Archer. We're from the Rocklin County Sheriff's Department."

"Oh, of course. I recognize you both from the newscast on TV tonight. Please, come in."

The two stepped into the foyer and took a quick look around. There was no one in the front rooms of the house but they could hear voices coming from the back.

"I'm Rachel Gillespie, Kendra's mother. Can I get you gentlemen something to drink?"

Mick started to decline the offer, but Mark jumped in. "That would be great. Coffee, if you have it. It's been a long day."

"Of course. Sheriff, would you like anything?"

"Sure, coffee sounds great."

"Come on back to the family room. We have some family and friends over. We're trying our best to deal with what happened today. We're all still in shock."

"That's certainly understandable," responded Mick.

The three walked through the house to the family room where a dozen or so people sat quietly sipping beverages stronger than coffee. Mrs. Gillespie made the introductions.

A man stood and walked to Mick, shaking his hand.

"I'm Tom Gillespie, Kendra's father. I just want to thank you and your department for saving my daughter's life today."

Mick nodded and replied, "I'm so sorry you and your family had to experience this. I'm just so thankful we were able to step in and prevent your daughter from being harmed. How is Kendra doing?'

Mr. Gillespie responded, "She's holding up fairly well. I think she's just overwhelmed by everything. We've contacted a therapist and she's going to meet with Kendra tomorrow morning."

Mark responded, "I think that's a great idea. It's really important for her to talk about her feelings about what happened. We deal with crime victims every day and the worst thing to do is keep everything bottled up."

Mrs. Gillespie offered, "And we're going to have her transfer to another high school. I don't think she'd ever feel safe on that campus again."

"Totally understandable," agreed Mick.

"Where is Kendra?" asked Mark, casually as possible.

Mrs. Gillespie replied, "She's upstairs with a couple of her girl-friends. They're going to spend the night here to support her."

Mick responded, "Good to have her friends around. Is there anything the sheriff's department can do to help you and your family?"

"I don't think so, at least not at this point. We just need to take it one day at a time and see how Kendra handles things. She's a strong girl, but this was a horrible experience for her, obviously. And this is all very unfamiliar territory to us," Mr. Gillespie answered.

Mark saw an opening.

"Listen, can we have a few minutes alone with the two of you?"

The Gillespies exchanged glances before Mrs. Gillespie answered, "Sure, we can go in the dining room."

Once they were seated, Mark spoke first.

"You mentioned that you watched the news tonight, so you know the incident today was the lead story on just about every newscast. Have either of you been contacted yet by any reporters?"

Mr. Gillespie replied, "No one has contacted us yet, but do you think that's a possibility?" he asked, looking at the sheriff.

Mick nodded at Mr. Gillespie.

"Yes, there is a high likelihood of that happening. But let me be clear—we will never release Kendra's name to the media. She's a victim of a violent crime and she's a juvenile. The media will not get her name from any member of the RCSO."

Mark jumped in, "The problem is there were lots of witnesses to what happened today. And the majority of those witnesses likely know Kendra, so it won't be a secret for very long. People talk and reporters will inquire. I'd be very surprised if reporters don't already have her name. I'm not saying this to scare you, but I think you should know, and at least have a plan for handling things if reporters begin knocking on your door."

"Jesus, that's just what we need," exhaled an irritated Mr. Gillespie.

Archer continued, "My primary assignment with the RCSO is to handle the media. I talk with reporters every day and I know most of them. If you'd like I can offer you my thoughts as to handling things once they reach out to you."

"Of course, we'd be grateful if you could help us with this," answered Mrs. Gillespie, looking at her husband, who nodded in agreement.

"Okay, well first off, you are under no obligation to speak to any reporters. Your daughter is a juvenile and is a victim in all this. So, they'll probably hound you for awhile but then things tend to cool off and they move onto the next story. However, this story could have legs, as they say, meaning it could take awhile for reporters to lose interest."

"Why is that?" asked Mr. Gillespie.

Mark hesitated for a few seconds before responding.

"Look, I don't mean to cause you any alarm, but this incident is already getting a lot of media attention. May I be brutally honest with you?"

"Of course, please do," replied both Mr. and Mrs. Gillespie.

Mark leaned in and lowered his voice, "As you know, the person that held your daughter hostage today is African American. Your daughter is obviously white. The deputy that shot the suspect is white. And I don't know if you are aware of this, but the deputy that very likely saved your daughter's life today is Sheriff McCallister's wife."

"Yes, we saw that on the newscasts. And from the bottom of our hearts, we know she saved our Kendra today. Sheriff, please thank your wife for us," answered Mrs. Gillespie.

"Thank you, I will let her know. She's having a very hard time with all this, as I'm sure you can imagine."

"I'd like to shake her hand, sheriff. She's a hero in my book."

It was clear that Mr. Gillespie didn't have much sympathy for Alex Washington. No one replied to the comment. It was understandable for the parent of a girl who had endured what Kendra had gone through to be bitter.

Mrs. Gillespie broke the silence, "So, what you're saying is that because Kendra is white and this guy was black the case will get a lot of attention?"

Mark replied, "Unfortunately, yes. And then you add to it that the deputy involved is married to Sheriff McCallister, and, well—it's going to get a lot of play."

"That's awful. I just want Kendra to get past all this and it sounds like that won't be easy."

"Another thing you need to be careful of is there are some unscrupulous reporters out there. They'll tell you one thing to get the story and then do something else. Not all reporters are like that, but there are a few. You need to be careful about who you speak to—that is, if you decide to speak about this at all."

"I say we just refuse to talk to anyone—that seems like the best approach," concluded Mr. Gillespie, still angry.

"That is one strategy. And it could work," Mark responded.

Mrs. Gillespie spoke up, "Is that what you'd recommend? I mean, are there other ways to handle this that might work better?"

"For Christ's sake, Rachel. We just shut them out. Screw the media—this is none of their business. We didn't ask to be in this position!"

Mrs. Gillespie responded calmly, "I understand that, Tom. But I want to make sure we handle this the right way and these gentlemen know more about this than we do."

Mark paused, waiting to see if Mr. Gillespie would respond to his wife's comments. Nothing. He saw his chance.

"Well, there is another way to handle this, but I'm hesitant to suggest it."

"What is it?" asked Mrs. Gillespie.

"Sometimes it can be helpful if you agree to do one interview—offer an exclusive to a specific reporter. If you agree to do that you can set the ground rules and they are obligated to follow them or you can just get up and walk out. It's not a perfect approach, but it usually works better than allowing any and all reporters access, or the other extreme—trying to keep every reporter at bay."

Mrs. Gillespie continued, "But who do we pick? I don't know any of these reporters. Is that something you could help us with, lieutenant?"

"Of course. I work with these people every day. I know who you can trust and who you have to keep an eye on. But you both need to be on the same page with this. And then you have to figure out who does the interview—do both of you do it? Is Kendra willing to talk to a reporter if you both are with her? These are all things that have to be considered . . . if you even want to do it this way. It's totally up to you."

"What do you think, Tom?"

It was clear to both Mark and Mick that Rachel Gillespie was on board with this approach. Tom was the issue.

Tom looked at his wife and slowly shook his head.

"I don't like it but given the circumstances, it may be the best thing we can do. The last thing we need is the media hounding us night and day. If this exclusive thing gets them off our back, then it's probably worth it."

Everyone looked at Mrs. Gillespie.

"Okay, let's do it."

CHAPTER 9

It was after eight by the time Mick returned home, and he found Mia and her dad talking in the living room. He walked in and immediately went to Mia, wrapping his arms around her. Neither spoke for a minute or so, and tears ran down Mia's cheeks.

"I am so sorry I wasn't there for you today. I hope you understand the position I was in."

"I know, Mick. Keller explained it to me. Don't worry about it."

"How are you doing?"

"I keep thinking I'm coming to grips with what happened and then ten minutes later I fall apart. It just seems so surreal to me."

"That's normal, Mia. It'll take some time, that's all. But remember—you saved that girl's life today."

"Maybe so, but I also took a life today and that'll be with me every day for the rest of my life."

Mick held her and the tears started again. Mick got choked up seeing his wife suffering. He hadn't known her when she went through the Columbine shooting but he knew she still had nightmares about it. He hoped the events of the day wouldn't have the same long-term effect on her.

He continued to hold her gently and spoke softly into her ear.

"I went over to the girl's house this evening. Her family is so grateful to you for saving her life today. They asked me to extend their deepest gratitude for what you did. They'll never forget your heroism."

Mia pulled away from the comfort of Mick's shoulder and looked at him.

"They really said that?"

"Absolutely. They're so grateful you were there."

"Well, that brings me some comfort. But I keep thinking—what if I hadn't run onto the campus? They told me to wait for backup, but I didn't. I was so scared that it would be Columbine all over again and I just couldn't let that happen."

"You did what you thought was best, Mia. You ran towards trouble when most people run away from it. That's law enforcement at its finest."

"But would Alex Washington be alive today if I had waited for backup?"

"We'll never know the answer to that question. But let me throw out a couple of possible outcomes if you hadn't run onto the campus today."

Mia looked up at her husband.

"First off, the deputies who did respond and set up a perimeter around the quad would have still done that. The news chopper would still have appeared and when the kid got rattled by that and made a sudden move while holding a gun to the girl's head, our deputies would have taken him out. If that had happened it would have been a much more chaotic scene, likely one with multiple shots being fired by multiple deputies, and the chances that the girl got hurt or killed would've gone up dramatically, not to mention innocent bystanders in the area. If bullets had started to fly it could have been disastrous."

Mia didn't say anything but she was taking it all in.

"Here's another scenario: the kid takes out the girl, then with nothing to lose he turns and fires on the other kids standing around the quad. He would probably get off a few shots before our deputies could take him out. Suicide by cop, but not before he exacts his revenge or anger or whatever it is that's motivating him."

Mia looked at her husband. Mick had gotten through to her.

"I guess it could have gone down that way, but we'll never know. But I can take some solace knowing that things could have been much worse."

"Exactly. You did the best you could given a very, very difficult situation. The family of that girl certainly thinks so. You need to keep that foremost in your mind."

"I know. I'll try to do that."

Mia changed the subject. "I'm almost afraid to ask, but what's the media coverage been like? I didn't want to turn on the news."

"Overall, it's been fine. Mark and I did a press conference from the campus this afternoon. I did release your name and inform the reporters that you're my wife."

Mia's eyes widened and suddenly the calm she was feeling seconds earlier vanished.

"You what?!"

"I made the decision to release your name. We would do it anyway in a few days, and I just wanted to get out in front of things and be totally up front about it. And the fact that you're my wife is an angle the media will likely play up. I just thought it was best to do it this way."

"Did you ever think of asking me?"

"There was no time, Mia. Mark and I were doing the press conference and I decided to release the information. It was going to come out anyway, and it's better that we put it out there rather than having some reporter figuring it out and then making a big story about it. I thought it was for the best, and so did Mark."

"You should have told me, Mick!"

"Look, I'm sorry Mia. But now it's out there and people can begin to move past it. I really think it was the right thing to do. I didn't mean to upset you."

Mia took a moment and considered what her husband was saying. Maybe it was best to release the information right away. It was just a surprise to learn that her identity was publicly known. She suddenly imagined thousands of people talking about her, judging her for the actions she had taken that day in the quad. It was a very uncomfortable feeling.

"I guess you're right. It's just that I feel like my privacy has been invaded."

"I also confirmed that you're pregnant."

Mia glared at her husband, "And why exactly did you tell them that?"

"Because a reporter from Channel Two asked me directly if you were pregnant. I guess she saw you before we got you in the patrol car."

"That's great, Mick . . . just great. I'm going to bed."

CHAPTER 10

After working out a media strategy with the Gillespies, Mark Archer made the thirty-minute drive to downtown Denver. He found a parking space and walked to the luxury high-rise apartment building adjacent to Coors Field. He rode the elevator to the twenty-eighth floor and was soon knocking on the door of unit 2830.

The door swung open and Archer walked in.

"Rough day, huh?"

"Yeah, you could say that."

Angela Bell stood in the entry of her apartment and gave her boyfriend a quick kiss.

"Come on in. I'll pour you a drink."

"Thanks."

As they walked to the kitchen, Angela turned to Mark and said, "For the record, I thought you and the sheriff handled a difficult situation very well today. And the sheriff coming clean about Mia being the shooter and her being pregnant was a very good move. Nothing whets a reporter's appetite more than a government official who appears to be hiding something. You guys did well to make a preemptive strike."

"Yeah, I give a lot of credit to Mick. Better just to take his medicine and get it over with. I really feel for him, but I especially feel bad for Mia. I'm not sure you know this, but Mia was a teacher in her former life. At Columbine. She was there the day of the massacre."

"She was at Columbine? I had no idea," Angela replied, handing Mark a glass containing an inch of very expensive whiskey.

"Yeah, Mia was in the library where a lot of the carnage took place. She saved several kids by huddling them out of harm's way. But she also witnessed a lot of what went down. She left the school that day and never returned. She applied at RCSO and we hired her almost immediately. Been with us ever since."

"Oh my God, that poor woman. And now this happens—on a school campus, no less."

Mark, looking haggard, took a long sip from his glass.

"I haven't had a chance to look at very much of the news coverage today. In your estimation, how was it?"

"It was the lead story everywhere, and the newspapers all had it at the top of their webpages. Overall, I think you did well, but we did do a live remote from the high school tonight. Not sure if you know, but there were some people out there holding signs that weren't exactly complimentary of the RCSO."

"Yeah, I did manage to catch that. Mick saw it, too. He wasn't pleased."

"I can only imagine. Your department being portrayed in a negative light, then add the fact that it's your wife who did the shooting, and she's seven months pregnant. Mick's had better days, no doubt."

"Hopefully the sentiment expressed on those signs doesn't spread. I know there will be people who try to turn this into a race thing, but Mia saved that girl's life today. I hope the media doesn't lose sight of that."

Angela gave Mark a little smile. "Duly noted."

"It's not you I'm worried about."

Mark thought about the reporter at the press conference who asked about Mia being pregnant.

"What do you know about Denise Elliott at Channel Two?"

"I know she's very aggressive. She's beaten us on a fair number of stories so we keep an eye on her. Why do you ask?"

"She picked up on Mia being pregnant. I don't think Mick was planning on mentioning it at the press conference, but when Elliott brought it up Mick did the right thing and confirmed it. To me, that information is borderline none-of-your-business, but it's going to come out eventually, so why not come clean with it?"

"Could the attorney that'll no doubt be hired by Alex Washington's family make it a fit for duty kind of issue? Can they say that Mia shouldn't have been working in a dangerous profession during the late stages of pregnancy?"

"Well, I suppose he could try. But it would be a boneheaded move— you'd have every female and a lot of males up in arms at such a sexist comment."

"Yeah, that's true."

"Hey, there's something else I want to run by you."

"Sure, what is it?"

Mark moved his glass in circles, staring at the whiskey as it swirled around.

"The sheriff and I paid a visit to Alex Washington's home today and after that we went to the home of the family of the young girl taken hostage."

"And how'd that go?"

"A mixed bag, as you'd expect. The visit to Washington's family was tough and we weren't exactly offered a warm welcome. We never got in the house to speak to the young man's mother; we were headed off in the yard by the his uncle."

"That's pretty understandable, they lost their seventeen year old today. And at the hands of the police and then you guys show up. I know what you were trying to do, but I'm not at all surprised that there was no welcome mat."

"Yeah, we weren't really surprised either, but we felt it was worth a try. What concerns us the most wasn't the uncle—he actually seemed pretty reasonable. It was the kid's cousin. His name is Jaquon. He confronted us in the yard and got in our faces pretty good. Threw down gang signs—the whole nine yards. A total dumbass."

"Okay, so you guys got reamed. No big deal. You deal with assholes all day every day."

"Speaking of assholes, during your newscast tonight you did a live shot from the quad. Your reporter showed the people marching around and one of the shots was a close-up of a couple of people carrying signs that were anti-RCSO."

"That's not unusual in police shootings."

"Yeah, well one of the people carrying a sign was none other than Jaquon. I have no doubt that the guy is a major shit stirrer and he's going to turn this into a race thing."

Angela nodded.

He continued, "You know the drill. The fury over these shootings is often fueled by people with their own agendas. I don't want that to happen here. And I suspect that there will be an effort by Jaquon and others of his ilk to do exactly that. And the family of Alex Washington, Jaquon included, are going to go after every penny they can get their hands on from the RCSO."

"Well, that's to be expected. Have you ever seen a case where the family doesn't sue?"

"Nope. But my concerns with this case aren't about money. It's public perception and ultimately public safety. If these idiots decide to make this into a racial thing and paint all cops as racist, then this is going to get really ugly."

"So, I guess we'll just have to wait and see what happens," Angela sighed.

"On a positive note, the visit to the family of the young girl went much better. They, of course, see us as heroes."

"How's the girl doing?"

"Pretty traumatized, but physically okay. Her parents are pretty shaken, understandably. I mean, you send your daughter off to school in the morning, just another day, and then this happens?"

"I can't even imagine."

Neither Angela nor Mark had children, but they both shuddered at the thought of what the Gillespies were going through.

"Mick and I talked with the Gillespies about the potential fallout from the shooting. They know Mia saved their daughter's life today and they don't want the RCSO to take it in the shorts."

"Not much they can do about that, really."

"They don't want their daughter's story to get lost in all the noise. That's a big concern of theirs."

Angela looked at Mark for a moment. "Do you think there would be any interest in them telling their side of the story? Maybe an exclusive interview where they could express their feelings?"

Bingo, thought Mark.

"I'm not sure, but I could ask them. Would this exclusive interview be with anyone I know?" he asked playfully.

Angela smiled. "I think I could be of service."

"They're pretty spooked and the dad especially has a suspicious nature when it comes to reporters. It would have to be handled the right way."

"I could make that happen. We could lay out ground rules with them ahead of time so they'd be comfortable with everything. Do you think we could get the daughter on camera?"

"That may be difficult. I could ask, but there's no guarantee."

"I understand, although it would give her a chance to tell her side of the story. She's the real victim in all this, and I would ensure that's highlighted in a big way."

"Well, all I can do is ask. Let me call them in the morning and see how they're feeling about everything If I can get them to agree to do it, I think the sooner we get it done the better."

Angela leaned in and gave Mark a little kiss.

"Absolutely. Thanks, Mark. I appreciate it."

CHAPTER 11

Mick gave Mia some time to cool off before he made his way to their bedroom. He understood she was very frustrated, confused, and afraid, and he needed her to know that he was on her side. He knew the coming days wouldn't be easy and Mia needed to understand what was going to happen. He also knew he needed to be careful about what the two talked when it came to the shooting. As the sheriff he wore one hat, but as a husband he wore another. The lines appeared very blurred to him, but one thing he was sure of—his wife came before the job.

As he walked into their bedroom he found Mia lying on top of the comforter with her head on the pillow. A pile of crumpled tissues covered the bed. She made no effort to look at him when he walked in. He sat at the edge of the bed and stroked her back. After a few minutes she turned and looked at him.

"Mick, do you understand why I'm angry?"

"I think so. You feel like no one's in your court, not even your husband."

"Exactly. Do you know what I went through today with all the interviews? They took my blood, my urine, treated me like a criminal. It was humiliating."

"I understand. But it's standard in officer-involved shootings and it'll benefit you in the long run. Your blood and urine will come back clean, and your statements to investigators will show that you feared for the girl's life. You were in an untenable position and you did what you had to do. I have no doubt that your actions will be deemed both lawful and within department policy. But it's a process, Mia—you know that. These things take time."

"I know, I know. But my God, I feel like I'm standing all alone in this. And then you tell me you have already named me as the deputy involved and told the world that I'm seven months pregnant."

"I understand. But take a minute and look at this from my position. We typically release the name of the deputy within a couple of days of the shooting. I didn't hold off this time for two reasons—a Denver reporter had already figured out it was you and knew you were pregnant. She asked me specifically about it at the press conference. You know I'm not going to lie, and you being pregnant is not something that we can really hide. Anyway, it's ultimately a non-issue. Second, if I didn't release your name today we would have people saying I was trying to cover it up. Now I know that doesn't make much sense, but we can't afford to have that perception out there. This is going to be difficult enough, so I wanted to be totally above board from the very start."

"What you're saying makes sense in my mind, but it still hurts. I can't help how I feel. It'll just take some time to process all of it and adjust to the reality that this happened."

"You need to focus on the girl whose life you saved today. You aren't responsible for Alex Washington's actions. You did your job and you did it well."

Mick felt the cell phone on his belt vibrate. He glanced down at the screen and saw that it was the watch commander's office.

"Hey, Jim, what's up?"

"Sheriff, we have a problem."

"What is it?"

"We've got several hundred people now at Wilson High School and they're getting pretty unruly. I'm getting reports from my sergeant on scene that several cars have been lit on fire. Someone tossed a Molotov cocktail into one of the classrooms and it's fully involved. Fire personnel are responding."

"Hold on a second, Jim."

Mick covered the mouthpiece on his cell and turned to Mia. "I've gotta go into the office. Try to get some sleep."

Mia nodded, too tired to ask why her husband had to go into work.

Mick slipped into the hallway and resumed his conversation.

"How many deputies do we have on scene?"

"Currently a dozen, but I've called for mutual aid and am expecting another forty personnel any minute."

"Good. Will the mutual aid be responding in riot gear?"

"Yes, sir."

"Good. We're going to send a very clear message tonight. Did you call Mark Archer and let him know?"

"I've left him a message and I've texted him but so far haven't had any response. I'll keep trying."

"Okay, I'm on my way."

⁓

Mick made the drive to Woodrow Wilson High School in less than five minutes. Once there he made contact with Fire Battalion Chief Kami Power.

"Give me the latest, chief."

"Fire personnel arrived about ten ago and they're making short work of the fire in the classroom. But the fire did spread to another classroom so we have two classrooms that are pretty much a total loss."

Mick looked out over the scene. The crowd, while vocal, was behaving. The mutual aid response was in place and doing a good job keeping things in check.

But as he was assessing the situation he saw someone in the middle of the crowd trying to incite the crowd, leading a chant. "Pigs in a blanket, fry 'em like bacon! Pigs in a blanket, fry 'em like bacon!"

Mick walked toward the group to get a closer look. Sure enough, the person leading the chant was Jaquon. This guy is going to be a major pain in the ass, thought Mick. He looked directly at Jaquon and they locked eyes. Realizing he had the attention of the sheriff, Jaquon changed the chant.

"Hey, hey, ho, ho, killer cops have got to go! Hey, hey, ho, ho, killer cops have got to go!"

Mick stared him down and watched as Jaquon, using his thumb and index finger, mimicked a gun and pulled the trigger. Then he turned directly toward Mick and mouthed, *Payback's a bitch.*

Mick instinctively began to move toward Jaquon, then thought better of it. This was not the time or the place.

As he stared out at Jaquon his attention was diverted by the voice of Chief Power calling out for him.

"Sheriff, we have a reporter on scene. They just parked their satellite truck and they're headed this way."

Mick looked toward the direction Power was pointing and could see Denise Elliott from Channel Two walking toward him.

"Sheriff McCallister, can we do a quick live interview with you on camera?" she asked.

Normally, Archer would handle these interviews, but he was nowhere to be found. Mick felt a live onscene interview would be an opportunity to send a clear message.

"Sure, where do you want to do it?"

"Right where you are, if that works for you."

Mick figured Elliott would want to do the live shot from that spot to include the crowd in the background, adding a feeling of controversy to the story. At first Mick was tempted to move the interview, but he wanted the viewers to see the damage caused by the protesters.

"This is fine, Denise."

"Great, sheriff. We really appreciate this."

Elliott's videographer clipped a mic to the sheriff's shirt and did a quick sound check. Within thirty seconds they were ready to roll. The anchor at Channel Two threw it to Elliott.

"Jackie, I'm on the campus of Woodrow Wilson High School in Castle Springs, where earlier today a violent confrontation ended with the death of a seventeen-year-old student at the hands of a Rocklin County sheriff's deputy. A large crowd is gathered here and the demonstration has turned violent. I'm here with Mick McCallister, sheriff of Rocklin County. Sheriff, thanks for joining us. What can you tell us at this time?"

"Our deputies were called to the scene after getting reports of a large, unruly crowd gathered here on campus. When we arrived we found several cars on fire in the parking lot as well as at least one classroom fully engulfed. Rocklin County Fire along with Castle Springs Fire responded and were able to extinguish the fire pretty quickly."

"Any injuries reported?"

"None that I'm aware of."

"Any arrests at this point?"

"No, but I fully expect some will be forthcoming. We will sort things out and determine who set fire to the cars and the classrooms. Those individuals will be arrested and will face appropriate charges."

"Sheriff, the lawlessness displayed here tonight is clearly related to the shooting earlier today. There are people here carrying signs highly critical of the RCSO. What do you say to them and to the community in general?"

"The tragic events that took place earlier today are being fully investigated. I have asked the Denver PD to come in and work with Rocklin County DA personnel. The residents of Rocklin County can rest assured that this investigation will be fair and totally above board."

Elliott continued, "Right now the crowd behind us is peaceful, but just a short time ago they were anything but. What would you like to say to those gathered here?"

Mick glanced over his shoulder then turned back to Elliott. "People have a right to assemble and express themselves as long as they don't break any laws. If they don't break the law we shouldn't have any problems going forward. But let me be clear—those who act outside the law will be dealt with quickly and will feel the full impact of the criminal justice system. We have zero tolerance for those who assemble for the purpose of being violent or destructive."

"Thank you, sheriff. Now back to you, Jackie."

With the interview over, Mick turned back to the crowd. There was Jaquon, smirking at him and throwing down 120th Street gang signs.

Angela and Mark had just finished a short but enthusiastic love-making session and were both lying in bed exhausted. Mark rolled over, grabbed his phone off the nightstand, and saw both the text and missed call from Jim Bailey.

"Shit. Turn on the TV. Channel Two."

Angela grabbed the remote and turned it to Channel Two.

"Ah, crap. Channel Two is doing a live remote from the high school. Looks like some major shit has been going down. And there's your boss on camera with Denise Elliott."

"Turn it up!" answered Archer.

Angela adjusted the volume but the interview was over and the anchor was already moving on to the next story. She and Mark sat on the edge of the bed, staring at the screen and trying to figure out what was happening on the campus. Angela flipped to Channel Eight to see if they were covering the situation at the school. The weather girl was busy discussing an upcoming storm.

Angela tossed the remote on the bed, frustrated.

Mark grabbed his phone and sent a text to the sheriff. At the same time Angela put together her own text asking her news producer how they missed the story. They sat and waited. A minute later, Mark's phone rang.

"Sheriff, I just caught the tail end of the Channel Two news story. How'd it go?"

"It was a shitstorm out here, but things have calmed down. Bailey should have called you; not sure how that breakdown happened. There's just one reporter, and as you saw, I handled the interview. Now that word is out I expect a flood of reporters to show up."

Archer dodged the comment about Bailey calling him. He could find an excuse if it came up again. He moved the conversation along. "It's ten thirty and all the newscasts are wrapping up so it's too late for them to get there. But tomorrow morning we'll get bombarded with media wanting the story. It'll go statewide, at least. I'll go in tonight and put together a press release so we can have it first thing in the morning."

"Sergeant Huber is on scene. Check with him for details. I'll let him know you'll be calling."

"Sounds good. Hey, how's Mia doing?'

"She's still pretty shaken. I talked to her a little bit tonight but then had to come out here to the high school. I told her to get some sleep and that we'd talk again in the morning."

"Give her my best. Talk to you tomorrow."

When Mick returned home he found Mia sound asleep. On the bathroom counter he saw an open pill container. He was surprised to see that it was Ambien, something he had never noticed before in the medicine cabinet. He picked up the container and read the label. It was a prescription written for Mia eighteen months earlier. The expiration date had passed, but just by a month. He thought about the baby and hoped Ambien wasn't harmful to an unborn fetus. But he knew Mia was very careful about what she put in her body during her pregnancy; having her first child at the age of forty-two had made her very conscientious.

With that in mind, he took a shower and went to bed.

CHAPTER 12

As Mark Archer predicted, the phone in his office began ringing very early. By six thirty he had already received five requests for interviews regarding the violence at Wilson High School the night before. Every morning news show in Denver had called. He managed to get all five scheduled before eight o'clock. He studied the press release he had written the night before, glad that he had taken the time to come into the station. The release covered all the basics about the events on campus occurring the night before. It included some strong language about the RCSO having zero tolerance for this type of criminal behavior. Mark had learned from the fire department that the two classrooms were a total loss, with damages estimated at more than a half million dollars, to be paid with funds from Rocklin County taxpayers. Throwing in the taxpayer angle always got people riled up, so it was mentioned near the top of the release. He needed to get people incensed by what a handful of unruly protesters had done to the only high school in Castle Springs, and it would be a point he'd be sure to hammer home in all his interviews.

When Mick awoke in the morning he found Mia was still sleeping. It appeared as though she hadn't moved all night. He had never taken

Ambien before, but had heard enough stories to know it was a very powerful sleep aid. At least she'll be rested, he thought, since she was going to have another very difficult day. He took a quick shower, and when Mia was still asleep when he got out, he decided to let her be. He made his way downstairs and found Chuck in the kitchen.

"Good morning, Mick. How's Mia doing?"

"Still asleep. I think I'll let her go for awhile. She needs the rest."

"Did she have a rough night?"

"She did in the beginning, but then I got called out. When I got back, which was a little after eleven, she was out like a light."

"I'm surprised. She was pretty upset last night."

Mick looked at his father-in-law and wondered if he should mention the Ambien. After a moment he decided to go for it.

"Evidently, she took an Ambien after I went in to work. I didn't even know she had a prescription for that."

Chuck replied, "I remember her doctor prescribed it for her after the two of you broke off your engagement. It helped her get through a rough patch. I don't think she's taken any for a long time, at least not that she's mentioned to me."

Mick thought back to their engagement. He had broken it off after discovering Mia had been keeping a secret from him—the fact that Jack Keller was Lisa Sullivan's father. Sullivan had been implicated a couple of years prior in a homicide, ultimately turning state's evidence against her married lover in exchange for no prison time. The decision, made by DA Dave Baxter, had been a controversial one. It took a long time for Mick to get past Mia's lack of candor, but soon they realized they couldn't stay apart.

"I didn't know any of that."

"I think she's fine now, or at least she was until yesterday."

"Look, this is going to be really hard for her and I don't want to be surprised by anything. Keep an eye on her; you may see things that I miss. We need to be on the same page."

"Of course. I'll watch her like a hawk. So, what's next?"

"Well, first off, she's on paid administrative leave. That's standard in all police shootings. We'll get some static for that; we always do. Many people think an officer should be immediately fired or at least punished after a shooting. Of course, a person is innocent until proven otherwise so paid leave is the right thing to do in these cases. Not to mention it's state law."

"Makes sense to me."

"But I'll be honest with you, Chuck—this is probably going to get pretty ugly."

"Why? Mia saved that girl's life yesterday. Won't people focus on that?"

"Most will, but there will be a vocal few that will be outraged. A white deputy shooting and killing a black teenager provides them with an opportunity to act out. Some will be so blinded by anger they won't be able to think straight. And they'll make this into a racial thing, conveniently ignoring the facts of the case. They have an agenda and they'll use this case to further that agenda."

"But who will listen to them? Are people really that gullible?"

"The media will jump all over this, and that fans the flames. Reporters like controversy and those vocal few I mentioned will stoke the fires of hate. After a while the media will get tired of this case and move on to the next controversy. But until that happens the heat on Mia and the RCSO could get pretty intense."

"What BS."

"As Mark Archer likes to say, 'The media is more interested in creating heat than shedding light.' There's a lot of truth to that, so we'll just have to deal with it. My callout last night was to the Wilson High School campus. We had a few hundred people out there protesting the shooting. Things got pretty ugly and they torched a couple classrooms, plus several cars."

"Oh my God."

The seriousness of the situation gripped Chuck. He had intentionally avoided the news the night before. He grew very concerned for his daughter.

Mick continued, "There will be more bullshit. I don't mean to alarm you, but I think you should know what to expect. It could help you with Mia."

"Go ahead, tell me everything. I need to know."

"Mia will be interviewed again today by investigators with both the DA's office and Denver PD."

"Why Denver PD? It happened in Castle Springs."

"I've asked them to do the investigation because I want it to be completely above board. If we do it, then those vocal few I mentioned could accuse us of whitewashing the whole thing. It eliminates, as much as possible, the argument that the police shouldn't investigate their own."

"But Mia didn't do anything wrong!"

"No, she didn't. But there may be a bit of criticism of her actions when critics say she should have waited for backup. And that she shouldn't have been so quick to fire her weapon on Washington."

Chuck looked exasperated. "But she only had a split second to try to figure out what he was doing!"

"Yep, and any reasonable person would have done the exact same thing. But there will be no shortage of opinions out there—she should have shot the gun out of this hand, or she should have shot him in the leg . . . all of which are not within the policy of the RCSO or any other police agency for that matter. Not to mention that it's virtually impossible to do those things in a situation like the one she faced yesterday."

"People watch way too much TV."

"Yeah, but Tom Cruise or Bruce Willis can do that, they'll say. But if you shoot the guy in the leg, he puts a bullet in that girl's skull. Or he fires off a few rounds while he falls to the ground and hits a couple of kids standing there in the quad. You have to shoot to kill in that situation. There are no other choices."

Chuck responded, "And if she had shot him in the leg and he then killed the girl, everyone would be saying she was a lousy shot and that she should have taken him out."

"Exactly. This is what law enforcement faces in virtually every police shooting that takes place in our nation."

"It sucks."

"Yes, it does. And then, besides all the public scrutiny, the RCSO will get sued. Mia will likely get sued, and I will certainly be sued. That also happens in pretty much every police shooting."

"Why would they sue you?"

"Because I'm the sheriff and the attorneys will say I've created an atmosphere that encourages this type of behavior from the deputies in the RCSO."

"Oh my God, that's ridiculous."

"It's our reality. Don't get me wrong—there are police shootings that aren't proper and in those cases the agency should be held to answer. But this is not one of those cases."

"And Mia can get sued?"

"Yes, but the county will provide her defense. It'll be long and drawn out and certainly won't be a pleasant experience. There will be depositions and possibly a trial. But most times these kinds of cases are settled out of court."

"But why settle out of court if she didn't do anything wrong?"

"It's typically just a financial decision. Generally it's cheaper to offer a sum of money to the family than deal with the expense of a trial. Attorneys are expensive and a case like this, if taken all the way to trial, could easily cost the county a couple million dollars or more. Then you run the risk of losing at trial—you never know about juries—and if things go wrong the county could be writing an even larger check. I've seen it happen."

"But Mia didn't do anything wrong—she saved that girl's life!"

"True, but like I said, it's just cheaper to settle most times. I don't know what'll happen in this case, but I can guarantee you that the family will sue. It'll be a wrongful death claim and they'll ask for millions."

Chuck just shook his head. He was getting quite an education.

Both men looked up when they heard a voice coming from the doorway. "What are you guys talking about?"

The men looked up and saw Mia slowly walking into the kitchen. She was a bit unsteady on her feet.

"Hey, Mia, how're you feeling?" asked Chuck.

"Like my world has been turned upside down."

Mick moved toward his wife and wrapped his arms around her.

"I know, sweetie, I know."

"Where did you go last night? I didn't hear you come in."

Mick looked at his wife and thought about dodging the question, but he knew she would find out soon enough.

"There were some people who showed up at the high school last night and they caused some damage. We responded and broke it up."

She pulled away from Mick's embrace. "They were there because of the shooting?"

"Yes, a few knuckleheads who were looking for an excuse to be assholes. We got things under control pretty quickly. It didn't last long."

"Great," she responded. "Just what I wanted to hear. How bad was the damage?"

Mick gave it to her straight. "A few cars were torched and they started a fire in the school. Two classrooms were destroyed."

Mia began to get weak in the knees. Mick helped her to a chair at the kitchen table.

"My God, this is like a bad dream that I can't wake up from."

"Mia, we'll get past this. It'll just take some time."

Chuck took a seat next to his daughter and grabbed her hand. He held it tightly.

"Honey, I hate to see you go through this, but I will be with you every minute of the day. We'll get through it, I promise."

She looked at her dad and put her head on his shoulder. It was apparent that some of the Ambien was still in her system.

"What time are you scheduled for your interviews today?" Mick asked his wife.

"I'm supposed to be there at ten. They told me it could take all day."

"A legal defense attorney will be provided to you by the deputies' union. Did they tell you about that?"

"Yeah, he was there yesterday. He told me to tell the investigators they couldn't talk to anyone until he arrived. You'll never guess who they sent."

"Who?"

"Danny Velasco. I had no idea he was on contract with the union."

"Neither did I," replied Mick.

"He was really good. I like Danny."

"Yeah, you could do worse. Just do everything he says and he'll represent you well," answered Mick.

Mia and Danny were acquaintances, but this was the first time they were on the same side, so to speak. As a prominent defense attorney in Denver, Danny had represented many clients who had been arrested by the RCSO. Most noteworthy among these cases had been the Lombard murder case which had gone to trial the year before. Velasco had represented Lisa Sullivan, an accomplice in what was the most publicized homicide case in the history of Rocklin County. He had worked a deal for her—she turned state's evidence against her former lover Scott Lennox, the mastermind behind the murder, in exchange for no jail time. It was a masterful move by Velasco and one that infuriated the RCSO, Mia included. But Velasco was just doing his job and the past would be put aside for now. Mia felt fortunate to have him representing her.

"I better get ready to go in," said Mia.

As she stood, she asked her husband, "Will I see you at all today?"

"Probably not. Technically we shouldn't be talking about what happened yesterday. And in reality, we haven't. But at the station we need to be above reproach so let's avoid any contact. People will be watching."

Mia looked blankly at her husband.

Mick turned to his father-in-law. "Get some food and coffee in her, Chuck."

"I will, don't worry."

CHAPTER 13

M ick left for the station, contemplating the challenge before him. He dialed Archer's number.

"Good morning, boss."

"So how's the media coverage of last night's incident at the school? Are you getting a lot of calls?"

"Yeah, I've done three interviews so far and I've got two more in the next thirty minutes."

"Any issues so far?"

"Not really. The reporters I've spoken to today have all been pretty good, pretty positive. When a couple of classrooms go up in flames the media is always going to play up that angle. Two of the reporters didn't even ask me about the reason for the protest, and no one mentioned the anti-RCSO signs."

"Good, but I don't expect to our luck to last long. Wait until Washington's family gets their smear campaign rolling. My bet is that they'll have an attorney by lunchtime today."

"No doubt. Are you on your way in?"

"Yeah, I'm about five out. Hey, do me a favor—contact Sergeant Cameo Tougas in the gang unit and have her see what she can dig up on our new buddy, Jaquon. I want to find out his story."

"Will do, boss."

"Thanks. See you soon."

Alex Washington's home was crowded with family members. Most had spent the night, grieving their loss. A half dozen cars were parked on the lawn and several more were parked illegally on the street in front.

Alex's mom, thirty-one-year old Danesha Washington, was still asleep, thanks to the Ambien her sister had brought to the house. Her older brother Floyd Liston was in the kitchen, helping to cook breakfast for those gathered at the house. The mood was tense and angry.

Liston was unaware that his nephew Jaquon had slipped out of the house and gone to Wilson High School the night before. He hadn't caught the Channel Two news at ten showing the destroyed cars and classrooms and the crowd that had gathered to protest. Jaquon had been questioned by police at the campus but with no hard evidence that he had set the fires, they had to let him go. They warned him that they would be looking closely at the campus security video and if it showed him playing a role in the violence they'd be back for him. What investigators didn't tell him was they really didn't know if such video existed. It was something the RCSO would actively pursue that day, but even if there were cameras, oftentimes they weren't operational; they were just there to serve as a deterrent.

As Liston was dishing out plates of scrambled eggs and toast, the doorbell rang. He didn't move to answer it; there were plenty of other people in the house who could tend to a visitor. Probably another family member coming to pay their respects.

"Floyd, there's a minister here to see Danesha. What should I tell him?"

Liston looked up at his brother-in-law.

"A minister? Did he tell you his name?"

"Yeah, Alvie something. You wanna talk to him?"

Liston didn't respond at first, considering carefully what his brother-in-law was telling him.

"Tell him I'll be with him in a minute."

The Reverend Alvie Rollins was a well-known African-American minister in Denver. He was revered by many in the black community and was thought to be a man of the people who represented those without a voice. He spoke out for the downtrodden, those poor souls who were taken advantage of by people in power, especially if those poor souls happened to be black. He had made his name on cable television, starting out with a rather amateurish show on public access, broadcasting from his small church in a tough east-Denver neighborhood. But the cable show had allowed him to gain a following and after a few years he was able to move to a larger church. He was a master with the media and knew exactly how to deliver a powerful sound bite. Colorful and dynamic, reporters loved him.

Liston washed his hands and moved to the living room. "I'm Floyd Liston. Can I help you?"

"Mr. Liston, my name is Alvie Rollins and I would like to speak to the mother of the poor young man who was gunned down by the police yesterday."

"That would be Danesha, but she's asleep right now. Is there something I can help you with?"

"Perhaps . . . are you related to the young man?"

"Alex was my nephew. Danesha is my sister."

Rollins looked around the crowded room.

"Very well. Is there somewhere we can talk?"

"Sure, we can go down to the basement."

Liston led Rollins downstairs and they took seats on an old sofa.

"What can I do for you?"

Rollins looked at Liston, sizing him up.

"Mr. Liston—may I call you Floyd?'

"Sure."

"Floyd, I'm a minister with a church in Denver and—"

"I know who you are, reverend. What I'm wondering is why you're here."

"I'll get right to the point. I am very concerned about the murder of your nephew and I want to offer you my help as your family is subjected to the chicanery of a very rigged criminal justice system. A system that is steeped in racism—something you are about to experience firsthand, I'm afraid. I believe I could be of some assistance to you and your family as you traverse the rocky path to justice."

"That's quite a speech there, reverend."

"I beg your pardon?"

"I don't think we'll be needing any assistance from you, but thanks for coming by," Liston responded, rising to his feet.

"But Mr. Liston, you're making a big mistake. You need my help, or you'll be taken advantage of by—"

Liston quickly interrupted, "I didn't ask you to come here, nor did my sister. My nephew isn't even in the ground yet and here you are, trying to make inroads with my family."

"Mr. Liston, I assure you my intentions are honorable. I have seen these kinds of situations more times than I can count. The wheels of injustice turn quickly and the police will do their best to sweep this tragedy under the rug."

"Reverend, do you even know what happened yesterday on that campus?"

"I've listened closely to news reports and I know that a deputy shot and killed a seventeen-year-old boy. I know that law enforcement kills an inordinate number of black people in this nation and something needs to be done. I don't want your nephew to be just another statistic. You and your family have an opportunity here—you can help us stop these needless deaths of our brothers and sisters. And I can help you do that."

"We don't know the whole story of what happened yesterday at the high school, so I'll need to know exactly what occurred before jumping on your bandwagon. Don't get me wrong, reverend—I understand what you're trying to do, and I'm not saying it isn't important or that my nephew's case is somehow different. The police may have killed my nephew needlessly, but just because a young black teenager was killed yesterday doesn't necessarily mean it was racism. I'm not willing to rush to judgment nor will I paint any group, police included, with such a broad brush. Especially one where race is the basis for everything."

"Mr. Liston, I have little doubt that if your nephew was white he'd be alive today. The deputy would have found a way to bring the situation to a peaceful conclusion. But this doesn't often happen when the person involved is African American. Those of color aren't offered the same benefit of the doubt, so to speak."

"I guess you and I have a different view of the world. I understand that racism exists today, but things today are better than at any time during my life. We had a black president for God's sake, and the opportunities for people of color are better than ever. The fact that many of my fellow African Americans don't take advantage of those opportunities might be something you could spend your time on and try to change. That might actually do some good."

Reverend Rollins looked long and hard at Liston. He didn't expect to encounter someone in Washington's family with these beliefs and he realized that he would need to bypass Liston and get directly to Alex's mother. That's where he could make some real inroads.

Rollins stood. "Very well, Mr. Liston. Thank you for your time."

∽

Mark Archer was returning emails from reporters when Mick stuck his head in his office.

"Let's get together and talk strategy for today. I want to stay ahead of this thing."

"Okay, give me a couple of minutes to finish up and I'll come to your office."

Mick left Archer's office and walked down the hall to his office where he was greeted by Lucinda, his administrative assistant.

"Good morning, sheriff. The phone has been ringing off the hook this morning. I made a list of all the callers and emailed it to you. Let me know what I can do to help."

"Thanks, Lucinda. It's going to be a crazy day."

"How's Mia doing?"

"She's hanging in there. Thanks for asking."

Mick opened his email account and read the list Lucinda had put together. Half a dozen reporters calling for a comment from him, a call from the chief administrative officer, or CAO, for Rocklin County, as well as a call from the chairman of the board of supervisors for the county. He could refer the reporters to Archer but he knew he'd have to return the calls from the two county officials. He could already predict their concerns. The CAO would be worried about the lawsuit from Washington's family that was sure to come and the chairman of the board, an elected official, would be concerned about potential political fallout from the shooting.

Archer walked into Mick's office and took a seat.

"Just looking at my messages from this morning. I'm going to need you to handle the media calls. I want to keep my distance from the press right now."

"Okay, no problem. Just forward them to me. Who else have you heard from?"

"The usual calls from our politicos. Worried about money and their political reputations, no doubt."

"Happens every time."

"Like clockwork. Did you talk to Angela about doing an interview with the Gillespies?"

"I did, and she's totally onboard with it."

"Great, and with what happened last night we should have a sympathetic public. People don't like thugs burning down classrooms. Let's hammer that point home today and get the Gillespies on camera. Maybe we can quell this thing before it gets going any more."

Archer continued, "I'll make it happen. I was also thinking that we should get some cell phone footage of the shooting. With a couple hundred kids witnessing it you gotta believe there are plenty of recordings of the whole thing. We can edit it so it doesn't show the actual shooting but we can show how Washington spun around and why Mia had to believe the girl's life was in danger."

Mick thought about what Mark was saying. "Let's hold off for now. Hopefully we won't need to do that. I don't want to vilify the kid."

"All right, but I'll check with investigators to see if they have footage that would work for us, just in case we need it later."

"That's fine. And we need to see what the autopsy shows today. Was this kid high? Was he on prescription drugs? Alcohol? We need to find out what set him off."

"I did speak to Jack Keller yesterday and he told me, preliminarily, that it looked like Washington was pissed off at the young lady for not wanting to be his girlfriend. There were text messages between the two prior to the shooting. An unrequited-love type thing."

"Wouldn't be the first time."

"Nope. I'll get busy returning your calls and get things moving with the Gillespie interview."

"Okay, thanks."

Mark returned to his office and called Angela on her cell. She answered on the first ring.

"Hey, Mark, I just got to my office. Can we set up the Gillespie interview today?"

"That's why I'm calling. What's your availability?"

"I'm anchoring at noon so anytime after one thirty or so. My producer wants to make it the lead at five, six, and ten. Wants to hit it hard."

It was just what Mark hoped to hear. "Okay, I'll call them right now and get a feel for what they want to do. You'll come to their home, correct?"

"Of course, whatever makes them feel most comfortable. And we really want the girl, Mark. The parents are good, but the girl is gold."

"I know. I'll do what I can."

Mark dialed the Gillespie home and Rachel answered.

"Good morning, Mrs. Gillespie, this is Lieutenant Archer calling. How are you all doing this morning?"

"Hello, lieutenant. We're holding up pretty well. Kendra had her friends spend the night and I think that had a real calming affect on her. She seems to be doing okay, thank God."

"That's great to hear. Listen, yesterday we mentioned the possibility of having you and Mr. Gillespie, along with Kendra, speak to a reporter about what happened. I've spoken to Angela Bell at Channel Eight and she's on board to do the interview personally. She was hoping to—"

Gillespie cut him off, "Well, there's been a change in plans, I'm afraid. I spoke again to my husband last night and he's really not comfortable doing this. I'm sorry, but I think we'll have to pass on the interview."

Shit. He'd really thought he had them onboard. He shifted to a sympathetic gear.

"I understand, Mrs. Gillespie. I just thought it would be much easier in the long run to get the media out of the way by doing just the one interview. But it's your call, obviously, and if you want to do this another way, that's fine, too."

Gillespie paused, then replied in a lowered voice, "Well, truthfully I liked your idea of doing this just one time and telling all the other reporters we're done talking about it. But my husband is really adamant about it and I wasn't able to change his mind."

"Sure, I can understand his reticence. It's not an easy situation and he just wants it all to go away."

"Exactly. We just wish the reporters camped out at our house right now would go away."

"Are they on your property?"

"Some are on our lawn and others are in the street and sidewalk."

"There's nothing we can do about them being on the sidewalk or in the street. That's public property and they have the right to be there. But we can get them off your lawn. Would you like me to do that for you?"

"That would be nice—at least give us a little breathing room. This is really intrusive."

"I'll have a couple of deputies come over and move them off your property. I can have them out there in ten minutes."

"Thank you, lieutenant."

"Not a problem."

Mark tried a different approach. "Did you happen to see the news about what happened last night on the school campus?"

"I did. I just can't believe this is happening. It all feels like a really bad dream."

"I agree. My concern is that this will become an even bigger story. As I explained to you and your husband yesterday, I have a pretty good feel for how big a story is likely to be. Judging by the number of calls I've already received this morning, this story is going to go national. CNN and the other national news networks are calling me. The destructive actions of a few individuals last night elevated this story from a local story to a national one."

Mark could hear a small gasp over the phone.

"Oh, God—I never even thought of that. You mean all this will be seen across the whole country?"

"Yeah, that's kinda how things work. I'm just afraid that this may focus even more attention on your daughter. But if you and Tom want to wait it out, I totally understand. Eventually, the media will get tired of the story and move onto the next big controversy. If we're lucky some big story will break and then you won't have reporters standing on your lawn anymore."

Mrs. Gillespie was exasperated. "This is exactly why I wanted to do the one interview and get it over with. I'm going to talk again to Tom and see if I can change his mind. Let me do that now and I'll give you a call back in a few minutes."

"That'll be fine, Mrs. Gillespie. Frankly, I think it's a good way to proceed. And while I'm waiting for your call back, I'll have my deputies get those reporters off your lawn."

CHAPTER 14

~~~

By the time Mark was able to get a couple of deputies dispatched to the Gillespie home, his phone was ringing. *Thomas Gillespie* appeared on the caller ID readout. Mark picked up the phone; it was the moment of truth.

"Lieutenant, this is Rachel Gillespie. I spoke with my husband and he's agreed to do the interview. Where and what time would you like to do it?"

Mark allowed himself a little fist pump before responding calmly.

"I can get it set up this afternoon. And I'm sure Angela Bell will come to your home, if that's all right?"

"Really? She'll come here?"

"If that's okay with you. There are a couple of advantages to doing it that way. First, you wouldn't have to leave your home and make it past the media parked in front of your house, and second, the media will see Angela Bell and the Channel Eight crew being let into your house and they'll get the message that you're doing an exclusive. And I'll be there as well to make sure the interview stays on course."

"Won't they be mad?"

"They won't be happy, but that's the way it goes. You have the right to speak to anyone you choose. How does two o'clock work for you?"

"That'll be fine. We'll see you then."

"Sheriff, we may have a problem."

Mick was back in his office, trying his best to focus on the budget report that had landed on his desk that morning. His heart and soul were with Mia and he couldn't get her out of his mind. It was just past ten and she was about to sit down again with the Denver PD and DA investigators. He felt helpless not being there with her, but he knew he couldn't be. He had to stay above the fray and remain a neutral player, just like in any other officer-involved shooting.

Now Jack Keller was calling with what sounded like bad news.

"What is it, Keller?" he asked bluntly.

"I'm at the medical examiners office and they just completed the autopsy."

"And?"

"The fatal shot was to the back of the head."

"Yeah, I knew that, Keller. That doesn't mean it wasn't justified."

Keller knew that better than anyone. But he also knew that fact could be a big problem for the sheriff. When the autopsy results got released and the public learned the young man was shot from behind, the perception would be that Mia killed the guy when she didn't have to. The public always had a difficult time understanding that there were many scenarios where an officer shooting someone in the back was acceptable and proper. But it was a hard sell to those who were looking for any opportunity to bash the police. Emotion typically won out over science or logic in these kinds of situations.

Mick continued, "Mia described the kid as twisting suddenly, so when she fired, one of the rounds must have caught him in the back of the head. It's easily explained given the situation."

Both men knew this case was anything but an ordinary situation, but Keller managed a small "Yeah."

"When will the toxicology work come back?"

"It'll take a few weeks so we don't know if the kid was on any drugs. But the early intel says the kid was on a lot of prescription drugs, anti-depressants, bipolar meds, et cetera . . . obviously he had a lot of psychological issues. Which may shed some light on his actions yesterday."

Mark Archer arrived at the Gillespie home at one thirty, slipping through a back door that Mrs. Gillespie had left unlocked for him. He didn't want any reporters thinking he had something to do with arranging the interview between the Gillespies and Angela Bell. Once in the house, he called out and Rachel came in and greeted him. Tom Gillespie was right behind her.

Tom glared at Mark. "This better work. I'm sick of these people."

"It should help. They'll eventually move onto another story. I expect them to be gone in a day or two."

Mark got right down to business. "I thought we could talk for a few minutes before the crew from Channel Eight arrives. Have either of you been on television before?"

Both shook their heads.

"Okay, I'll give you some tips. Also, I spoke with Angela Bell this morning and she's agreed that if she asks you a question you aren't comfortable answering you can just let her know and she'll drop it."

Rachel replied, "That's more than fair. Thank you for speaking to her about that."

"No problem. I think you'll like Angela and I certainly trust her more than some of the other reporters that cover our stories."

"Like the assholes standing on my lawn?"

Mark looked at Tom Gillespie and tried to figure out if the anger was directed at the reporters standing in his yard or at the young man who nearly murdered his daughter. He needed to make sure the anger was aimed at Alex Washington. He didn't need a loose cannon.

"Is there somewhere we can sit and talk?"

"Sure, let's go into the dining room," answered Rachel.

The three took seats around a large mahogany table and Mark, wasting no time, jumped right in.

"Let me explain how this'll work. The crew will set up in your living room since it has the best light. There will be two cameras and a floor director, and, of course, Angela. The rule of thumb is to not look at the camera, just look at Angela. There's a temptation to look at a monitor they'll have set up near you to see what things look like, but it's really best if you don't do that."

Mark continued, "Let Angela ask you the questions and just answer them as you see fit. And as I said before, if you don't like the question, just let her know and she can skip it or maybe try to rephrase it in such a way that you'll be more comfortable."

As Mark was finishing his sentence he noticed a teenaged girl peeking around the corner. She was blonde and very pretty. Rachel invited her to come in the room.

"Lieutenant, this is our daughter, Kendra."

Mark stood and offered his han.

"Nice to meet you, Kendra. I'm sorry it's under these circumstances. How are you doing?"

She shook Mark's hand and managed a quiet reply. "I still can't believe this is happening. I didn't really even know Alex. I don't know why he did what he did. Now he's dead and it's all my fault."

Mark looked directly into Kendra's eyes and said, "Kendra, this is not your fault. You're a victim in all this. You did nothing to cause it. You need to remember that."

Kendra lowered her head and began to cry. Her mother stood and put her arms around her. Tom didn't move from his place at the table, which didn't go unnoticed by Archer. What was this guy's problem? Mark wondered.

"Lieutenant Archer is here to help us prepare for the interview I told you about this morning."

Kendra nodded, but didn't respond.

"You're welcome to sit here with us if you'd like," Rachel offered.

"No, I think I'll just go back upstairs. Is it okay if Miranda comes over?"

"Sure, sweetie. That's fine."

Kendra left the room and Rachel sat back down at the table.

"Will you be in the room when we do this interview, lieutenant?"

"I can be, if you'd like."

"Yes, I think that would be helpful. I feel like you're our advocate in all this. Tom and I are very appreciative of your assistance."

"Happy to do it."

Just then the doorbell rang.

"It would be best if you answered the door. I'd rather the reporters not see me here. I hope you understand."

"Of course," replied Rachel, as she stood and moved toward the front door.

Mark looked at Tom who was sitting with his arms folded across his chest. When Rachel reached the door she looked through the peephole to make sure it was Angela and the Channel Eight crew before opening the door.

Angela and the crew quickly stepped inside. Mark looked at her and said, "I think you guys will want to set up in the living room. It's got the best light and it's out of view from anyone outside."

She nodded toward her videographers. "Marvin, Henry, check the living room and see if that'll work. If so, we'll need three or four chairs."

"I'd say three at this point," whispered Mark.

"We can't get the daughter?" Angela asked quietly.

"I spoke with her a few minutes ago and she's still pretty spooked. I'd suggest you build rapport with Mrs. Gillespie and see how things go."

"What about the father?"

"He's a tough nut to crack. You might have to work your charm, Angela."

"Thanks for the heads up."

⟨∂⟩

Mick McCallister had been sheriff of Rocklin County for less than three years and had quickly learned it was the politics of the job he hated most. At heart he was a cop, but as the sheriff he spent a considerable amount of his time studying budgets and learning the dynamics of Denver-area politics.

He had met the governor and most of the congressional representatives in the state. He had met all the state reps in and around Denver as well as the Rocklin County Board of Supervisors. While the supervisors were relatively low in the political hierarchy, they were an important group to Mick because they controlled his budget. The chief administrative officer of the county, Luis Centeno, was appointed by the board to carry out its policies. As such, Centeno was a powerful figure and, like many bureaucrats, he resented the large amounts of money it took to operate a sheriff's department. He looked for any opportunity to strip the RCSO of the funds they re quested to run the agency. And whenever the RCSO was involved in a controversial incident, such as a deputy-involved shooting, Centeno became particularly difficult to work with.

To further complicate things, Centeno wasn't technically Mick's boss. The sheriff was elected by the people of Rocklin County, so Mick answered only to them. But the county structure called for the board of supervisors to allocate the funding for RCSO. So, while Centeno wasn't Mick's boss, he did control the purse strings, and Mick had to be cognizant of that.

Mick stared at the phone message Lucinda had taken from Centeno earlier that morning. Might as well get it over with, Mick thought, and he dialed Centeno's extension.

"Good morning. This is Sheriff McCallister returning Mr. Centeno's call."

"Good morning, sheriff. One moment and I'll connect you."

Mick waited and finally heard Centeno's voice. "Mick, how are you doing?"

"Doing okay, thanks."

"Hey, look, I'm sure you're swamped with everything that's happened but the board of supervisors wanted me to touch base with you on the Wilson High shooting yesterday."

"Okay, what do you want to know?" he replied.

"I know you don't have a crystal ball but any thoughts about how much liability we could be facing on this case? I don't need to tell you how tight things are financially and the board is very concerned about the prospects of paying out a large sum to the family of the kid that got shot. Now, we have insurance and all, but we're still on the hook for the first million. And that's no chump change."

"Look, it's still really early, but I think we're on solid ground. The kid took a girl hostage, held a gun to her head, and looked, by all accounts, like he was going to kill her. We took the action we felt appropriate, but unfortunately it cost the kid his life. But the deputy did what she needed to do, and I really believe most people will view her actions as heroic."

"What about the damage to the cars and the classrooms last night? I hope the school district doesn't come after us to cover those costs. They could say their losses were as a result of what the sheriff's department did . . . You know how this goes, Mick."

Mick was growing angry. "The losses at the school last night were due to a small handful of thugs who decided to take advantage of the situation and be assholes. Nothing more, nothing less. I think the school district would be hard pressed to come after us for that. Besides, they have insurance as well. It should be covered."

"I have a call into the school board president. I'll ask about the insurance. Hopefully they do, but again, who knows what kind of deductible they have. But with the damage estimates of a half million bucks, they may have to cover the losses because it doesn't exceed their deductible."

Mick had had enough. "Is there anything else?"

"No, but keep me posted. I need to keep the board apprised of what's happening here. They're very concerned."

Mick hung up the phone before saying out loud, "Thanks for asking about my wife, asshole."

CHAPTER 15

⤬

The Gillespies were impressed by the efficiency of the Channel Eight crew turning their living room into a small sound stage. Three chairs and a coffee table had been set up in the center of the room and several lights had been brought in. Large silver reflectors were placed around the room for a softer, diffused look. Angela had quietly instructed one of the crew to have a fourth chair and microphone nearby in case Kendra could be persuaded to join them.

Angela made small talk with Tom and Rachel before the interview, doing her best to put them at ease. Rachel was definitely the one she would focus on; Tom seemed very uncomfortable with what was happening. She assured them that the interview would be friendly and the goal was simply to tell Kendra's story of what had transpired on campus.

"We're ready when you are, Angela."

Angela nodded to the crew member and motioned for the Gillespies to take their seats. She grabbed a mirror from her purse and did a quick check of her makeup. The crew attached small mics to each of the three and they were ready to go.

"Before we start, there are a couple of things to remember. First, forget about the cameras, just look at me. The cameramen will get the shot—it's not your worry. Secondly, just relax and tell your story. If you aren't comfortable with something I ask or if you don't like your response to any question we can reshoot it. Now, there's a monitor off to the side," she said, pointing it out. "There is always a temptation to look at it, but try not to. Also, the director may signal me from time to time, but you don't need to worry about any of that. Just ignore him."

Both Gillespies nodded.

"Camera's rolling," said the director.

"Hello, I'm Angela Bell and I'm here with Tom and Rachel Gillespie, parents of the seventeen-year-old student who was taken hostage yesterday on the campus of Woodrow Wilson High School in Castle Springs. Thank you so much for speaking with me today."

Rachel nodded, while Tom stared straight ahead.

"Yesterday must have been a horrible day for the two of you. How are you holding up?"

Rachel took the reins. "It was a nightmare. What started out as just another day turned into a parent's greatest fear. We are just so happy that things turned out the way they did. We have our Kendra back and we're so grateful."

"And how is Kendra doing?"

"All things considered, she's doing well. She's surrounded by family and friends and we're just trying to let her feel safe again. Give her some sort of normalcy."

"So, how did you learn about what was happening yesterday on the school campus?"

Rachel answered, "I actually got a text from a friend who was watching the TV coverage on Channel Eight. The helicopter was zooming in on what was happening. The friend told me that it was a blonde girl being held at gunpoint and that she thought it looked like Kendra."

"That must have been horrifying."

"At first I thought my friend was just mistaken but I turned on the television and within a few seconds I knew it was Kendra. There was no doubt about it."

"And so what did you do?"

"I immediately called my husband, who was at work. I told him what was happening, but he doesn't have easy access to a TV, so he left work and went directly to the school. I was at home so I drove to the school as well."

"I can't imagine what you must have been feeling. What happened when you arrived on the campus?"

"It was bedlam, and just as I arrived I heard gunshots. Two or three, I think. My heart sank and I just totally lost it. I think I fell to my knees and started sobbing. Several students saw me and came over to try to help me. They didn't know I was Kendra's mom."

"So at that moment you believed your daughter had been shot?"

Rachel didn't respond. Tears began flowing and the cameraman zoomed in for a closeup. Angela knew better than to interrupt the moment. It was television news at its best and she knew this moment was their ticket to getting picked up by the networks and going national. After several seconds Angela reached into her pocket, fished out some tissues, and handed them to Rachel. After a few more seconds Tom reached over and put his arm around his wife.

Rachel regained her composure somewhat and was able to respond feebly, "Yes."

Angela turned her attention to Tom to try to bring him into the conversation and give Rachel some time.

"Tom, where were you at this point?"

"I was stuck in traffic, unaware of the shooting. It was another fifteen minutes before I reached campus and located my wife and daughter."

"And that's when you learned what had happened?"

"Yes. The deputies took us to Kendra. Then they put us in a patrol car so we could have some privacy."

"What was that moment like? When you saw Kendra and realized she was safe?"

"Obviously, it was a huge relief."

Mr. Gillespie had the emotional range of a rock, thought Angela. Time to get back to Rachel.

"And for you, Rachel? The time between hearing the shots and learning that Kendra was safe . . . that must have seemed like an eternity."

"It was the worst few minutes of my life. They say you see your life flash before your eyes when you're about to die. Well, I saw Kendra's life flash before my eyes. From her birth, first communion, graduations . . . all of it."

"I can't imagine what you went through."

Angela caught some movement in the corner of the living room. She was able to take a surreptitious glance and saw it was Kendra. She had come in to watch the interview. Mark Archer was standing with her, whispering to her and pointing to the set.

"I want to shift gears for a moment. The Rocklin County sheriff's deputy that was involved in the shooting—did you have an opportunity to speak with her after this horrifying event?"

"No, we were put into the patrol car right away so we didn't have a chance."

"Is there anything you'd like to say to her now?"

Both Tom and Rachel nodded. Rachel once again took the lead.

"I want to thank her for saving our Kendra's life. Without her heroic actions yesterday I really think our daughter would have died. Kendra is alive today because of her."

Angela continued, "As you probably know, the deputy involved in this incident yesterday was the wife of the sheriff of Rocklin County. She's seven months pregnant and just happened to be near the campus when she heard the commotion coming from the quad. She was actually coming from a doctor's appointment when this all transpired."

Rachel nodded. "We did hear about that and thank God she did what she did. It would have been easy for her just to leave and let other deputies handle the call, but the fact that she took it upon herself to run onto that campus . . . that's pretty amazing."

Bingo, thought Archer. Angela had delivered the goods.

Kendra leaned toward Mark and whispered, "I didn't know any of that."

He whispered back, "The deputy's name is Mia. Would you like to meet her sometime?"

Kendra nodded. Peripherally, Angela could see that the conversation was continuing between Mark and Kendra. She didn't want to interrupt the flow of the interview but decided to take a chance, so she feigned a cough.

"Let's take a short break. I'm battling some allergies and I need to take a minute. Could I get a drink of water?"

"Take five, everybody," ordered the director.

Angela unhooked her mic and stood. One of the crew handed her a bottle of water and she took a small sip. She looked around the room and saw Mark and Kendra still chatting in the corner. She caught Mark's eye and he knew what she wanted.

"Kendra, have you met Angela Bell?"

"No."

The two walked over and Mark made the introductions.

"Kendra, it is so nice to meet you. And I am so happy that you're safe and sound."

Kendra managed a small smile. "Thanks."

"Have you ever watched a TV interview before?'

"No, this is my first."

"Well, let me explain what all goes on during an interview."

Angela took her around and introduced her to the crew, explaining what all the equipment and lighting was for. Kendra seemed interested and was asking questions before long.

Mark sat down with the Gillespies and chatted with them while Angela was giving Kendra the grand tour.

"How long have you been on TV?" Kendra asked Angela.

"Almost twenty years now. I started out as a field reporter at a little station in Wichita Falls, Iowa and then kept moving to larger and larger stations. I finally ended up in Denver about ten years ago and I was given the anchor job four years ago. I love it. No two days are the same."

"That's really cool."

"Do you know what you want to do after you finish up with school? Ever give any thought to going into the news business?"

"No, I never have. I don't really know what I want to do."

"Think about it . . . it could be a great career for you."

Kendra looked intrigued. "I'll do that. Thanks."

While they were talking, Angela had carefully walked Kendra closer to where the interview was being conducted, subtly trying to get her to consider being part of it. Angela turned to the Gillespies sitting on the sofa and said, "You both are doing great, by the way."

They nodded but didn't say anything. Angela continued, "And Kendra here is such a sweetheart. I'm trying to talk her into being a news reporter when she gets a little older."

Kendra smiled, the first real show of any kind of positive emotion since before the ordeal on campus had unfolded.

"What do you think of that, sweetie?" asked Rachel, pleased to see a little bit of the old Kendra.

"I think it's kinda cool. But I dunno," she answered, shrugging her shoulders.

"You know, Channel Eight offers internships to college students who want to get a taste of what working in the news business is really like. The positions are unpaid and you do a lot of the grunt work but it would be a great opportunity to see what being a reporter is all about."

"Really? Maybe I could do something like that once I'm in college."

"Wow, Kendra. That sounds like a great opportunity," encouraged Rachel.

"I'm sure we could make that happen. We need to stay in touch and as you get closer to graduation we could talk more about it."

CHAPTER 16

"Sheriff, I have some information on the kid you wanted me to check on."

Mick was in his office going over budget reports when Sergeant Tougas of the Gang Unit stuck her head in his office.

"Come in. Tell me what you got."

Tougas took a seat and opened her notebook. She was still old school; no fancy electronic gadgets for her.

"At this point I can tell you that Jaquon's last name is Jackson, he's twenty-three years old, DOB 8/23/94, and is a member of 120th Street. He's been arrested twice but nothing stuck."

"What was he arrested for?"

"Small stuff—theft from a vehicle in twenty-fourteen and disturbing the peace a few months ago."

"Tell me about the disturbing the peace collar."

"It was that rally in Denver for the guy running for congress. I forget his name but he was a pretty conservative candidate. Anyway, there was a group that gathered to protest at the rally and things got out of hand. A half dozen protesters were arrested, including Jaquon, but no charges were filed. I think Denver PD just wanted to take the ringleaders out of the equation in an effort to quell the protests, so they popped 'em. But a couple cars were torched and charges were filed against two of the six protesters. But Jaquon wasn't one of them."

"Interesting that cars were set on fire at that protest. The same thing happened at the high school last night and Jaquon was clearly one of the instigators. Could be a coincidence but I doubt it. The guy is a righteous asshole. How about his family life?"

"We've heard it before . . . dad's in prison and mom's a druggie. Jaquon did manage to graduate from high school but there's no sign of any further educational efforts on his part."

"Any employment history?"

"A few months at Mickey D's while in high school, but nothing since then."

"No tax returns, no evidence of supporting himself the past several years?"

"Nope. But as you know, 120th Street is heavy into the meth trade. Our friend Jaquon may have dipped his toe into those waters."

"Wouldn't surprise me any."

"Anything else?"

"No, that'll do it for now. But let's keep this between ourselves for the moment."

∾

Mick picked up his phone and dialed Tim Dekker, commander of the RCSO Narcotics Unit.

"Sheriff, how are you today?"

"Doing okay, Tim."

"How's Mia holding up?"

"As well as can be expected."

"Give her my best. She's a hero in my book."

"I'll do that, thanks."

"What can I do for you?"

"Does the name Jaquon Jackson ring any bells for you?"

"Not offhand. Got a DOB for your friend? I'll run him through our narc database."

"I had Cameo Tougas do a quick preliminary on him, but yeah, run him for me. His is DOB is 8/23/94."

"Hold on a sec . . ."

Mick waited patiently while Dekker ran the name. He came back on the line a minute later.

"Yeah, we have an entry for the kid in our gang file. Nothing in the drug offender database."

"Smith said he was tied in with 120th Street."

"Yep, he's listed as an affiliate gang member. Not much contact with him, just some field interviews our deputies have filled out on him. He looks like someone who hangs with 120th Street but isn't one of the primary players."

"I'm guessing he might be a little more active than we know. I also suspect he could be involved in the meth business."

"Want our guys to take a closer look at him?"

"Yeah, I'd appreciate that, Tim. He's popped up on my radar screen and I'd like to know what Mr. Jackson is up to these days."

"I can put a tail on him and give you regular reports on his day-to-day movements if you'd like."

"Yeah, let's do that. And I'd like daily updates at this point. Call my cell; don't put it in email. I'd like to keep this quiet for now. No electronic trail."

"No problem, boss. You got it."

"So, how is Kendra holding up after this horrible ordeal?"

The interview had resumed, but now Kendra had moved from the corner of the living room to a chair about ten feet from Angela, but still out of the shot. She was watching intently.

Rachel responded, "She's doing okay, I think. She's a strong girl and

I'm hopeful she'll be able to move past all of this."

"I can't imagine going through what she's gone through. Tell me, did she know Alex Washington very well? Was he a friend? Just a classmate?"

"From what Kendra tells me he was someone she barely knew. She said he was new to the school, that he transferred from another school just a month or two ago. I think Kendra talked to him a few times—you know, being friendly, but they never spent any time together."

"Sounds like Kendra may have just been in the wrong place at the wrong time."

Rachel glanced over at her daughter and could see her shaking her head.

"I'm sorry, Angela, but can we stop the interview for a moment? Kendra is shaking her head at me. Maybe I have this wrong."

"Of course, we can do that. Would you like a few minutes to speak to her?"

"Yes, and Tom, why don't you join us?"

The Gillespies stood, unhooked their mics, and walked Kendra into the dining room. Angela gave Mark a keep-your-fingers-crossed kind of look, then walked over to him and whispered, "If we're going to get Kendra on camera, now is the time."

"I think you made some good inroads with her during the break. She's definitely calmer now than when she first came into the room," replied Mark.

"She's a sweet girl. I really feel awful for her. I can't imagine what she's going through."

"How are we doing on time? It's almost three now . . . you wanted this in time for the five?"

"If we can wrap up by four we should have enough time. There won't be too much editing; it's pretty much a straight shot. If we manage to get Kendra on camera and we run long, then I'll let my producer know and we can tease it for the six. It'll be worth the wait."

Angela looked up as the Gillespies returned to the living room.

"Angela, Kendra would like to be part of the interview. She thinks she should tell what happened."

Angela smiled at Kendra. "Oh, that'll be great, Kendra. I know people want to hear from you about what happened. Marvin, can we get another chair for Kendra? She'll be joining us."

CHAPTER 17

Mia spent the morning at the station going through yet another series of interviews with investigators from Denver PD and the Rocklin County DA's Office. Mia's attorney, Danny Velasco, was at her side throughout the proceedings. Mia and Danny were acquaintances, but this was the first time they were on the same side, so to speak. As a prominent defense attorney in Denver, Danny had represented many clients who had been arrested by the RCSO. Most noteworthy among these cases had been the Lombard murder case which had gone to trial the year before. Velasco had represented Lisa Sullivan, an accomplice in what was the most publicized homicide case in the history of Rocklin County. He had worked a deal for her—she turned state's evidence against her former lover Scott Lennox, the mastermind behind the murder, in exchange for no jail time. It was a masterful move by Velasco and one that infuriated the RCSO, Mia included. But Velasco was just doing his job and the past would be put aside for now. Mia felt fortunate to have him representing her.

By late afternoon Mia was finished with the interviews and was set to meet with Dr. Analee Lusetti, a local psychologist under contract with the RCSO. Dr. Lusetti's duties included assisting RCSO deputies with any psychological struggles they might have. The job of a deputy was a difficult one and having a psychologist available to talk things through was a huge benefit to the department. The doctor also assisted any deputy who was part of an officer-involved shooting. In fact, it was mandatory that any deputy involved in such an incident go to Dr. Lusetti for at least one session. By making it mandatory, the department eliminated the "I'm fine, I don't need a shrink" position that many deputies resorted to in an attempt to maintain their dignity. If you were involved in an OIS then you knew you had to visit the shrink; this way there was no possible stigma.

The reality was that most, if not all, deputies benefitted from their visit with Dr. Lusetti. Many times deputies would feel like they were handling things pretty well following an OIS but once they started to talk about the incidents, their true feelings would come out. Some of the most macho deputies fell the hardest, with tears flowing freely. The funds RCSO spent keeping Dr. Lusetti on retainer were money well spent.

Mia had no issues with the idea of going to a psychologist. She had spent some time with one seventeen years earlier following her experience at Columbine. She had not personally met Dr. Lusetti, but had heard good things about her from deputies who had used her services.

The doctor's office was in Castle Springs in a new medical arts building near downtown. Mia decided to walk the six blocks from the station for her three thirty appointment. She was exhausted from the nearly five hours of questioning and thought the fresh air would do her some good. As she walked through the downtown area she passed by restaurants and shops, many of which had been built in the past few years. The area, which had become somewhat rundown over the years, had gone through a revitalization period and was now a vibrant part of Castle Springs.

Mia was a little early and took her time walking along Fifth Street, stopping and perusing some of her favorite stores. As she left a maternity clothes store she encountered a group of half a dozen African-American men loitering on the sidewalk. They were all dressed the same—white t-shirts and Dickies that sagged well below their hips.

They stopped and turned their attention toward her when they saw her exit the store. Mia didn't think much about it and turned up Fifth

Street and continued walking toward her appointment. A half minute later her intuition kicked in; something wasn't right. She glanced back over her shoulder. The men were following her and weren't far behind. She quickened her pace, but the men sped up as well and quickly reached her.

"Hey there, don't I know you?"

Mia spun around, "No, I don't think so . . . sorry."

She continued walking. She was only half a block away from the medical offices.

"Yeah, yeah, we know you. You're the one who shot our homie's cousin. Oh yeah, that be you."

Mia didn't answer, she just kept moving as quickly as she could.

Two of the youth moved into the street and then darted back onto the sidewalk a few feet ahead of her, blocking her in.

Mia reached into her purse for her phone. "Whatcha gonna do, bitch? Shoot us like you did Lil' Alex? One nigger ain't enough for you?"

The reality was that her service weapon had been taken from her after the shooting; it was standard procedure. She was unarmed, but she wasn't about to correct their assumption.

"Get out of my way, gentlemen."

It was the moment of truth. The six men closed ranks and surrounded Mia, careful not to touch her. The leader, a tall lanky man with bad acne, pointed his finger in her face.

"Fine, but remember, pretty lady—you can run, but you can't hide. We know where you fucking live."

They moved aside to let her pass, but not without additional comment. "Oh yeah, I'd like a piece of that ass. It's fiiiiine." Several of them displayed 120th Street gang signs as Mia walked past.

Once they were behind her she heard more whooping and hollering. She darted into the entrance of the medical building and found her way to the elevator. She rushed in, closed the door, and burst into tears.

After a couple of minutes, Mia was able to gather herself and walk to the check-in desk for Dr. Lusetti's patients.

"I'm Mia Serrano-McCallister. I have a three thirty appointment."

Once Kendra was mic'd, Angela resumed the interview.

"Kendra, I'm so sorry to meet you under these circumstances. Tell us, how are you doing?"

"I'm doing okay."

"What a horrible ordeal you went through yesterday. If you don't mind, I'd like to ask you a little bit about what happened. Would that be okay?"

"Sure, I guess so."

Clearly, Kendra was battling some nerves and Angela knew she would need to do her best to put her at ease. She'd start with some fluff questions that would be edited out later. She reached over and grabbed Kendra's hand.

"Okay, we'll go slow. Take your time."

"Thanks. I will."

"Tell us a little bit about yourself, Kendra. What grade are you in, school activities, you know—that kind of thing."

"I'm seventeen and a senior. I'm a cheerleader and I play softball . . . not sure what else you want to know."

"What position do you play on the softball team?"

"Shortstop and left field. I'm not a starter, though."

"How's the team going to be this year?"

"Not really sure. Last year we made playoffs but we had some really good seniors on the team and now they're gone, so I guess we'll see," she replied with a shy shrug.

"And how long have you been a cheerleader?"

"This is my fourth year. I started as a freshman."

"Wow, good for you."

"Yeah, it's really fun."

"It sounds like it!"

Angela paused for a few moments, lowered her eyes a bit, then glanced up at Kendra.

"So, let's move on to the subject we're here to talk about. Would that be okay?"

"Sure, I guess so."

"So Kendra, did you know Alex Washington?" she asked softly.

"Not really. I mean, I've met him but we weren't friends or anything. A group of us went to the movies a couple weeks ago and he was part of it. But there were like twenty kids and he was just one of them."

"And that was the extent of your time with him?"

"Yeah, but right afterwards he started texting me."

"What were the texts about?"

"At first, it was just stuff . . . nothing big, just chatting . . . you know."

"You say 'at first' . . . does that mean the tone of the texts changed?"

"Yeah, they started to get more personal. You know, sorta like he liked me."

"Kendra, you are a very pretty, popular girl. I'm sure lots of boys are interested in you."

"But I wasn't really interested in him and so I was really nice, and I let him know we could be friends, but that's it."

"And how did he react to that?"

"He was really persistent and so I kept trying to tell him I just wanted to be friends . . . and then his texts got, I don't know . . . meaner, I guess," Kendra replied, starting to tear up.

"How so?"

"He never really got the message so I had to finally tell him I wasn't interested. And that's when he got pretty angry."

"What did he do?"

"He sent me some really nasty texts. They scared me so I decided

I'd just totally avoid him."

"Did you tell anyone about the texts?"

Kendra hung her head. "No, I wish I had. Maybe then none of this would have happened."

"Kendra, it's not your fault. You didn't deserve this."

Angela knew that speaking this way to someone she was interviewing was overstepping her bounds as a journalist, but she also knew it could be edited out. Only parts of the conversation would make the newscast. It was important to keep her talking and Angela felt the best way to ensure this was to offer personal support.

"In my mind I know that, but I just feel so bad. Like his death is all my fault."

"It's not your fault at all. He did this to you, and sadly he paid the price. You can't blame yourself."

Kendra nodded, but didn't respond. She was looking down at her hands folded in her lap. Angela decided to move in a different direction.

"So, a deputy from the Rocklin County Sheriff's department responded as things were unfolding on campus. Tell us what you know about that."

"I didn't see her at first. But then she was just kinda there and started talking to him. Telling him to let me go."

"She talked with him?"

"Yes, she was hiding, I guess. But then she came out and really tried talking to him. I couldn't believe it."

"But he wasn't having any part of that?"

"At one point I think she was really getting through to him, but then the news helicopter got his attention and he kinda freaked out. And that's when it happened."

Tears began again, rolling down Kendra's cheeks. Rachel stood and moved toward her daughter; she leaned over and gave her a hug. It was great television and Angela let it play out. That part about the news helicopter would need to be edited out, she thought. Angela didn't want the blame for the shooting pinned on Channel Eight. She knew they were first on scene and it was their chopper that had caused Alex to get distracted.

"Is there anything you'd like to say to the deputy who responded to the scene?"

Kendra regained her composure and looked directly into the camera.

"Yes, I want to say thank you for saving my life."

CHAPTER 18

～

Mia sat in the waiting room thumbing through six-month-old magazines, trying her best to calm down after the altercation with the gang members. She cursed to herself about not having her gun; she would have to talk to Mick about getting a personal weapon that she could carry until she went back on duty. She knew it was standard to take the gun that had been used in an OIS, but she really felt naked without a weapon.

After a few minutes in the waiting room, Dr. Lusetti appeared and introduced herself to Mia. They walked back to her office and Mia took a seat on a sofa while Dr. Lusetti sat down on a chair a few feet away. The office looked more like someone's living room than a doctor's office, but that was by design, Mia thought. Get the patient comfortable and talking.

"Can I offer you some coffee? Bottled water?"

"Actually, water would be great."

Dr. Lusetti went to a small refrigerator in the corner of the office and pulled out a bottle. Mia noticed a Keurig coffee maker on top of the mini-fridge. On the other side of the office was a large aquarium filled with dozens of small, colorful fish.

"Here you go."

Mia took a long drink from the bottle and the doctor started in.

"So, I understand you were involved in a OIS yesterday at the high school. Why don't you tell me about it?"

Wow, she doesn't waste anytime, Mia thought.

Mia recited the whole story, from being at the doctor's appointment, to running onto the campus, and ultimately to shooting Alex Washington. She was surprised at how quickly she was talking, like she wanted to get it over with. It didn't go unnoticed by Dr. Lusetti.

"So, you were off duty when this all happened?"

"Technically, I was using my sick time, which is allowed by the department . . . you know, for doctor's appointments and things."

"But you chose to run onto that campus. You were off duty and you ran toward trouble. No one would have thought less of you if you hadn't done that. I mean, you were at a doctor's appointment. You really went above and beyond yesterday. It just didn't end well."

"I guess that's true. But *not* running onto that campus never entered my mind."

"That's remarkable. Mia. I mean, here you are, seven months pregnant, off duty at a doctor's appointment and you hear and see commotion coming from the campus. Instead of getting in your car and going to lunch, you take it upon yourself to run toward the trouble. It's what great law enforcement people do."

Mia shrugged. She hadn't thought of it like that.

Dr. Lusetti leaned in toward Mia and asked in a lowered voice, "So tell me this . . . do you regret what you did? Do you wish you could redo the whole thing and not run onto campus? Just get in your car and meet your husband for lunch as planned?"

Mia thought for a few seconds. "Well, that would have simplified things for me, obviously. But then the girl he took hostage might have been killed. I mean, who knows what would have happened if I didn't do what I did. I don't know what the deputies who responded would have done. They would probably have handled the situation in the proper way, but with a scene that's fluid like that . . . "

"Exactly. Unfortunately, we'll never know the answer to that question. But what we do know is this: you were in the area, you heard the commotion, you responded when you didn't need to, you rushed to help a young girl who was potentially just seconds from being murdered, and you saved her life. Now you had to take action that was very, very unfortunate, but from what you described here today, I don't see what other choice you had."

"I don't know . . . that young man is dead, and he's dead by my hands."

"Yes he is, but not by your hands, as you put it. The bullet you fired at him came from your gun, but the reality is that bullet was on its way long before you pulled the trigger. That bullet started its journey when he decided to bring a gun to school, to take a girl hostage, when that news helicopter flew over, when he realized the other deputies were there . . . do you see what I'm saying?"

Mia nodded, taking it all in.

"Now, you need to prepare yourself for the fallout that's on its way. I'm sure your husband has been through a lot of negative stuff. As sheriff, crap lands on his doorstep every day. You're lucky—he can help you through a lot of this."

"That's kind of a double-edged sword. Yeah, it's nice that my husband can lend a supportive ear, but he's also in a really awkward position. He needs to be above board with the public and the media, but at the same time he wants to support me. He just can't appear to be showing me any favoritism or he'll get blasted for it. He can support me privately, he just can't defend me publicly—at least not till the report is issued on the shooting. And that will be six months or more from now, and that's assuming I'll be cleared. The damn things take forever to complete."

"From what you've described to me today, it sounds like you did what you needed to do. Unfortunate, yes, but necessary under the circumstances."

∽

The interview with Kendra was gold, and Angela knew it. Once it was over she and the crew rushed back to the studio so the footage could be cut and prepared for the newscast at six. They had missed the five, but Angela felt the story would likely go national, so it was worth the delay.

Mark watched as the crew in the edit bay performed their magic. He was always amazed by a skillful editor could do with raw footage. People could be made to say almost anything. It was the primary reason he didn't pay much attention to interviews on prime time national news shows. He knew from experience that the longer someone spoke on camera the chance of an unscrupulous editor putting words in their mouth grew exponentially. He had learned to say what he had to say and do it quickly; the proverbial sound bite was crucial. Most people didn't understand that and on more than one occasion he had someone tell him how pleased they were after doing an interview with a reporter. "I spoke for a half hour with so and so" they would say, happy they were able to get so much of their story out, blissfully unaware that they had little control over which fifteen seconds would be used . Mark prided himself on telling the story in as few sentences as possible, leaving editors and reporters with little to use except for what he had actually said.

"How long will the edited piece run?' asked Mark.

"Probably four, four and a half minutes," replied Angela.

That was an eternity on a local thirty-minute newscast, but Mark knew Channel Eight would milk the story for all it was worth. And that was fine with him; the whole point of this was to show that Mia had acted properly and had saved the girl's life.

"Are you going to use any of Rachel and Tom's comments? Or just go with Kendra?"

"No, we'll use a little bit of the parents. I don't want them to think we've pulled a fast one. They can set the stage and then Kendra delivers the goods."

All eyes fell on the edit screen as Kenny, Channel Eight's best video editor, put the interview together.

"How much longer, Kenny? It's five fifty and I need to get on set," asked Angela.

"Give me three minutes and I'll send it to Eileen in the control room. I've even cut a little something they can use to tease the story at the top of the six."

"Fantastic. Thanks so much for the quick turnaround."

"No sweat, Angela. It's a great interview."

Mia glanced at her watch and was surprised to see that it was nearly six. Dr. Lusetti noticed and offered, "Don't worry about the time, Mia. You're my last patient of the day."

Mia knew Mick would likely be at the office until at least seven; that was his normal workday schedule. It felt good talking with Dr. Lusetti and Mia found some of the guilt she had been feeling was lifted from her mind. Then she remembered the encounter with the gang members on Fifth Street. She recounted the story to Dr. Lusetti.

"Unfortunately, that's to be expected," she replied. "You're going to be in their crosshairs. You just need to ride it out."

It wasn't really what Mia wanted to hear but she knew the doctor was right. She hoped things would calm down soon but she knew that was unlikely. Things would take time to play out and that time would likely be very uncomfortable for both her and Mick.

Mia spent another half hour talking with Dr. Lusetti before thanking her and taking an Uber home. She didn't want to chance another encounter with the gangbangers.

CHAPTER 19

〜

"Hey, Mia, is that you?"

Chuck was in the basement watching television. Sasha, the family dog, jumped from his lap and raced for the stairs.

"Yeah, it's me!" she yelled down the stairway, leaning down to pet Sasha, a Jack Russell/Beagle mix, who was very excited to see her.

Chuck stood and made his way up the stairs to greet his daughter. He was quite concerned about her and wanted to see how she was holding up.

"Hey, I'm glad you're home. How'd your day go?" he asked, giving Mia a hug.

"It was okay, for the most part. More interviews at the station and then I had an appointment with the department's shrink. A young woman named Dr. Lusetti. She was really good."

"You went to a psychologist?"

"Yep, it's actually required by the RCSO for any deputy involved in an OIS. It's a good policy."

"And this woman was able to help you?"

"Yeah, she did, actually. It helps to talk things out and she offered me some insights I hadn't considered before."

"Mia, you know you can always talk to me," responded Chuck, feeling a bit hurt.

"Oh, I know, Dad. And it's great to discuss things with you, but this doctor has helped a lot of deputies process what they're going through after an OIS, so she has some really good perspectives."

"Okay, I just want you to know I'm always here for you."

Mia gave Chuck another hug and kissed him on the cheek. "I know, Dad. And I truly appreciate that."

"Any idea when Mick's coming home?" Chuck asked, changing gears.

"No, I haven't heard from him all day."

"Should I start on dinner? I was going to make some pasta."

"Let me text him and get his ETA."

"I've got salad stuff in the fridge, too. We can have that with the pasta."

Sasha suddenly ran for the front door. Mick was home.

"Hey, just got your text. My ETA is one second. How's that for timely?"

Mia smiled and gave Mick a hug and a kiss.

"Are you hungry, Mick? I'm thinking pasta and salad," said Chuck.

"Perfect."

"Okay, both of you outta my kitchen. I've got everything handled in here."

The two moved to the living room sofa. Mick started, "So, how'd the interviews go today?"

"Pretty much like yesterday. They keep asking me the same questions over and over again, like I might suddenly remember something new."

"It's just part of the process; they need to be thorough. I don't think there's any worries about the shooting being ruled anything but justified, but the county is always worried about the liability side of things."

"But if it's ruled a justifiable shooting, then we're good, right?'

"Yes and no. It certainly takes a bite out of the civil suit. And with you ultimately being cleared there won't be a criminal case. But the family will sue, and the county will very likely write a relatively small check so this all goes away. It's purely an economic decision, so don't take it personally."

"It's hard not to, but I understand the realities of it all. When you say a 'relatively small check,' what are we talking about?"

"It can vary, but with Washington being so young the check could reach seven figures, maybe a little more, but that's just a guess. It will also depend on how much publicity the case gets. If it ends up on the front page of the paper every day the county elected officials will want it to go away ASAP and they're likely to write a larger check."

Mia shuddered at the thought of the story being played out over and over again on TV and the front pages of newspapers.

"So a million bucks?"

"Just a guess. And who knows, maybe the county takes a stand and fights it. That happens, too, but typically they just write the check. The county has insurance for these kinds of things so a portion of the settlement would be paid through that. Look, I just want you to know what can happen in these cases."

Mia was conflicted by the idea of giving money to Washington's family. On one hand she felt horrible about what happened and if some money could ease their loss, she was fine with that. On the other hand, she was sure she hadn't done anything wrong and didn't feel like her actions should cost taxpayers any of their hard-earned money.

"Okay."

"So how'd it go with Dr. Lusetti?"

"She was great. I pretty much went in thinking I wouldn't get much out of it, but I really felt better when we finished."

"That's great to hear. I've heard a lot of good things about her."

"She's really insightful and she didn't mince words, which I appreciated."

"So, overall your day went pretty well?"

Mia considered not telling Mick about her encounter with the gang members on Fifth Street; she didn't want to worry him. But if she was going to carry a weapon she needed an official approval from the sheriff.

"Yeah, it was okay. Although I did have a little issue this afternoon with some gangbangers."

Mick stared at her. "What? What do you mean?"

"I decided to walk to my appointment with Lusetti. On my way there I was confronted by a group of gangbangers—120th Street, based on the gang signs they threw down. Anyway, they eventually let me through, but they certainly recognized me—from the media coverage, I guess."

"What exactly happened?" Mick asked, his voice rising in anger.

"They just hassled me a bit. Told me they knew who I was and what I had done to their little homie Alex. It was over in like, two minutes. No harm, no foul."

"Assholes! I'll let our gang unit know and they can deliver a message that this won't be tolerated. They aren't going to pull this shit. Not on any of my deputies, and certainly not my wife!"

"Mick, I'm fine. The only reason I brought it up was to ask if I can be allowed to carry a weapon. I know my Beretta can't be returned to me but can I carry another firearm? I just feel better if I have some protection with me. I feel naked without it."

"Absolutely. I have several guns you can use. Pick out the one you like and then head to the range to get comfortable with it. Damn it, this really pisses me off."

Now it was Mia's turn to calm her husband down. "I know, Mick, but over time this will all fade away. Then we can get back to normal and get ready for the baby."

Mia looked at Mick and reached out for his hand. She pressed it to her belly. The baby was active and he could feel the movements. It was still such a miracle to him that a living human being was inside Mia's body—a little person they had created together. He focused on that and tried to forget about what Mia had told him.

⚬

Danesha Washington was at home, surrounded by family and friends, all trying their best to comfort her. She had barely been able to function since learning her son had been killed by police the previous day. The Ambien had done its job and she had managed to get some sleep the night before, but she was still in a trance-like state. Her family had demanded she eat a couple of times, but she was just going through the motions and didn't really get much down.

The television in the living room was on, the sound turned to low, just providing a bit of a distraction to those present. They sat mindlessly watching another episode of *Family Feud*, smiling occasionally at the antics of the host, Steve Harvey. As the episode ended, the credits rolled and a tease for the six o'clock news flashed across the screen.

It was an image of a pretty young girl with a graphic crawling just beneath her face.

Channel 8 EXCLUSIVE - Hostage Speaks Out!!!

"Turn it up," yelled one of the young men in the room. "That's about Alex!"

All attention turned toward the big-screen TV while someone grabbed the remote and adjusted the volume.

"Coming up next on Channel Eight News at six—an exclusive interview with Kendra Gillespie, the student taken hostage yesterday on the campus of Wilson High School. You'll only see it here on Channel Eight . . . stay tuned!"

Danesha's brother, Floyd Liston, moved to the center of the room, arms folded, his eyes focused on the television.

"Good evening, I'm Amy Johnson. We start tonight's newscast with an exclusive interview with the young woman who was taken hostage yesterday on the campus of Woodrow Wilson High School in Castle Springs. That incident resulted in the death of seventeen-year-old student Alex Washington; he was shot and killed yesterday by a Rocklin County sheriff's deputy. Our Angela Bell has the story."

"Thanks, Amy. As our viewers probably remember, yesterday's

tragedy played out on the campus of Wilson High School in Castle Springs. Watch as we recap those events . . . "

The coverage from the day before was displayed on screen, including the video from the news chopper that captured the actual shooting. Editors fuzzed the footage, blocking out the fatal shot that struck Alex Washington. The story went on to identify Mia Serrano-McCallister as the deputy involved and highlighted the fact that she was pregnant and the wife of Sheriff Mick McCallister. When the package ended, Angela continued.

"Amy, I was able to get an exclusive Channel Eight interview with Kendra Gillespie and her parents, Tom and Rachel Gillespie. They sat down with me just a few hours ago, and as you are about to see this was a very traumatic event for all involved. Here's some of that interview . . . "

Floyd Liston and more than a dozen other people, including Danesha, gathered around the television and watched as Kendra and her parents told their side of the story. Slowly, anger boiled to the surface. Tears began rolling down Danesha's cheeks and she walked out of the room before the interview was over. Floyd followed her into the kitchen.

"Sis, you okay?"

"No, I'm not okay. They're portraying my Alex as some kind of monster. He had his problems, but he was trying. God knows we were all trying to help him. And then this happens and they're demonizing him! So, no, I'm not okay!"

Floyd walked over and put his arms around his sister to comfort her. The interview was bullshit, he thought, and he needed to do something about it. He couldn't let people draw their own conclusion about what happened based on a one-sided interview on some television news station. After calming Danesha he walked out onto the front porch of the house and took out his cell phone. He googled Reverend Alvie Rollins and the phone number to his Denver church popped up on the screen. Floyd hit the call button and waited.

CHAPTER 20

~≈~

Mick and Mia headed off to bed early, both exhausted from the events of the past two days. Mia fell asleep almost immediately, without Ambien, but Mick was unable to quiet his mind and he tossed and turned. They had seen the Channel Eight interview and were pleased by how well it had turned out. Angela Bell was certainly an asset for the RCSO, thanks in large part to Mark Archer. Mick kept going over the fallout of the shooting in his head, trying to determine what, if anything, could be done to keep things under control. He knew it was a powder keg that could blow at any moment.

A chirp came from his cell phone on the nightstand. He grabbed it and switched it to silent so Mia wouldn't wake up. It was a text from the on duty watch commander:

> More trouble . . . a molotov cocktail was just thrown through the window at Channel 8 studios in Denver. Small fire, no injuries

Shit, he thought. He climbed quietly from the bed and threw on his clothes. He went downstairs and called the watch commander for more details. A few minutes later he was headed to the Channel Eight studios in Denver. On the way he dialed Mark Archer.

"I'm guessing you know about the Channel Eight incident tonight?"

"Yep, I'm headed up there now."

"Me, too. What's your ETA?"

"I'm about ten away."

"You're a little ahead of me. Have you talked to Angela?"

"Yeah, she called me right after it happened. It went down during their ten o'clock newscast. Scared the living shit out of everyone."

"I can imagine. But no one injured, correct?"

"Fortunately, no. It was thrown through the front window, near the entrance. That area is empty after hours; everyone is in the back where the studio is. So they all heard it, but no one was too close. Several crew members were able to put out the fire with a couple of fire extinguishers. Not much damage, just a burned up sofa and the broken window. If this had happened during regular business hours it could have been different. That front office area is usually filled with people."

"Fucking pricks. This has Jaquon written all over it. Is there anything left of the Molotov cocktail? Anything to get prints or DNA from?"

"I doubt it, but I'm sure the Denver CSI people will look into it."

"Okay, I'll see you in a few."

Mick searched his contacts list and located the number for Narcotics Commander Tim Dekker. Dekker picked up on the first ring.

"Hey, Tim, have you heard about what just happened at the Channel Eight studios in Denver?"

"No, sir. Whatcha got?"

"Someone threw a Molotov cocktail through the front window of their studios. This sounds like something that asshole Jaquon might do. Are your guys following him tonight?"

"Yes sir. We've been on him every minute since your call this afternoon. If he'd been up to something like this my guys would have called me, pronto."

"Just the same, can you check in with them and make sure he's been accounted for tonight? I'd love to find out he was the prick behind this and lock his ass up."

"Sure, I'll make that call right now. Be back with you in a couple minutes."

"Thanks, Tim."

Mick pulled up to the studio and saw a half dozen Denver black and whites in the parking lot, along with a Denver Fire Department truck. He parked and saw Mark and Angela standing outside in the parking lot.

"Angela, how are you guys holding up?"

"We're all fine, sheriff. Thankfully these idiots chose the front window and not the ones around back."

"Yeah, thank God for that."

"That would've been interesting—getting firebombed during a live newscast. Would've been a new experience for us," she added with a small chuckle.

"No doubt."

Mick felt his cell vibrate in his pocket.

"Excuse me for a moment."

He walked away and answered the call.

"Sheriff, it's Dekker. My guys have been sitting on Jaquon's apartment and he hasn't gone out at all tonight. So it looks like someone else is responsible for the fireworks show up there."

"I'm surprised, but he still could have orchestrated it. Stayed home and just called the shots."

"It's possible, but from what you told me earlier this guy seems like the type who wants to be in on the action. More of a player than a shot caller. But who knows?"

"Let's hope Denver PD can get something from the scene. It's probably a long shot, but we can hope. Let your guys know what happened tonight; maybe they can pick up some intel from their sources. We need to find the people responsible for this bullshit."

"I'm on it, sheriff."

"Thanks, Tim, and keep me posted on anything you hear."

"Will do, boss."

Mick walked back to where Mark and Angela were standing.

"So, Angela, the obvious question is: was this in retaliation for the interview you did with the Gillespies or just one hell of a coincidence?"

They all knew the answer but Mick thought it was important to air it out.

Angela jumped right in. "Of course it is—I have no doubt. But if these thugs think this is going to intimidate us, they're sorely mistaken. I was a war correspondent in Afghanistan for a year. These punks don't scare me."

Mick glanced at Mark, who was hiding a small smile. This was a side of Angela Mick hadn't seen before. He liked it.

"I can appreciate that, Angela, but we need to be cautious just the same. I'll call Chief Hookstra at Denver PD and ask him to put some resources out here for a few days. Keep an eye on things."

"That's fine, sheriff, but keep in mind that tonight's footage of the Gillespie interview was just part one of a three-night package. We're in sweeps and we fully plan to proceed with the interview the next two nights. If these dirtbags don't like it they can go to hell."

Both men smiled and Mick decided to call it a night. On the drive back to Castle Springs he dialed up Chief Hookstra to tell him about the bombing, although he was sure he would already know about it. The firebombing of a television station within the jurisdiction would certainly garner a call from the watch commander. Chiefs liked to be kept informed of anything that could bring attention to their agencies.

"Thanks, Mick, we're already on top of it. We'll have a couple of uniforms stationed there around the clock. They'll be highly visible and should be a good deterrent to anyone wanting to cause more problems."

"I appreciate that, chief. I think it's safe to say that this bombing is retaliation for the interview Channel Eight did with the family of the girl held hostage yesterday. Did you happen to see it?"

"Yeah, I did. They sure jumped on this story in a hurry. I was surprised they got the girl and her parents to talk so soon after such a horrible experience."

Mick paused for a second, trying to read into the chief's comments. Was he asking, in a subtle way, if the RCSO had something to do with setting up the interviews? Mick wasn't going to take the bait.

"Yeah, I was surprised, too. But I know Angela Bell fairly well and she can be very persuasive. It's also sweeps week and all the news stations are scrambling for news that will win over viewers."

"Well, I'd say she hit a homerun with this story. The ratings will be huge, and now with this incident they'll get even more attention and more viewers."

"Yeah, no doubt. Let's just hope this is an isolated incident. Hey, on another note, would you have any problem with us releasing some cell phone footage of the shooting? There's a ton of it; just about every kid in the quad was taping it. I'm thinking that putting it out to the news media could show the public a little bit of what happened out there."

Mick knew he was asking a lot; typically investigators held evidence very close to the vest, at least until the investigation was complete and all the facts could be put forward at once.

"I'd rather not, Mick. I'm sure you understand why. It could look like we're trying to garner public support for the RCSO. We need to be completely above board on this and I think releasing cell footage could be perceived as something less than that."

"Sure, I understand, but you and I both know how these things go. Law enforcement is always held to a higher standard, and rightfully so. Meanwhile, the Washingtons' attorney won't play by the same rules. All bets are off and they'll pull shit that makes us look bad. I had a case a few years back where an attorney showed the media a toy handgun and told them that was the weapon his deceased client flashed at deputies. 'Just a toy,' he would always say. Sure, it was fake but it looked very real to our deputies. And our guys don't have the luxury of taking a close look at the gun to see if it's real or not before they have to take action. And the public, over time, starts believing the attorney. It's bullshit, chief."

"Tell me about it, Mick. We've had more than our fair share of cases like that in Denver. But we gotta be above board and in the long run it pays off. We just gotta be patient."

It was clear that Hookstra wasn't going to budge on the issue so Mick let it go.

It was after midnight by the time he got back home. Mia was still sound asleep and appeared to be unaware that he had ever left. Good, thought Mick. She had enough to worry about.

CHAPTER 21

~~~~~~~~

Mark Archer arrived at the station the next morning holding a triple latte. He was operating on four hours of sleep and knew he had a chaotic day ahead of him. He sat down in his office and turned on his computer so he could go over the coverage of the various media outlets in the greater Denver area. It was an important part of his job, seeing what the news agencies were covering, and a routine he carried out three or four times a day.

He logged on to the Channel Eight website and saw the headline banner:

Channel 8 Studio Firebombed!!!

He clicked through and read a lengthy story highlighting the events of the night before. He was surprised by the detail in the story. It was very thorough, not typical of stories he generally read in the early morning. Someone must have stayed late at the studio putting it all together, he thought. That made sense, given the magnitude of the event. It wasn't often the media became part of the story. Channel Eight would milk the hell out of it, he reasoned. Whoever did the fire-bombing did quite a favor for Channel Eight. Ironic, he thought.

He checked the other Denver-area media sites and saw that no one else was picking up the story. No big surprise; there were no injuries in the blast and the competition certainly didn't want to direct any unnecessary attention to Channel Eight during sweeps week. He clicked back to the Channel Eight site and reread the story. After a third read through, it hit him—Angela had written the piece. But it didn't make sense; she never wrote copy for the website. That task was left to more junior reporters, editors, and the website editor. But he knew Angela's writing style and this story was clearly hers. He stared at the screen and uneasy thoughts began creeping into his mind. He put those thoughts aside and did a quick check of his voicemails. He had only one.

"Hello, lieutenant, this is Rachel Gillespie. I just wanted to thank you for helping us through the interview yesterday with Angela. We watched the story last night and we understand more of the interview will be played tonight and tomorrow. We all think it went really well. Anyway, there was something else I wanted to discuss with you . . . I know how busy you must be, but I was wondering if you might have time for coffee sometime this morning. Anyway, if you can't, I understand. My cell is (303) 555-7631."

He jotted down her number and checked the calendar on his computer. A couple of department meetings were listed but they were both in the afternoon. His morning looked clear, at least for the time being. He glanced at his watch and saw that it was still before seven. He'd wait a little while before he called back Mrs. Gillespie.

Mia was the first one awake in the McCallister household and decided to make breakfast for everyone. She put on a large pot of coffee and started some scrambled eggs. She turned on the small TV on the kitchen counter and began searching the refrigerator for bacon but couldn't find any. As she considered what else she could serve with the eggs, she heard a newscaster tease the top of the news with a story about a "firebombing at the Channel Eight television station." She turned her attention to the TV and saw news footage showing the exterior of the Channel Eight studio. The window was broken and the inside was black with soot. The story cut to Angela Bell, who was being interviewed by one of her co-workers at Channel Eight. It was odd seeing Angela on camera, Mia thought. She turned up the volume.

"We were live doing the ten o'clock newscast when the bomb came through the front window of the studio. Thank God, no one was there at the time and our staff was able to put out the fire before it spread to other parts of the building. We are very, very lucky."

"Any idea why someone would want to firebomb Channel Eight?" asked the reporter.

"Not really . . . I mean, there are always some people that are unhappy with how we cover a story or don't like what they perceive to be an editorial slant to our coverage, but who knows what might have set this person off."

The reporter lowered his voice a bit and said, "Now, Channel Eight aired an exclusive interview last night with the high school student taken hostage on the campus of Wilson High School a couple of days back. Any chance this could be related to that?"

"Oh, I don't know. It could really be anything. But now that you mention our exclusive with Kendra Gillespie and her parents, I suppose there might be some people not happy about that. But that's just speculation on my part."

"Has anything like this ever happened to you in your broadcast journalism career?"

"No, this is a first . . . and I hope it's the last."

The reporter turned back to the camera and wrapped the story.

Mia stood there, stunned by what she had just heard. More fallout from the shooting—it was like a nightmare that just kept repeating. She sat down at the kitchen table and stared at the wall, oblivious to the the eggs burning on the stove.

"Mia, the eggs!"

It was Chuck, with Sasha at his heels. He grabbed the pan from the stove and moved it to the counter.

"Oh my God. Dad, I'm so sorry. I forgot about the eggs."

"You didn't smell them burning?"

"No, I'm sorry. Just kinda got lost in my thoughts for a minute. I'll make some more."

"That's okay, Mia. I'll make breakfast."

Chuck got busy cooking. Once the eggs were in the pan he turned his attention back to his daughter.

"What's going on, Mia? You looked spooked."

Mia looked up at her father and slowly shook her head. "Channel Eight got firebombed last night. They think it might be because of the interview they did with the girl taken hostage."

"They got bombed?"

"Yeah, last night during the ten o'clock newscast. The bomb went off in a different part of the building, and thankfully no one was hurt. But, my God, this is all because of me."

Chuck walked over and put his arms around Mia.

"Sweetie, you didn't do anything wrong—all this stuff is people acting out. They're responsible for this, not you."

"It doesn't feel that way, Dad. It was my actions that set all this in motion. If I hadn't done what I did the other day none of this would be happening."

"Maybe, maybe not. A family might well be planning their daughter's funeral today if you hadn't acted. And if you hadn't responded to the scene the other deputies would probably have done the same thing that you had to do. Or there might have been an exchange of gunfire and innocent people could have been hurt or killed."

Mia listened to her father. She had heard it all before, but it didn't ease her pain.

"Hey, good morning," said Mick, walking into the kitchen. "I think I smell eggs."

Chuck looked at Mick. "Yep, got scrambled eggs and toast coming up in a few minutes. Here, sit down with your wife, Mick."

Mick took a seat at the table, but Mia barely looked over at him.

"What's wrong, Mia?'

"Channel Eight got firebombed last night. They think it might be related to the shooting."

"Yeah, I know about it."

"How did you know? Did you hear it on the news?"

"No, I actually got called out on it last night. I went to Denver and met with the Channel Eight crew. Archer was there, too. Look, they don't know for sure that it was in retaliation for the Gillespie interview. We'll just have to see."

"Oh, come on Mick. What else could it be?"

"We just don't know at this point. I spoke with Chief Hookstra last night and he's got his people on the place twenty-four-seven. Nothing more is going to happen out there. It'll pass in a few days, but the bottom line is that this is not your fault, Mia!"

Mia didn't respond. She was thinking back to her session with Dr. Lusetti, trying to remember all the coping mechanisms she had learned.

Chuck slipped plates of eggs and toast in front of Mick and Mia, then backed out of the kitchen and retreated to the basement with Sasha.

"Maybe I'll see Dr. Lusetti today."

Mick looked at his wife. She was obviously very troubled by the incident at Channel Eight.

"I think that's a great idea. You know she's there whenever you need her. You should give her a call this morning and set something up."

"I think I will."

CHAPTER 22

The Reverend Alvie Rollins was quite pleased but not surprised to receive the phone call from Floyd Liston. Floyd's anger came through loud and clear; he was stunned by what he described as the one-sidedness of the Channel Eight interview. His dead nephew, who wasn't even yet in the ground, was being demonized by both the news media and the Gillespie family. Liston said he could understand the Gillespies not being particularly fair or rational at this point, but the actions of the news media were simply inexcusable. Just two days earlier, Liston had blocked the reverend's access to Alex's mother but now the family was willing to talk to him. They were coming around to his way of thinking, he thought.

Rollins arrived shortly after ten and parked in front of the house. The crowd had thinned considerably since the day of the shooting and there was no one standing on the front lawn. He walked up to the front door and knocked loudly. Thirty seconds later a young man answered, saw the reverend's collar, and let him in.

"I'm here to see Danesha Washington. She's expecting me."

"Wait here and I'll see if she's awake."

Rollins took a quick look around the living room. Lower-class household, he thought, almost certainly living paycheck to paycheck, with a good chance the family was receiving some form of public assistance. That was the government's way, getting everyone feeding at the public trough. No worries, he thought; a nice, large settlement from Rocklin County would lift this family out of this existence. He would help them obtain that; they deserved it.

After a few minutes, a large, disheveled woman stood appeared before him; her eyes were red from two days of crying.

"I'm Danesha Washington. Who are you?"

"Good morning, Ms. Washington. I'm Alvie Rollins and we have a ten o'clock meeting scheduled. I spoke with your brother Floyd Liston yesterday—"

"So much has happened the last two days, I'm sorry, I can't remember . . . "

Danesha looked confused and for a moment Rollings considered rescheduling the meeting. But he approached the woman, his arms extended toward her. As they came face to face he gently placed his hands on her shoulders.

"May our Lord, Jesus Christ, take your heavy heart into his hands. Dear Jesus, fill this woman with your love and grant her peace during this most trying of times. Bless the soul of her beloved son, Alex . . . and please, dear Jesus, allow her family to find justice in this hate-filled world. In Jesus' name we pray."

Danesha lifted her head and looked at Rollins. Tears rolled down her cheeks as Rollins gently embraced her.

"It'll be alright, Danesha. It's all in Jesus' hands now."

The two moved to a nearby sofa and began to talk.

☙

"Thanks so much for meeting me this morning; I'm sure you're a very busy man."

"No problem at all."

Mark Archer and Rachel Gillespie were sitting at the Bean Crazy coffee house in Castle Springs.

"Look, I really want to thank you for everything you did to help us get the interview with Channel Eight. It really allowed us to tell our side of the story, and guess what—all the reporters on our lawn are gone!"

Mark smiled and replied, "That's great! I figured it would do the trick. Our next step would have been to blast them with a firehose."

"Oh, that would've been something!"

"Don't think I haven't had that thought a few times."

Rachel laughed, looked at Mark, and continued. "Look, I wanted to meet with you today to offer my apologies."

Mark look surprised. "Apologies for what?"

"For my husband's rude behavior. He wasn't exactly cordial to you, or to Angela for that matter. This situation has been extremely hard for all of us and it's Tom's usual way of handling things—just kind of shutting down and acting like a jerk. You and Angela did us a favor with this interview and I just want you to know how much I appreciate it."

Mark didn't really know how to respond. In reality, the Gillespies had done the RCSO a huge favor by doing the interview, not the other way around. Of course, Rachel didn't know this.

"Oh, there's no need to apologize. You guys have been through a very traumatic experience and I totally understand his reaction."

"Well, I wasn't happy with him and I let him know."

"I'm sorry to hear that. I hope he's calmed down now."

"Not really. He'll just find something else to be angry about. To be honest, life with my husband is not very easy."

Mark wasn't sure where this was going. He looked at Rachel and tried to get a read on her. She was a very attractive woman and certainly didn't look old enough to have a seventeen-year-old daughter. Her husband was a lucky man; too bad he didn't know it.

"So you're saying we can sue the sheriff's department for killing my Alex?"

"Yes. They need to pay the price for what they did. They deprived you of your son and they need to be held accountable. Ms. Washington, look at it this way—the sheriff's department and law enforcement throughout this nation need to get the message that their abhorrent behavior and total disregard for those in minority communities will not be tolerated. Don't let your son die in vain. This could be a turning point in police community relations. Your case could be the catalyst for change."

Alvie Rollins and Danesha Washington had spent nearly an hour talking on the living room sofa. At first reluctant, Danesha was starting to come around to the reverend's way of thinking. He had worked his magic on her, talking about improving the relationship between police and the African-American community, although the idea of getting a large cash settlement from the people who killed her son didn't hurt. Rollins was throwing out figures as high as ten million dollars and Danesha was hanging on every word.

"So, what do we have to do to make this happen?"

"First thing's first, and that is you need a good lawyer."

"Do you know any?"

"Yes, I happen to know an excellent attorney who has done this kind of thing before."

"Do you think he might want to take my case?"

"I can speak to him on your behalf if you'd like. In fact, I happen to be having lunch with him today. I can bring it up then."

"But I don't have any money to pay him. Would he still want to do this for my Alex?"

"Yes, I'm sure he'd be willing to take the case. And the best part is that you don't have to pay him a dime. Once the case settles he'll just take a small percentage off the top and then you and your family can keep the rest. Maybe use some of the money to put up a nice memorial for Alex. My Lord, Danesha, he'd be so proud of you for that."

"This seems too easy. I really don't have to pay him?" Danesha was having trouble with the concept.

"Leave all that to me. Sometimes you just gotta put all your faith in Jesus. And I think this is one of those times. Trust me, Danesha, trust me."

CHAPTER 23

⤡

Mark was clearly getting a vibe from Rachel Gillespie. He still wasn't sure why she had wanted to meet; the reason she gave about wanting to apologize for the actions of her jerk husband seemed weak to him. He knew he should just end the conversation and tell her he had to get back to work, but he couldn't quite bring himself to let her go. She was easy to talk to and once she'd gotten past bad-mouthing her husband they had settled easily into other subjects. He had learned that she and Tom were high-school sweethearts and had been married for eighteen years. Kendra came along quickly after they married, making them parents before either was twenty years old. Tom was a successful financial planner and Rachel had only recently gone back to work. She had found a part-time job at a hospital in Littleton, where she worked in the human resources department. She enjoyed her work, but Tom often grumbled that it took too much of her time—time she should be devoting to him.

"Oh, look at me—taking up all your time. I'm so sorry, Mark."

"No, no, don't worry about it. My schedule's pretty flexible."

Rachel continued, "Well, I better run. I've got to get to work. But look, I've really enjoyed our time together this morning."

"Yeah, me too."

Rachel hesitated for a half second and then reached over, put her hand on Mark's, and gave it a little squeeze. "I hope we can get together again. I'd like that very much."

The good reverend left Danesha Washington's home and drove directly to the office of his friend, attorney Leland Simpson. The office was in a downtown Denver highrise, complete with spectacular views of the greater Denver area. It was a crystal-clear day and the mountains off to the west looked close enough to touch.

The rent for the penthouse office, while exorbitant, was chump change to Simpson given the rather large settlements he had earned for clients in the past few years. He had carved out a lucrative specialty suing law enforcement agencies in excessive force cases, netting more than thirty million dollars for his clients and, most importantly, some fifteen million for himself. Much of his business came from referrals, and Alvie Rollins was his top scout. In just the past three years Rollins had brought him four cases, yielding a profit of more than two million dollars each. For his efforts Rollins was paid a five percent finder's fee, a princely sum for a minister. So far, his take totaled over half a million dollars, which wasn't bad, given not a single case had gone to trial.

Rollins waved to the receptionist seated in the fancy office and walked right through to Simpson's office.

"Alvie, my friend, what brings you downtown this morning? Got some good news for me?"

"Yes, I believe I do. Could be a good one, Leland."

"Sit, sit. Can Elaine get you a latte or espresso?"

"No, I'm fine," he replied, too excited to sit. He walked over to the ten-foot-high window and gazed out at the Denver skyline. Down below he could see the Rockies getting ready for an afternoon game. Batting practice was underway.

"So, what have you got for me?"

"Did you see the news about the high school kid that was shot to death down in Castle Springs? A deputy with the Rocklin County SO took him out."

Of course Simpson had seen the story; it was to his benefit to keep his eyes open to any potential police brutality cases.

"Yes, I've been following it. The case has caused quite a stir."

"With good reason. The kid was shot in the back of the head in front of hundreds of high school kids."

"Yeah, I saw that. Of course, he had taken a hostage and was threatening her life . . . "

"Yeah, there's that."

"Easily overcome—just a minor inconvenience."

"I met with the victim's mother this morning, Danesha Washington. She's quite distraught, as you can imagine. I explained that she would have a very strong case against the RCSO, should she want to pursue things legally."

"And her response?"

"Quite positive after I explained to her how it works. I think she's onboard. Might be a good idea for you to meet with her before some unscrupulous attorney gets to her."

Simpson chuckled. "Yeah, we don't want that to happen. Can you set something up for this afternoon? I can clear my calendar."

Denise Elliott was pissed off. Her station had been royally scooped by Channel Eight on the Wilson High shooting. First, Angela Bell landed an exclusive interview with the Gillespie family and then Channel Eight garnered headlines for getting their front window blown out. Big fucking deal, she thought; a little Molotov cocktail wake up call. She would gladly be the recipient of a lousy bottle filled with gasoline in exchange for getting the story. And she had spent two days on the Gillespies' front lawn, trying to get someone from the family to go on camera with her, till she got shooed off by the RCSO. She had nothing, a big fat nothing, for her efforts. Then Angela Bell gets invited into their living room and she delivers the goods. What the hell, she thought. How did she pull that off?

Sure, she had been the one to break the news that the deputy involved in the shooting was the wife of the sheriff and that she was pregnant, but most of her thunder was stolen by McCallister when he went public with it at the news conference that day at the school. She couldn't catch a break on the story; it was like she was jinxed.

She sat at her desk reading the story on the Channel Eight website, which highlighted all the details about the firebombing. Once again, Channel Eight was all over it. The story was quite extensive and detailed, not at all like the hastily-written story typically posted to a TV news website in the middle of the night. They must have had a reporter stay after hours to write the piece, she thought. She reread it, trying to find some angle to the story that she might play off that wouldn't draw more attention to Channel Eight.

Then she saw it. The timestamp on the website story: *10:48 pm.*

"So, what's going on, Mia?"

Mia was seated in Dr. Lusetti's office, sipping a bottle of water. She had called the doctor soon after telling Mick she wanted to arrange an appointment and Dr. Lusetti had told her to come right in.

"Did you see the news this morning?'

"No, I didn't get the chance. What did I miss?"

"Channel Eight got bombed last night. Someone threw a Molotov cocktail through their window during a live newscast. They think it was in retaliation for an interview they did with the family of the girl held hostage."

"Okay, I can understand why you might be upset, but remember what I told you yesterday—this is not your fault."

"Yes, of course it's my fault. I started this whole chain of events when I shot Alex."

"These things are out of your control and you are not responsible. Period."

"I know what you said, but this shit is real. And I'm having a hard time believing what you said. I mean, it all sounds good, but when bombs start being thrown into buildings, it gives one pause," Mia answered, giving a bit of a glare at the doctor.

"I can understand you feeling that way, Mia. But we need to move you away from that kind of thought process and toward new ones."

Mia looked at Dr. Lusetti. What she was saying sounded like mumbo jumbo psycho babble. She hoped she hadn't been wrong about the doctor.

"I've got to be honest, I'm having a hard time with you telling me just to move past this and develop new ways to think about things. This event really happened and a kid is dead."

"I'm not saying that and I'm certainly not minimizing what happened on that campus. Mia, it won't be easy, and it'll take some time and hard work, but you need to develop these skills or you may suffer flashback-type feelings anytime something reminds you of what happened on that campus. I can really help you with that."

Mia paused for a moment, her thoughts suddenly settling on her experience on the campus of Columbine High School so many years earlier.

"What do you mean, flashback-type feelings?"

"Oftentimes when someone goes through a traumatic event they'll have flashbacks. Usually they come on when you don't expect it, typically triggered by other events. You were probably doing okay this morning until you saw the news about Channel Eight and then you flashed back to the shooting. But it can often be much smaller trigger events. I've counseled deputies who have flashbacks when they hear a loud, unexpected noise, for instance. Their mind immediately goes back to their OIS, or whatever the primary event was, and they almost relive it. It can be terrifying."

"I'm familiar with PTSD—I mean, that's what you're describing, essentially."

"Yes, but until you actually experience it you don't realize how upsetting it can be. I've had deputies tell me they dive for cover when they hear a car backfire in the Walmart parking lot."

Mia hesitated, not sure if she should proceed.

Lusetti picked up on it. "Mia, what's going on? Do you have something else you want to talk about?"

She blurted it out. "I was at Columbine."

CHAPTER 24

Floyd Liston dialed the cell number for his nephew Jaquon. He picked up after a few rings.

"Hey, Uncle Floyd, what's happening?"

"Jaquon, I just saw on the news that someone threw a firebomb through the window at Channel Eight last night. You wouldn't happen to know anything about that, would you?"

"What? Someone put the hurt on those assholes? Did you see that bullshit interview with blondie last night?"

"Yeah, I saw it. But that doesn't give someone the right to throw a damn bomb through the window. Someone could have been killed."

"True dat. But come on, Uncle Floyd—doesn't a part of you just wanna high five that doer?"

"No, I don't want to high five the guy. I wanna slap him upside the head, to be truthful."

"Ah, come on man—you gotta loosen up. Shit happens, you know dat."

"Do you know anything about the bombing, Jaquon?"

"No man, I'm clean on it. But I'd like to buy the guy who done it a forty ouncer."

Mick McCallister was determined to find out who did the bombing at Channel Eight. Mia was clearly upset by it, and rightfully so. He hated to see his wife suffer; she was going through enough already. He worried about the pregnancy; she was seven months along so if the stress from all that happened somehow caused the baby to come early, it would have a pretty good chance for survival. He was thrilled at the prospect of becoming a father and now all this mess was clouding things up for him and Mia and their unborn child.

Technically, it wasn't his responsibility to find the bomber—the crime had been committed in Denver, outside the jurisdiction of the RCSO. But that didn't mean he couldn't quietly do his own investigation. His interest centered around Jaquon, even though his undercover guys had reported that Jaquon was at home when the bomb was tossed. But the little shit had been a problem since the moment he had met him at the Washington home the night of the shooting. And then seeing him on the campus of the high school inciting the crowd to carry out violent acts—he'd had his fill of Jaquon.

He picked up the phone and dialed the direct line to Chief Hookstra in Denver. He picked up on the first ring.

"Good morning, chief. Did you manage to get much sleep last night?"

"Yeah, a little bit, but our CSI team was out there until dawn this morning. We also called in the Denver Arson Task Force to take a look."

"Did they find anything?"

"Nope. There wasn't that much left to find. The bottle shattered when it went through the window and the gasoline started the fire, which destroyed a lot of the potential evidence. So we're working it from the other side, going through lists of potential perps, seeing who has done this kind of thing before."

"Well, I've got a name for you. Jaquon Jackson, DOB 8/23/94."

"And how does he tie in with all this?"

"He's Alex Washington's cousin. We've already had a couple runins with him. He's definitely taking his cousin's death personally. I think the interview Angela Bell did with the family was the trigger and he decided to take action against Channel Eight. To my way of thinking he's suspect number one."

"Makes sense."

"But there's a problem. My guys have been tailing him since the night of the shooting and they tell me Jaquon was settled in for the night when the bombing went down. It's possible he slipped my guys and did the thing himself, but a more likely scenario has him putting this thing in play and having some buddies carry out the mission."

"Okay, I'll have my guys run him through our system and see if anything pops. Now we just need to make sure there isn't a repeat of last night's events at Channel Eight. They told us they're planning on airing part two of the interview tonight and another part Monday night. I've got my guys planted very visibly outside the studio twenty-four-seven so that should fend off anyone with a stupid idea."

"Okay, that sounds good. Keep me posted if you learn anything about Jaquon."

"Will do, and give my best to Mia."

Denise Elliott wrestled all morning with feelings of angst about Channel Eight getting the interview with the Gillespie family; the bombing at their studio was just the icing on the cake. Now, all eyes were on her rival station and it couldn't be happening at a worse time—sweeps week for all Denver-area news agencies.

The timestamp of the website story, 10:48 pm, was really puzzling to her. Ten o'clock Denver-area newscasts ended at 10:35, allowing for the late night shows to start. The bomb was thrown sometime during the news-cast. The story didn't specify the exact time, but how did they get the story written and posted so quickly? She could understand if the story had just been a quick hit, listing just a few facts, but the story had depth—way too much depth, in her opinion, to have been put up at 10:48 pm. And who wrote it? By ten at night most of the newswriters had gone home.

She picked up the phone and dialed Henry Beltran, her former videographer, who now worked at Channel Eight. Elliott was still on good terms with Henry and hoped he could share some insights.

Beltran recognized Elliott's number on his screen.

"Hey, Denise. How goes it?"

"I'm doing well, Henry. Just trying my best to stay ahead of the competition. How are Cindy and the kids?"

"All fine, thanks."

"Good to hear. Hey, listen, I was wondering if you were around last night when the bomb went through your window?"

"Yeah, actually I was. They have me pulling a couple of late shifts each week, covering stuff that happens after the other cameras go home."

"So, what happened?"

Henry chuckled, "Don't tell me, Channel Two's going to do a story about it?"

Elliott fibbed, "Yeah, my editor thinks we should do something on it. Personally, I think it's bullshit . . . not sure why we want to give you guys any play on our newscasts, but you know how assignment editors roll."

"Yeah, tell me about it. As far as last night goes, I was in one of the edit bays cutting footage for a story when I heard a loud boom. A bunch of us ran out to see what it was and we saw the sofa and the drapes on fire. So we grabbed a fire extinguisher and doused it. Thank God the assholes did it while we were on air. If they had waited till the middle of the night the whole damn building might have gone up in flames."

"Yeah, I thought the timing was interesting. If their intent was to do some real damage to the building they would have tossed it when no one was there. But they did it while the ten o'clock was in progress. I guess they wanted to scare the hell out of you guys. Probably in retaliation for the interview you ran with that girl and her family. What time did the bomb get thrown?"

"It was during Ray's sports report, so probably around 10:25 or so. That interview with the family was an interesting deal, too. I was one of the cameras on it."

"How so?'

"It happened really quick, like the very next day after the shooting. Angela Bell landed the gig, and it was all rush, rush, rush. I know it's sweeps but the whole thing seemed almost fixed. The media guy for RCSO was there, too."

"Mark Archer? He was there during the interview with the family?"

"Yeah, he stood off to the side and watched the whole thing. Then somehow they got the girl to talk. They even had an extra chair nearby in case she decided to join them—"

Beltran paused, realizing he was probably saying too much, even if Denise was a good friend.

Elliott, sensing her friend's sudden apprehension, let him off the hook, "Okay, I appreciate your help. I may be calling Angela Bell later to get her feedback. Or maybe my editor will come to her senses and kill the story . . . not give you guys more attention than you've already got with all this."

"Sounds good, Denise."

Elliott sat at her desk and considered what she had learned. The bomb was thrown at 10:25 and the story was up twenty three minutes later. No fucking way, she thought. And Mark Archer was at the interview at the Gillespie home? Something wasn't right and Denise Elliott was determined to find the truth.

Dr. Lusetti took a moment before responding to Mia's revelation about being at Columbine High School. It certainly added a layer of complexity to the incident at Wilson High.

"I didn't know that, Mia."

"Yeah, well, it's not something I go around talking about very much. Only a few people know. It's just something that happened and I've put it behind me. It was seventeen years ago."

"Are you okay talking about it with me now? This is a safe environment, Mia—no one will ever know what we talk about in here."

Mia considered what Dr. Lusetti was offering. Mia had spoken briefly to a couple of counselors after Columbine, but neither were much help. Ultimately she had given up and just dealt with the aftermath on her own. Except for some recurring nightmares, she seemed to be managing her life. But she liked and trusted Dr. Lusetti and maybe she would feel better about things if she did open up a bit about it.

"I was there—in the library where a lot of the trouble took place."

Interesting way to describe what happened, Dr. Lusetti thought. A sign that Mia was still struggling with the events of that horrible day.

"Tell me about it, Mia."

Mia didn't respond. She was staring at the fish tank on the far side of the office.

"It's safe here, Mia. Let me help you."

Several more seconds ticked by. Then Mia closed her eyes and started in, "It was my prep period and I was in the library looking at some books for my English lit class. It was just before lunch and I remember hearing some commotion coming from the hallway outside the library. It sounded like balloons popping. I didn't think much of it—probably kids fooling around, I thought."

"That's understandable."

"The noises continued and I just thought it was strange . . . so I walked to the front of the library and looked down the hall. That's when I saw them."

"The shooters?"

"Yes. Their attention was directed at something in the hallway but they were pretty close to the library entrance. They had shotguns with them. I couldn't believe what I was seeing and I froze for a second or two. It was like a dream, or like a scene from a movie playing out before my eyes. And for that split second I thought maybe it was some kind of senior prank. But then they fired a few rounds in the direction of some kids in the hallway and I saw the shell casings being ejected. I knew it wasn't a prank."

"My God, Mia. That must have been terrifying."

"It was, but it wasn't. I mean, of course it was . . . but my mind just kicked into gear and I went into survival mode. I turned away from the entrance and looked around . . . there were two boys just a few feet from me. I told them to hide. At first they didn't understand what I was saying, but then more shots rang out and they ran for cover. I knew one of the boys, I'd had him the year before in my English honors class. The other boy I didn't know."

"And what did you do next?"

"The boy I knew . . . he didn't make it. They came into the library and started looking around. They shot him point blank while he was cowering under a desk."

Dr. Lusetti studied Mia—she was speaking in an almost trance-like state. It was apparent to her that Mia had very likely never spoken in detail to anyone about any of this before.

"I'm so sorry, Mia."

Mia continued, "When I saw that happen I knew that they would kill others. It all seemed so indiscriminate. Like they were just casually picking who would live and who would die. Like they felt they they were God. But what could I do? They were just moving around the library and I was taking cover like everyone else."

"Do you feel like you should have done more, Mia?"

"In my mind, no . . . but in my heart, yes. I mean, I know that if I had acted I would probably have been targeted. No one in that library was moving around—I would have been an easy target if I had tried to stop it."

"A helpless feeling, no doubt."

Mia nodded, and tears began to roll down her cheeks. Dr. Lusetti offered her a tissue and put her arm around Mia's shoulder. The two sat in silence.

CHAPTER 25

Jack Keller was busy dictating reports on the Alex Washington shooting when he glanced down at his watch and realized it was time to go. It had been an incredibly busy week, one spent collaborating with investigators from several other agencies on the OIS case. It was Friday night and he looked forward to spending the weekend with his daughter.

His flight wasn't scheduled to leave until ten but he knew that traffic on a Friday night in Denver would be hellish. He merged onto the freeway and the traffic began moving at a good pace. He made good time until he was a mile from DIA, when things slowed considerably, but he was still ahead of schedule when he pulled into the long-term parking lot. Soon he was at the terminal where he checked his bag, went through security, and headed for the gate.

He had forty-five minutes till boarding so he looked around for a bite to eat. There was no shortage of choices in the terminal, and soon Jack was settled into a place that had a reputation for good burgers. He ordered and sat back to watch the people hurry by. It felt good to sit and relax.

After he finished his meal he walked to the gate and was soon on the plane. He settled in and was asleep before the plane left the ground. Dreams soon followed, playing out in Jack's mind, as always, in black and white.

A beautiful young girl running through a backyard toward a slip and slide, laughing hysterically . . . He chased her from behind, pretending he couldn't catch her. Burgers grilling on a nearby barbecue, friends sitting around a fire pit talking and laughing. Colorful balloons anchored around a large table, with one oversized balloon shaped into the number three.

He recognized the scene—his daughter's third birthday party at their home in St. Louis. Those were happy times, before alcohol took over his life and ultimately ended his marriage. More scenes from his previous life played out in his mind, all centered around his daughter, Lisa.

Jack felt a hand on his shoulder and jerked awake.

"Sir, we're about to land. You'll need to put your seat in the upright position."

He opened his eyes and took a few seconds to remember where he was going. He looked around at the half-empty plane and refocused. A voice came over the loudspeaker.

"Ladies and gentlemen, we're on our final approach. Should be on the ground in just a couple of minutes. Welcome to Puerto Peñasco."

∽

Mark called Angela to see if she was available for a quick dinner during her evening break. Her schedule called for her to do the five, six, and ten newscasts each weeknight, typically giving her some free time between seven and eight thirty. They agreed to meet at a small bistro they frequented a few blocks from the station. It was Friday night and the start of a weekend for both, barring anything serious requiring a callout on Saturday or Sunday.

Mark arrived first, grabbed a table, and carefully began putting together his thoughts. He was bothered by the story about the fire-bombing appearing so quickly on the Channel Eight website, and that the article appeared to be of Angela's hand. Maybe he was making too much of it, he thought. Angela was an experienced reporter who had written hundreds, if not thousands, of stories. But that timestamp really gave him pause . . . could the time listed be wrong? He didn't know how online stuff worked exactly, but the chance of a computer listing an incorrect timestamp was probably slim.

"Hey, stranger, want some company?"

The voice startled him, then he smiled. "Aren't you that famous newscaster—don't tell me . . . aren't you Katie Couric?"

"Watch it, big boy!" she answered, leaning in and offering a quick kiss. She slid into the booth next to him.

"So, how was your day?" she asked.

"Compared to the last couple, it was pretty uneventful."

"That's good. Nice to throw in a slow day once in awhile."

"How about yours? Did you air part two of the Gillespie interview?"

"We did, at the five and the six and we'll go again at ten. It's huge, and our prelim numbers for the week show our viewership up thirty percent. That translates to some pretty big ad dollars for the next quarter. Management is quite pleased."

"I can imagine. After all, it's all a ratings game."

"Well, it's not all about ratings. We actually try to put out a fair and accurate reporting of the news as well."

"No doubt."

Angela glanced sideways at Mark, unsure what he was insinuating.

"Something on your mind tonight, Mark?"

"No, I just know how things work in your business. And I'm not saying there's anything wrong with that. It's just that—a business."

"Well, not to get all high and mighty on you, but this country was founded, in large part, on something called freedom of the press. And I think reporters generally do a pretty good job of informing people about what's happening in their world."

Mark, sensing a fight looming, changed the subject.

"So, what looks good tonight? I'm in the mood for a steak."

Angela stared at Mark, still trying to figure out what was going on.

She let it go.

"Probably just a salad. I've got another newscast to do. If I have a steak I'll be snoring before Kaitlyn gets through the weather segment."

Mark motioned for the waiter and they placed their orders.

"So, I talked to the sheriff today and he was asking me about the Channel Eight website."

It was a lie, but Mark thought it might get him the information he was seeking.

"What about it?"

"He was asking me if Channel Eight people run it or if it's farmed out to some webcast company?"

"We do it. It would be impossible to rely on a third party to run it. When we get breaking news we have to get it up as quickly as possible. To have a third party do that would be time consuming and just not practical. Why would he ask you that?" Angela asked, looking puzzled.

"I'm not really sure. We got interrupted before I could ask him more about it."

"Who does the RCSO website?"

"Same as you guys—we have our internal IT guys run it. We wouldn't farm it out either, except our reasoning is different than Channel Eight. You guys are interested in speed; we have security issues."

"Yeah, I can see that. But you guys do have a breaking news tab. All those webcasts you do at crime scenes—those need to be timely."

"That's true, but we're not competing with anyone like you are."

"I remember when you first started doing the webcasts, like ten years ago—so many in the media were up in arms about it. 'It's not the RCSO's job to report the news' was the cry. 'They can't be fair!' Do you remember all the uproar?"

"Oh yeah, I was clearly stepping on some toes."

"Well, as I hope you recall, I wasn't one of those caught up in the 'media are the only purveyors of the truth' crap."

"I didn't really know you then, but thanks for that. You hadn't been in Denver that long when I started doing the webcasts. When did you arrive, like 2006 or 2007?"

"November 2006. Right during sweeps week."

"Ah, yes, sweeps week."

Angela shot him a look.

"Jesus, Mark—there you go again. What the hell is wrong?"

Mark took a deep breath and started in.

"Look, I noticed the story on the Channel Eight website about the bombing last night was posted really quickly after the firebombing. And it looked to me like you wrote it."

Angela stared at him, her anger growing.

"What the hell are you saying?"

Mark leaned in to her and whispered, "Did you write the story, Angela?"

"No! I'm sure a staffer wrote it, and they did a hell of a job getting it up that quickly!"

Mark sat back in his chair, placing his hands flat on the table.

"Yeah, they got it up quickly, I'll give them that."

Angela stood. "I've lost my appetite."

Mark replied, "Well, I guess I have my answer."

She stormed off without a reply. Several patrons noticed her as she left, and began whispering among themselves, "Wasn't that Angela Bell, the newscaster?"

Mark sat alone at the table, contemplating what had just happened. The waiter brought him the steak he ordered and then, with Cobb salad in hand, looked around for Angela.

"She's not here. Just wrap up her salad to go."

"Very well, sir."

CHAPTER 26

⤛⤜

Jack could feel the warm Mexican breeze as he walked through the open air terminal. Even though it was almost midnight the temperature was still nearly eighty degrees. The beautiful port town of Puerto Peñasco, located on the Sonoran coastline some sixty miles south of the Arizona-Mexico border, was very familiar territory to Jack. He owned a condo on the beach, purchased following his retirement from the St. Louis PD more than a dozen years earlier. Back then Puerto Peñasco was a small, little-known fishing village, but over the years things had changed considerably. It was now a haven for movie stars and celebrities, embraced by many as the new Cabo San Lucas. The airport was new, and the first and only privately-owned airport in Mexico. Jack made his way through the terminal and out to the loading zone out. He instantly saw his daughter.

Lisa Sullivan ran to her father and threw her arms around him, hugging him tightly. They hadn't seen each other in more than three months and Jack held her in a bear hug.

"It's great to see you. It's been too long," Jack whispered in her ear.

"I know, Dad. I'm so glad you're here—I've missed you so much. Come on, let's get to the car so we can get down to the Marbella. We've got you booked into the same suite as last time."

"That sounds great. Where's Peter?" he asked.

"He's waiting in the car."

The Marbella was a world-class luxury resort on the sands of Puerto Peñasco that had been built a decade earlier by Peter Donnelly and his wife, Marbella. Just prior to the opening of the resort Marbella passed away from cancer. Peter named the resort in her honor.

As they approached the Lincoln Town Car, Peter climbed out from the back and shook Jack's hand.

"Welcome, Jack. It's great to see you again. How was your flight?"

"It was good, I think. I slept the whole way here," he replied with a shrug and a smile.

"Look, next time I'll send the jet for you. You mustn't be so stubborn about it."

"No, no—flying commercial is fine for me. I don't mind it at all."

"Well, I'm going to keep working on you. At least take the jet back home on Monday night."

"We'll see, but I already have my return ticket. Wouldn't want to waste it."

Peter shook his head and smiled. Jack was a practical man and his daughter had inherited the trait. It was refreshing after all the gold diggers Peter had encountered over the years.

The three climbed into the Town Car while the driver went to collect Jack's suitcase.

"So, how are the wedding plans coming along?" Jack asked Lisa.

"We've got a few details still to work out. It'll be nice to get your input on some stuff. The wedding is in less than three months. Yikes . . . still so much to do!"

Jack nodded at his daughter. He wasn't sure what he could add to the planning, but he was happy to be included.

"Hey, did I ever tell you what happened when your mother and I got married?"

Lisa looked at her father. They had only reconnected a few years earlier, following a thirty-year separation. No doubt there were many things she hadn't heard about.

"No, I don't think so . . . what happened?"

"So during the reception the people working the event wheeled in the wedding cake. It was supposed to be a big deal—all your mother's idea, believe me. There was music, special lighting, on and on, like a Broadway stage production. I have no idea why this was so important to your mother. Anyway, they started wheeling the cake in and somehow it hit a bump, and—"

"Oh my God, don't tell me, Dad," replied Lisa, covering her mouth with her hand.

"Oh yeah, the damn thing slid right off the cart and hit the floor with a big *splat*."

Peter burst out laughing, then caught himself. "I'm sorry, Jack. But I can just picture it all happening in my mind's eye. All in slow motion, like a car accident."

"Don't apologize, Peter. Hell, I probably laughed the loudest of anyone. Of course, I was drunk at the time, something that was pretty commonplace for me back then."

"Gee . . . somehow Mom failed to tell me that story."

"It was pretty much a foreshadowing of our marriage, I'd say. But I lay all the blame at my feet for the marriage."

"I find that hard to believe, Dad."

"Oh, it's true. But thanks just the same. Now let's talk about happier stuff."

CHAPTER 27

~

A ngela Bell was still angry when she returned to the station to do the ten o'clock newscast. She tossed her purse on her desk and punched in Channel Eight's URL on her computer. What exactly was Mark insinuating with all his questions about the website story? She scrolled through the posted stories until she found the one about the bombing. And there it was—*10:48 pm* listed at the bottom of the article.

Shit, she thought.

The phone on her desk began to ring and she turned her attention to the screen to check the caller ID. Maybe it was Mark calling to apologize, she thought. Those thoughts were quickly dashed when the screen read Channel 2 Newsroom.

Why would Channel Two be calling? She let the phone ring a couple times before letting her curiosity get the better of her.

"Angela Bell."

"Angela, this is Denise Elliott over at Channel Two. How are you doing this evening?" she asked cheerfully.

"Good, Denise. What's up?" she responded, trying to keep her voice from sounding suspicious.

"Hey, I'm putting together a story about the firebombing over there and was hoping to ask you a few questions."

"Channel Two is doing a story about it?" she responded, surprised.

"Well, yeah—it's news, Angela. And 'we keep you covered . . . Channel Two is your news source for the greater Denver area' . . . you know that!" she said mockingly.

"Yeah, right. Splashy slogan and still number two in the ratings. All hat, no cattle, as they say in my native Texas."

"Whatever."

"So, what do you want to know?" Angela asked, getting Denise back on topic.

"Well, you were anchoring the ten o'clock when the thing went through your window, correct?"

"Yep."

"And it was thrown through a window in the front of the building, where the admin offices are?"

"Yes, the studio is in the back. You know that, Denise—you've been here."

Where was she going with this, Angela wondered.

"But there are windows much closer to the studio than the one the bomb went through, and yet the perp chose to toss it where there were no people?"

"Yeah, I guess they did. Maybe they didn't want to hurt anyone. Ever think of that?"

Angela was getting frustrated with Denise's inane questions. Her anger from the exchange with Mark was also still simmering, and Denise was the unfortunate recipient of some of that anger.

"Yeah, I did, actually. But think of the attention this would have gotten if the thing was thrown through a window closer to the studio, interrupting a live newscast. Seeing the reaction of everyone on set . . . that would have been good for a couple million YouTube hits, don't you think?"

"I don't know, Denise. I can't look into the heart and mind of someone who tosses a Molotov cocktail into a building with a bunch of people inside. You got me there."

Elliott didn't respond at first, letting an awkward silence sit between the two, hoping that Angela might jump to fill the void. It was a trick many reporters used, but how often were the tables turned and the tactic used on a reporter? Angela didn't fall for it.

"Got any other questions, Denise?"

"Yeah, just one more. I noticed the timestamp on this story on your website was 10:48 pm. I gotta ask—how did you guys get the story posted that quickly?"

Jesus, Angela thought . . . again?

"We're just really good, Denise. Once that thing went through the window we jumped on it and got the story written and posted. Just good reporting. Nothing more, nothing less."

"Angela, I'm sorry, but there's no way the timeline works. That story was twenty paragraphs. I could understand a quick headline and brief appearing that quickly, but that story had pretty good depth, almost like it was written before the bombing and then posted just minutes after the bomb went through your window."

Angela sat stunned and unsure how to respond.

Elliott waited patiently on the line, waiting to see what, if anything, Angela would say in response to her allegation. It was serious business, essentially accusing Channel Eight of planting a story. Or worse, creating a story.

Angela wasn't sure why, but a hint of her Texas accent somehow sneaked into her voice as she answered. "Denise, you've got yourself quite the imagination. I've never heard of a more ridiculous thing."

"Really, Angela? It makes perfect sense to me. You guys land a great interview with the Gillespie family and you want to do everything possible to pimp the story. It's sweeps week so the timing is perfect. You promote the hell out of it, and rightfully so. But that wasn't enough. You had a home run but you wanted a grand slam. So you arrange to have someone toss the bomb during a live broadcast then go public with it twenty-three minutes later. That was your mistake, Angela.

That damn timestamp."

The accent disappeared. "You're fucking crazy, Denise! Do you know that? And if you go with that story you and your two-bit station will be on the receiving end of a libel suit that'll knock you into Kansas. Got it?!"

Angela's over-the-top response told Denise that she was on the right track.

She hammered away, "And another thing—why was Mark Archer present at the Gillespies' house when you did the interview? Did he help Channel Eight land that deal?"

"I'm done with you, Denise. You and your little tinfoil hat can go to hell."

She hung up the phone and stared at the wall, sensing her world was about to crumble around her.

Mark tossed and turned most of the night, unable to shake from his mind the scene that had played out with Angela about the website article. He didn't like confronting her like that, but he had to know the truth. Was she somehow responsible for the firebomb going through the window? Would she do something like that just to win ratings points? He thought he knew her really well, and it certainly didn't seem like something she would ever do, but who knew? She was a very successful television journalist, driven by ambition. Many other prominent journalists had been caught up in scandals, compromising their journalistic ethics—was it that far-fetched that Angela might as well? Their business was so competitive; reporters were constantly looking for any possible advantage.

If she was guilty of arranging the bombing, then she could be facing felony charges if caught. Her career would likely be over, and prison was a possibility. Probation would be a more likely sentence, but who knew what some judge might do? Someone wanting to look tough on crime could try to make a name for themselves in what was sure to be a high-visibility case. What a frickin mess, he thought as he rolled out of bed.

He grabbed his cell on the nightstand and took a quick look at the screen. No missed calls and no significant personal emails. He checked his RCSO email and read the *Summary of Activities* report filed by the evening watch commander. The reports came to him three times a day, highlighting anything unique or unusual that transpired during the shift. It gave him a heads up as to what he'd be facing with respect to media calls. The evening shift had been quiet and there were no significant events to report. Good, he thought.

Denise Elliott had more than thirty years under her belt in the television news business, most of which had been spent in the greater Denver area. A longtime fixture at Channel Two, there were few people in the industry more respected than Elliott. Her body of work included six Emmys and three Peabody Awards. She had a great nose for news and when she got hold of a story she pursued it relentlessly.

Like Mark Archer, Elliott couldn't shake the concerns she had about Angela Bell and the firebomb story. It was Saturday morning and she grabbed her cell phone. She rarely called Jessica Valenzuela, her newsroom director, especially on a Saturday morning, but she needed to talk about the firebomb issue with her boss. This couldn't wait till Monday, she reasoned.

"Whatcha got, Denise?" Valenzuela asked, sitting at her kitchen table sipping her third cup of coffee. Valenzuela wasn't much for idle chatter.

"A good one. Need to run it by you though—it could get a little dicey."

"I don't mind dicey. Tell me about it."

"So Channel Eight had a Molotov cocktail thrown through their window two nights ago night during their ten o'clock newscast. It was thought to be in retaliation—"

Valenzuela interrupted, "Yeah, yeah—I know about it."

"I have reason to believe that Channel Eight, namely Angela Bell, arranged to have the bomb tossed through their window in an effort to get a ratings boost."

"Whoa. And you know this how?"

"A lot of things, really. And last night I talked to Angela and asked her about it. She was very defensive and threatened to sue. Which leads me to believe even more strongly that she's up to her eyeballs in this."

"Give me specifics. Why exactly do you think she did this?"

Elliott spent several minutes running everything down to Valenzuela, who listened intently to what Elliott reported. They discussed the timing of the story on the website, Mark Archer's presence at the Gillespie interview, and the fact that the story looked to be written by Angela Bell.

"It's all circumstantial, Denise. You gotta have more than this. I can't go and accuse a rival news station of this kind of underhandedness unless we're absolutely sure. If we don't have proof then it just looks like we're taking a shot at the competition, which happens to hold the top spot in the Denver television market."

"I think we do have enough. How do you explain the timestamp on the story?"

"I don't know, but I'll bet Channel Eight will come up with something. A computer glitch, human error, who the hell knows. But that timestamp is not enough proof. Get me more and we can talk."

Elliott, frustrated by her boss's response, ended the call. She grabbed her laptop, typed in the Channel Eight URL and began looking again through the posted stories. After scrolling through more than a dozen entries she realized she was looking at stories from earlier in the week.

The firebomb story was gone.

CHAPTER 28

⌇

Alex Washington's funeral was scheduled for Monday morning at eleven at the Sonrise Community Church in downtown Denver, with the Reverend Alvie Rollins presiding. The Washington family members were not regular churchgoers, so when Rollins offered his church and his services at no cost, they quickly accepted. At first the family said they weren't ready to bury Alex, that they needed a few more days. But Rollins was insistent, saying the sooner the better, so the family could begin the grieving process. Eventually, the family acquiesced and agreed to the Monday service. The truth was that Mondays were typically slow news days and the funeral would likely attract far more media attention on a Monday morning than later in the week. It was attorney Leland Simpson who had suggested Monday, but Rollins didn't share any of this with Danesha or Alex's other relatives.

Over the weekend Simpson had spent considerable time reviewing the extensive press coverage the shooting had received. There were no official reports to review, it was much too early for that, but Simpson was able to glean some information that he felt he could exploit. It was critically important to keep the case on the front page of the newspaper, holding the RCSO's toes to the fire. The public had a short memory and anything he could do to keep the public interest would help him secure a larger settlement from Rocklin County. He certainly didn't want the case to go to trial—he had never taken a wrongful death case against the police to trial—he was just looking for a quick settlement that he could split with the family. Forty percent of a couple million bucks was a very nice payday for him, even after giving Rollins his finder's fee.

Simpson was intrigued by the fact that Mia Serrano-McCallister was seven months pregnant. The sheriff had confirmed this fact at the press conference right after the incident and Simpson contemplated some way to capitalize on it. Media reported she had been leaving a doctor's appointment when the situation began, and that she responded directly to the campus after hearing the commotion. She was in plain clothes, but that was not unusual for an investigator. It wasn't clear if Alex realized she was a deputy, but he would have no reason to assume that she was.

By most eyewitness accounts, Serrano-McCallister was actually making some progress with Alex when the Channel Eight news chopper appeared and startled Washington, starting the fatal chain of events. Simpson considered that for a moment, given that news agencies had both money and insurance policies. Should he name Channel Eight in the lawsuit he would be filing? The RCSO was the deep pocket, but going after Channel Eight might be something to consider. But the more he thought about it the less he liked the idea. He would need the media to put pressure on the RCSO so the case could be settled out of court as quickly and as quietly as possible. Alienating them would work against that objective.

Another consideration was Alex Washington's mental condition. He was clearly a troubled young man, and there were medical records to prove it. Since he was a juvenile, getting access to the records might prove problematic, but with help from the family he should be able to get what he needed. Danesha had told Simpson that Alex was on medication for both depression and bipolar disorder. But Alex wasn't always good about taking his meds, and when he skipped his meds, all bets were off. Even still, maybe the drug companies could be held partly responsible, he thought.

Simpson shifted gears and began drafting a press release giving the details of Alex's funeral. He planned to send it out a couple of times over the weekend and again first thing Monday morning to ensure a good media presence. Reporters loved covering a funeral, especially when the deceased was a seventeen-year-old minority gunned down by police.

Danesha Washington could hardly climb out of bed Monday morning, dreading what would be one of the worst days of her life. Burying her son was something she couldn't quite get her head around. He had been gone for five days, and each morning she had awakened hoping the entire thing was a nightmare. But it was real and now the day had arrived to bury Alex. There was something so final about putting him in the ground—a truly permanent separation.

She put on her robe and went into the kitchen. There were still several family members staying over, and people were lying about the small living room. Danesha managed to put on a pot of coffee, then took a seat at the kitchen table. She thought about what she would wear to the service and suddenly realized she didn't really have anything appropriate. Somehow this had slipped her mind, and she started to panic. The funeral was in less than four hours and she had no dress and really no money to buy anything. She thought about asking her family members for help, but quickly surmised that most, if not all, were in the same financial straits. She considered asking one of her cousins if she could borrow a dress, but none of them was her size.

Danesha looked up when she heard someone enter the kitchen.

"Good morning, sis."

"Hey, Floyd."

Floyd walked over and put his arm around his sister's shoulder. He didn't say anything, there was no need; the moment didn't call for words. She reached up and grabbed his hand.

The coffee maker shut off and Floyd walked over to pour a cup.

"Can I get you some?" he asked, looking back over his shoulder.

Danesha managed a nod and Floyd filled two large cups, adding a heavy dose of cream to Danesha's.

She looked up at her brother with tears in her eyes. "I don't have anything to wear, Floyd. I'm burying my son today and I don't have a proper dress for the service. It never even crossed my mind till a minute ago."

Floyd looked at his sister. She didn't need to be worried about this, he thought.

"I'll take care of it, sis. What size do you wear?"

"Sixteen. What are you going to do, Floyd, go shopping for me?"

"No worries, Danesha. I'll have something for you in a couple of hours."

Danesha looked at her older brother.

"Thanks, Floyd. Thanks for everything you've done for me."

He handed Danesha her coffee and replied, "Anything you need, sis—just ask."

Leland Simpson's administrative assistant faxed out the press release outlining the details of Alex Washington's funeral. It was the third time sending it out, all from a fax machine that had no trace back to his law office. The fax had simply come from *The Family of Alex Washington*, according to the header. He didn't want the media believing that he was orchestrating things, although he did plan to hold a press conference on the steps of the church immediately after the service. It would appear to be impromptu, but it was anything but. He had carefully crafted what he was going to say.

"The fax has been sent. I'm going to run out to Macy's to get the dress. I'll drop it off at the Washingtons' and be back by ten."

"Thanks, Peggy."

"No problem, boss."

Alvie Rollins had called Simpson a few minutes earlier telling him about the phone call he had received from Floyd Liston. Danesha needed a dress and Simpson had immediately agreed to handle it. Anything to keep his newest client happy. Peggy Sandoval would know what to buy.

Denise Elliott read the fax from the Washington family and quickly deduced it wasn't written by anyone related to Alex Washington. She googled the fax number listed at the bottom of the page but came up with nothing. Had to be an attorney's office, she thought. She had seen this kind of thing before. The more attention the media paid to the death of someone killed at the hands of law enforcement, the stronger the wrongful death case would be. One of the factors of wrongful death settlements was pain and suffering. A well-attended funeral that received full media attention helped build the case. If the family had an attorney, and it was quite likely they did by now, he or she would be doing everything possible to attract attention to the case.

Elliott was still upset with her news director over the discussion about the Angela Bell story. Although she understood her boss's apprehension, Elliott was certain she was right. Bell had arranged for someone to throw the bomb through the window in an effort to increase ratings. Her boss wanted more proof, so it was on her to find it.

She planned to attend the funeral at eleven. She knew every Denver media organization would be sending a reporter and the church would be mobbed with people and cameras. It was sure to be an emotional scene, and she would make it a top priority to get Alex's mother on camera. Nothing paid off more than a grieving mom, she thought. She wondered if Angela might be covering the funeral for Channel Eight.

If she was there, it would give Elliott a chance to speak to her again.

Angela Bell had spent the weekend consumed with worry about her phone conversation with Denise Elliott on Friday evening. The fact that she had accused her of doing something totally improper was very upsetting to her. She was the anchor of the number-one rated newscast in Denver—how dare she go after her like that. She had a certain standing in the community and she wasn't going to let someone push her around. If Denise Elliott wanted a fight, she'd give her one.

She'd be covering the funeral at eleven. She, too, had received the fax outlining the details of the funeral. And like Denise Elliott, she thought it odd that there was no real header on the fax, leaving people to wonder who exactly had generated it.

She called the videographer who had been assigned the story and let him know to be ready to leave the studio by ten. It was just a short five-minute drive to the Sonrise Community Church but Angela wanted to get there early to stake out a good position on the front steps.

Peggy arrived at the Washington home at nine thirty with three dresses in hand. All were black but differed in style. Peggy had never met the young mother, so she was purchasing the dresses based only on the dress size she had been given. Danesha seemed appreciative of Peggy's efforts and tried on all three dresses. After selecting the one she wanted she gave the other two dresses back to Peggy, who headed back to the law office.

A large, black limousine, compliments of Leland Simpson, arrived at the Washington home at ten, and the driver went to the door to let them know he was there. He estimated it would take thirty minutes to get to the church, allowing for any hitches they might encounter with

Denver traffic. The limo seated just ten passengers, but the Washingtons had fourteen family members leaving from the house to go to the service. They agreed they'd all manage to cram in.

～

Mark Archer had no plans to attend the Washington funeral. He had made that mistake early in his career, attending a service for someone killed by the RCSO, and had nearly caused a riot. While the shooting in that case appeared by all accounts to be justified, the family resented the presence of anyone from the agency that had "murdered" their son. He was simply there to pay his respects and to express his sympathies, but the family wanted no part of it. At one point, when the mother of the deceased saw Mark in his uniform sitting near the back, she began screaming for him to get out. The minister stopped the service and politely but firmly asked Mark to leave. He was only too happy to accommodate the request and quickly exited the church. He was followed out by more than a dozen people who essentially chased him to his car. He hadn't been to a funeral for anyone killed by the RCSO since.

It was nearly ten and Mark was in his office, thinking about Angela. He didn't like the way things had gone between them at dinner Friday night and had considered calling her several times over the weekend. But he'd never called and now he was feeling like maybe he should reach out to her. He still had serious concerns about Angela's possible involvement in the firebomb that hit Channel Eight, but keeping an open channel of communication was always better than having things shut down between them.

He grabbed his cell and put together a text message, thinking it might be the best way to start a dialogue.

Thinking about u…how are u doing?

Angela checked the message after hearing her phone chirp. She typed back.

On my way to the funeral. . .can't talk

Mark looked at the screen and tried to interpret her text. She either didn't have time to talk or she was blowing him off . . . it was always dicey trying to interpret someone's feelings from a text. As he was looking at the screen the phone chirped with a new message, this one from Rachel Gillespie.

Hi Mark, I'm off today and am going to be downtown,
any chance we can meet for lunch?

He considered Angela's text—she was going to be in Denver at the funeral. What harm would there be grabbing some lunch with Rachel? He typed back:

Sure, when and where?

The service for Alex Washington was thirty minutes late getting started. Pastor Rollin's church had a capacity of just over five hundred people, but there were close to a thousand crammed in. Every seat was taken, every aisle was full, the back was standing-room only, and people were overflowing each of the side doors. If the Denver Fire Department had known about the crowd in the church they would have ordered hundreds to leave. But neither Pastor Rollins nor the family of Alex Washington minded the huge crowd. The family saw it as a nice tribute to Alex, while Pastor Rollins saw it as a way to increase the pain and suffering award the county was sure to offer the family. Five percent of a larger number.

Angela Bell and a half dozen other television reporters were in attendance, each accompanied by a videographer. Typically, there would be just one camera allowed in events like this, a pool camera, and all the news stations would share the footage. This was done to reduce the distraction of having several different cameras shooting the funeral and taking away from the dignity of the service. But both the family and Pastor Rollins had informed the media that all were welcome and so they came. The happier the reporters were the better the coverage, Rollins figured. Many reporters didn't like using pool cameras; they wanted to shoot their own stuff.

The service ran nearly two hours, with an abundance of gospel music and scripture readings. Rollins gave a thirty-minute eulogy, which was quite a feat considering he had never met Alex. At the conclusion of the service Danesha spoke, but she was only able to get through a few lines before she was overcome with emotion and helped back to her seat. The media cameras captured her every move.

Leland Simpson sat in the pew directly behind the family, offering support with the occasional touch of his hand to Danesha's shoulder. On more than one occasion she grabbed his hand and held the embrace, seemingly appreciative of the attorney's support.

Denise Elliott stood at the back of the church. She had her camera guy capture all the poignant moments of the service, but she was most determined to get video of the family coming out of the church. Raw emotion was what she wanted; it made the best television.

Angela Bell was outside, staking out a position on the front steps of the church, ready to talk to Alex's family and friends as they left. Other reporters took various positions outside, each careful that the backdrop of their shot didn't show a reporter from a rival station. It created a sense of exclusivity.

At the conclusion of the service the family filed out first, directly behind the casket. Elliott's videographer angled for just the right shot while Denise darted out of the church and took a position on the steps. She was careful to show a proper level of respect for the situation and wouldn't try to talk to Alex's mother until she was outside. Once the family passed by Denise's videographer he quickly joined

Denise outside. They both managed to station themselves in front of Angela Bell and two other reporters with the same idea. Seeing Elliott suddenly positioning herself on the steps angered the other reporters and infuriated Angela Bell. She told her videographer to maintain his position and quickly ran up the steps to where Denise was standing.

"Excuse me, can we get a little professional courtesy?"

Elliott glanced back and saw it was Angela.

"Professional courtesy? That's a laugh coming from you, Angela."

"Really? You get beat on a story and this is how you react? What are we—in third grade?"

As this exchange was taking place, Danesha Washington, surrounded by her family, came outside and started down the stairs.

"Excuse me, Angela, but I have a story to cover. Maybe you should just call Mark Archer and see if he can get you an exclusive with the family," replied Elliott, forming air quotes with both hands to emphasize the word *exclusive*.

Angela, not wanting to make a scene, resumed her position with her videographer as he shot some usable footage. Denise was able to corral the family and do a quick interview with Danesha on the stairs outside the church.

"Zoom in tight on the mom," Angela told her video guy, angling her mic toward the woman. "We can edit it later and make it look like our interview. Make damn sure you don't get any of that bitch, Elliott."

While Angela wouldn't be in the shot, having Danesha offering her thoughts and feelings about her son could be edited and included in her package.

At the bottom of the steps of the church stood a man who was starting to speak loudly. He was tall, African American, in his early sixties, and very well dressed. A couple of reporters noticed and moved to set up around him. Both Angela and Denise saw what was happening and headed down the steps. The man began speaking.

"Good afternoon. My name is Leland Simpson and I am the attorney representing the family of Alex Washington."

Simpson paused, allowing all the cameras to be positioned properly before he continued. He wanted to give the family enough time to get down the steps and gather behind him. A minute later Danesha and several of her relatives, including her brother Floyd and her nephew Jaquon, were all in place.

Denise Elliott recognized Simpson—he had sued law enforcement agencies before and Denise had covered the stories for Channel Two. Angela, being on the anchor desk, didn't cover the stories in as much depth as Elliott and she didn't know Simpson.

Once everyone was in place, Simpson continued speaking.

"Ladies and gentlemen, my name is Leland Simpson and I have been retained as legal counsel by the family of Alex Washington. Just five days ago Alex was a typical seventeen-year-old high-school student whose biggest concerns in life centered around grades, girls, and the Denver Broncos. But today we bury young Alex, taken from his loving family much too soon. All this at the hand of a Rocklin County sheriff's deputy, whose primary job is to ensure public safety. And yet, here we stand, once again ready to bury yet another young person of color, killed at the hands of the police."

Here we go, thought Denise.

Simpson continued, "It is my job to make sure that young Alex didn't die in vain. Alex's death must be a turning point, not only here in Denver but across the nation. Enough is enough—this has got to stop!" shouted Simpson.

There was a burst of applause from the crowd that had gathered near the bottom of the steps.

"If you are an African-American male living in the United States of America, make no mistake about it—you are at risk. Every time you are confronted by police you are at risk. If you are African-American, police are trained to shoot first and ask questions later. But if you are white and live in a nice, rich neighborhood the police don't stop you. They just wave at you and say, 'Good morning.'"

More applause. Simpson, fueled by the crowd, continued.

"Alex Washington was gunned down by police on the campus of his high school, shot in the *back* of the head! No judge needed, no jury needed—just *bam*, let's take him out! Where is the justice?!"

Denise Elliott looked around at the crowd and saw they were getting fired up by Simpson's antics. She leaned over to her videographer and said, "Get some crowd shots."

Simpson continued, "And then we learn the deputy who murdered our Alex is none other than the wife of the sheriff. What kind of justice do you think we'll see in this case? I'll tell you what we'll see—they'll whitewash the investigation and then just brush the whole thing under the rug—that's what we'll see! You can bet this deputy will be cleared of any wrongdoing, in fact she'll probably be promoted! It's the RCSO way!"

The crowd booed and hollered, clearly under Leland Simpson's spell.

"But there's more! This deputy, Mia Serrano-McCallister, is seven months pregnant! And she's still on duty? What factor did her pregnancy play in this outrageous act? Was she fearful for her unborn baby? Did it cause her to take steps she might not otherwise take? Did hormones cloud her judgment?"

Whoa, thought Elliott. Did he really just mention hormones?

The crowd buzzed, but Elliott couldn't quite read their reaction. Did they agree with Simpson or were they surprised he would say such a thing? Elliott decided to take a shot.

"Mr. Simpson, Denise Elliott with Channel Two News. Are you saying you believe that because the deputy is pregnant, hormones may have been a factor in this shooting?"

Simpson looked into the crowd and located the origin of the voice. Play to the camera, he thought.

"Yes, I do. I don't believe the deputy should have been on duty in her condition. She shot the young man in the back of the head. There was no need for it."

Elliott had a decision to make—continue to ask Simpson questions or let it go? Normally she would pursue it, but she was standing on the steps outside of a church where a funeral had just taken place for a young man killed by police. It wasn't really the time or place, she thought. On the other hand, Simpson had called this impromptu press conference, so he was fair game. Then there was the crowd factor. There had been violence on the campus of the high school the night of the shooting; did Elliott really want to risk stirring something up with the family and friends of Alex Washington?

Her reporter instincts took over. She forged ahead.

"Early accounts have the deputy actually talking to Alex and making some headway. It was only after he was distracted and made some sudden movements that the deputy took action. And you're saying it was because of hormones?"

The crowd became silent and turned their attention to Elliott. The mood had changed quickly, with the crowd not liking Elliott's line of questioning.

"Yes, that's exactly what I'm saying. Deputies that are seven months pregnant shouldn't be on the streets."

The other reporters on scene all captured the comments. Each knew it would be their lead. *Family attorney claims hormones played role in shooting.* The story was getting juicer by the minute.

Simpson's assistant, Peggy, was standing a few feet from her boss as he made the comments. Realizing he was on thin ice she gently grabbed his arm and whispered, "Time to wrap it up, Leland."

Simpson ignored her; he was enjoying being the center of attention. But when she pulled on his arm again, he got the message.

"That's all for now. Thank you for your time, everyone."

Denise Elliott and her videographer left the church steps and headed straight to the station.

CHAPTER 29

Mark Archer agreed to meet Rachel Gillespie for lunch at a small cafe in the city of Parker, several miles northwest of Castle Springs and outside the RCSO jurisdiction. He had suggested the location, not wanting to meet her in town. There was nothing wrong with having lunch with someone, but somehow he thought meeting in Parker made more sense. And given Channel Eight's three-day exclusive interview with the Gillespies, he thought it possible she could be recognized. People in Parker were less likely to recognize him and somehow put things together. Maybe he was a bit paranoid but why take chances?

He thought about Rachel as he drove to the cafe. She was a beautiful woman married to a man who, by all appearances, didn't appreciate her. So what did she want? This was the second time she had reached out to him. The purpose of the first meeting, she said, was to apologize for her husband's actions. But they had talked that day for nearly two hours and once they got past the apology for Tom's behavior, they fell easily into conversation. Now they were meeting again at her request, this time with no reason given for the meeting.

His thoughts drifted to Angela. Things had been strained between them since the conversation a few days earlier about the firebomb story. Mark was pretty sure she had faked the story, and this truly concerned him. The television news business was very competitive but reporters had an obligation to be fair and truthful, and if Angela had indeed arranged for the bomb to go through the window then she had failed at both. He had more faith in her than that, but the facts pointed to her doing something both unethical and illegal. Could he be associated with someone like this? His relationship with her wasn't widely known, but if it did come out then where would that leave him? And then there was Denise Elliott, who evidently was aware of his presence at the Gillespies' home during the interview. Elliott was no dummy; she would put two and two together, and could possibly make trouble for both Mark and Angela.

He glanced at his watch. It was a few minutes before noon and he thought about the Washington funeral that had started at eleven. He had asked the watch commander to keep him informed if any issues popped up. Even though the funeral was out of the RCSO jurisdiction, the department had sent a couple undercover deputies to attend to keep an eye on things. It was not uncommon to do so and with the explosive nature of this case it was a wise move. So far, so good, he thought, glancing down at his phone. There were no texts indicating any issues or problems at the service.

He pulled into the cafe parking lot and saw Rachel getting out of her car. She waved and waited for him to park. He walked toward her and was surprised when she gave him a hug and kiss on the cheek. He glanced around the parking lot as she wiped the lipstick from his face.

❧

Angela Bell arrived back at the station just after the noon newscast had wrapped. She and her videographer went immediately to the edit bay and began piecing their story together. What they had intended to be a story about the funeral was now a story about Leland Simpson and his remarks about Mia Serrano-McCallister and her pregnancy. Angela was surprised at Simpson's misstep, given his experience. Clearly his objective had been to draw public sympathy for Alex Washington as his grieving family buried him, but now the focus would be on something else entirely.

Denise Elliott was also busy at work back at Channel Two putting together her story about the funeral and the Simpson comments. She, like Angela, couldn't believe what Simpson had said. A bonehead move by an experienced attorney—it would make for great television.

"So, how was your weekend?" asked Rachel.

"It was nice and quiet, the way I like it."

"Do you get called into work a lot after hours?"

"I do, actually. Nights, weekends, it's all fair game. You never know when the proverbial shit will hit the fan."

"I don't know how you do what you do. My experience with reporters is limited to what happened last week. I can't imagine dealing with that every day."

"You get used to it. And if you're smart you forge relationships with reporters so things go more smoothly. The last thing you want is to have an ongoing battle with a reporter or particular TV station or newspaper. Those don't typically end well."

"I can imagine. I mean, they can report whatever they want. You don't have much recourse."

"There's an old expression that I always keep in my mind: 'Don't argue with people that buy ink in twenty gallon drums.'"

Rachel laughed, "Yeah, I guess that's true."

Changing subjects, she leaned in a bit.

"So tell me, what's your relationship with Angela Bell?"

The two RCSO undercover officers assigned to Alex Washington's funeral had been giving twice-hourly updates to the watch commander, who in turn had been keeping Mick updated. So far so good, they reported, except for Leland Simpson's escapades on the steps of the church following the service. But while the crowd got a bit riled up during his antics, they had dispersed peacefully once he was finished pontificating.

Mick was relieved that things had remained peaceful, although he had not expected any real difficulties during the funeral. The trouble, if there was to be any, would come later, after the services were complete. He told the watch commander to keep the two UCs in place to attend Alex's burial. He was not at all surprised to hear the family had retained an attorney. Mick was certainly familiar with Leland Simpson; his reputation was well known. He made a nice living suing the government, in particular, law enforcement agencies.

Mick was also keeping a close eye on Mia. Given the new round of attention the case would receive as the media covered the funeral, he wanted to be sure she was holding up. Her session with Dr. Lusetti on Friday had gone well and she had seemed much better over the weekend. He, of course, was careful not to ask her about what they covered during the nearly two-hour long session, but she had mentioned to him that they had discussed her experience at Columbine. He was surprised, given that she had hardly ever spoken with him about what happened that day. But what mattered most was that she seemed better, and he just hoped that it continued.

He called Mark Archer's cell to check if he had received any media calls regarding the Washington funeral. It kicked to voicemail but he didn't leave a message. It was two thirty; Mick knew that Mark would see the missed call and give him an immediate call back. He was really good about staying in contact.

He had also been informed by Lucinda that he had received another call from the county administrator, Luis Centeno. Mick knew what that would be about. He dreaded making the call but wanted to get it over with so he dialed the number.

"Sheriff, I'm assuming that you've seen the news coverage of the funeral today?"

"I have," he lied.

"What do you make of all this? We've dealt with Leland Simpson before but what is up with the guy going after Mia and the fact that she's pregnant?"

Mick was at a loss and had no idea what Centeno was talking about.

"Mr. Centeno, I'm sorry but I've just been told of a situation that requires my immediate attention. Let me get right back to you."

Mick disconnected the call before Centeno could object. He dialed Mark's number but it again went to voicemail. "Damn it! Where the hell are you, Mark?"

Mark finished showering and dressed quickly. It was nearly three and he'd been gone from the office since before noon. He grabbed his cell phone and saw the missed calls from the sheriff.

"Shit."

He sat at the edge of the bed and dialed Mick's number.

"You called?"

"I just spoke with Luis Centeno and he said the Washingtons' attorney was talking about Mia and the fact that she's pregnant. What do you know about this?"

"I don't know anything about it."

"Well, the goddamn chief executive for the county knows about it. Why is it my media guy doesn't?"

"I'm sorry, sheriff. Give me five minutes and I'll call you right back."

"Where are you, Mark?"

"I'll call you back in a few," he replied, disconnecting the call before Mick could ask any more questions.

"What's the matter, Mark?"

"I don't know, but I'll know in a minute."

Mark considered calling Angela, but thought better of it, given the circumstances.

He tapped the Channel Eight website address in his phone and there he saw it.

Attorney Says Deputy's Pregnancy a Factor in Alex Washington's Shooting

"What in the hell?" he wondered aloud. He clicked on the story and quickly read through the copy.

"My God, what an idiot."

"What is it?"

Mark grabbed his sports coat and headed for the door.

"I gotta go."

"But—"

Mark didn't answer, and Rachel poked her head out the door of the hotel room and watched him sprint down the hallway.

❧

Once in his car, Mark dialed the sheriff.

"Okay, this is what I've got. The family has an attorney, none other than that asshole Leland Simpson. He held court on the steps of the church after the funeral today. Not surprisingly he blasted the RCSO, but then he specifically talked about Mia and the fact that she's pregnant. He talked about how he believes hormones may have played a role in her shooting Washington. It's unbelievable."

"You gotta be kidding me."

"It's no joke. He's getting blasted on the blogs. People are calling him a misogynist and worse."

"Well, Centeno called me and imagine my surprise when I didn't know anything about it. Usually my media guy keeps me informed on these kinds of things, ya know?"

"Yeah, about that . . . I'm sorry, it got past me. It won't happen again, boss."

"Where the hell are you?"

"Over in Parker. I had some personal business to attend to. I'm heading back now; my ETA is twenty minutes."

"When you get back, check in with me. We need to strategize a bit with this Simpson development."

"Will do."

Mick sent a text to Mia; he needed to let her know what was happening.

Call me when you get a minute.

CHAPTER 30

⌘

The Black Lives Matter movement had a significant number of activists in the greater Denver area. A handful of high-profile police brutality cases against African Americans involving the Denver Police Department had given rise to the movement and the shooting death of Alex Washington, while not in Denver, had certainly attracted the attention of those involved.

More than a dozen of the more active Denver-area BLM members gathered inside the Sonrise Community Church following the funeral service for Washington. They were agitated with the RCSO, and Leland Simpson's comments had simply added fuel to the fire.

Darius Curry, coordinator for the Denver-area BLM, tried to calm the group.

"Listen, you all know our mission is to bring about change in a peaceful manner. We can't go and act out with violence every time we see injustice taking place. There are avenues to follow; think about MLK. Change through peace."

A voice rang out near the back.

"That don't work, man. You know it and I know it. MLK tried that and got his fuckin' head blown off. We gotta make a statement and the only thing that gets their attention is when we do shit to their neighborhoods."

Curry looked up to see a young, tall black man walking toward them.

"Jaquon, welcome. We're happy to have you join us, but you gotta tone it down a bit, my friend. Meaningful change comes through peaceful movements."

"Fuck that, Darius."

Darius looked at the angry young man. He understood Jaquon's pain, having lost a younger brother himself a few years earlier. Stephan had been shot by Denver PD, and the officer involved was not charged in the case. Instead of acting out against the police, Darius decided to channel his anger and frustration into the Denver BLM movement.

"Jaquon, come in and take a seat. We're planning a demonstration protesting your cousin's death. We're going to do it in a peaceful but powerful way."

"That don't work, we all know dat. You gotta put it to the man. We been held down for long enough."

Darius was becoming concerned about Jaquon. Darius had worked very hard to keep the Denver BLM chapter focused on pursuing peaceful resolution to the problems faced by young African Americans. Jaquon, who had attended a handful of BLM meetings prior to his cousin's death, posed a definite threat to those efforts.

"In the words of John Lennon, you gotta 'give peace a chance,' Jaquon. It's the only way we can enact positive and long-lasting change."

"I ain't gonna believe nothin' some white guy from England said a hundred years ago. Those times are behind us and we gotta take this shit to the next level."

Darius looked around the room. Jaquon had his share of supporters; he certainly wasn't the only one in the room who believed violence was a necessary component to what they wanted to accomplish. Darius didn't want the group to lose its focus.

He said, "The time is right to speak out against Alex Washington's death. Tonight we march on the RCSO in Castle Springs. We'll time it so we get live news coverage during the ten o'clock newscasts. We need at least fifty people willing to march peacefully and stage the protest. Who's in?"

Every hand went up.

"Okay, a block west of the RCSO station there's a Bean Crazy coffee house. We'll assemble there at 9:30 tonight and then march to the station. I'll put out a press release to the media a couple hours before so they can get their reporters out there to cover it. Jada, can you help put together some signs?"

A young woman in the front row nodded.

"Great, now we just need everyone to get the word out. I'll start making calls to our regular supporters and get them out there tonight. And if each of you brings a couple friends we should have a good turnout. Any questions?"

No hands went up, and people stood to leave the church. As the group dispersed from the church, one of the young men reached into his pocket, fished out his cell phone, and clicked off the recorder.

Mark Archer returned to his office and closed the door. He needed a few minutes to compose himself before he went to see Mick. He reached up and touched his lower lip; it hurt and felt a little swollen. He pulled out a small mirror he kept in his desk for unexpected on-camera interviews and looked. Great, he thought. It was a little puffy and had some red marks. No one had bitten his lip since high school.

Mick was talking on the phone with the RCSO office manager when Mark stuck his head in his office. He waved him in, ended the call, and turned his attention to Mark.

"Geez, what happened to you?"

"What do you mean?"

"Your lip—it looks like you got punched in the face."

Mark reached up and touched his mouth.

"No, nothing so dramatic as that. Just a little accident, that's all."

"An accident?" Mick responded, suspiciously.

"Yeah, it's no big deal. Let's talk about Leland Simpson—I can't believe he said that about Mia."

"Yeah, me neither. So the question is, how do we capitalize on it?"

"I'm not sure we have to do anything. The reporters are already going crazy, so it's probably better if we just stay clear, above the fray."

Mick glanced at his watch. "The four o'clock newscasts are going to start in a minute; let's see how this is all playing out."

Mark nodded and Mick grabbed the remote from his desk, flipping on the TV in his office. They sat quietly, waiting for the news to begin.

"An accident, huh?"

"Yep, an accident. Now can we just drop it?"

"Sure, whatever you say."

Both turned their attention to the TV.

"Hello everyone, I'm Angela Bell, Eyewitness News at four. There are new developments this afternoon regarding the shooting death of Alex Washington. We have Melanie Higashi standing by with a live report."

"Angela, I'm standing on the steps of the Sonrise Community Church in downtown Denver where, just hours ago, services were held for young Alex Washington. As you may remember, Washington was killed last week by a Rocklin County sheriff's deputy on the campus of Wilson High School in Castle Springs. Washington had taken a fellow student hostage and Mia Serrano-McCallister, wife of Rocklin County Sheriff Mick McCallister, tried to de-escalate the situation. Despite her best efforts, Washington was ultimately killed by Serrano-McCallister. The young female hostage was physically unharmed. Here's a look at the highly emotional funeral service."

The screen filled with footage from inside the church of the Reverend Alvie Rollins officiating. Mick looked away from the TV and directed his attention back to Mark.

"While they're running that footage, go to Channel Two and see what Denise Elliott is doing with the story," Mark suggested.

Mick changed channels and sure enough Denise Elliott was doing her story live from the same steps as Melanie Higashi. But they weren't rolling footage of the funeral; Elliott was going right into Simpson's pregnancy comments.

"... so after hearing Mr. Simpson make the comment about Deputy Serrano-McCallister's pregnancy, I checked with a prominent Denver OBGYN who had this to say on the subject."

A physician, in his mid-fifties and wearing the obligatory white coat, appeared on the screen.

"It's my experience that hormones, while they might cause some mood swings in a pregnant woman, shouldn't play much of a role in a deputy's decision-making process."

Denise Elliott appeared again on the screen. "So the question is, will the attorney for Alex Washington's family hang their case on the deputy's hormones? It'll be interesting to see how this all plays out. Now back to you in the studio."

Mark reached over and gave Mick a high five.

"I'd say Leland Simpson just had his hormone ploy shoved up his ass."

Mick's cell phone rang and he saw it was Mia.

"Hey, sweetie. You didn't happen to catch the news just now, did you?"

"No, I've been avoiding the news. I know the funeral was today . . . I don't want to see any of it."

"I know, honey. But we actually had some good come out if it."

Mia couldn't see how anything good could come from the funeral service for the young man she had killed. She didn't respond.

"The family has retained an attorney."

"Oh, and that's the great news?" she asked, sarcastically.

"No, listen—he spoke after the funeral today and really stuck his foot in his mouth. The media attention has shifted away from the shooting and landed on him. And that's a good thing."

"So, what did he say?"

"He said he thought your hormones played a role on the shooting, and that—"

"He said *what*?!"

"Look, Mia, this is a good thing! He's saying that you being seven months pregnant affected the way you handled the shooting."

"Jesus, Mick, I'd hate to see what you considered bad news," responded a very angry Mia.

"No, no—listen to me. Doctors don't agree with his assertion. He's making a big thing out of something that isn't true. It puts a big hole in his credibility."

Mia considered what her husband was saying. She understood his point, at least to a certain extent, but was still horrified that her hormones was now part of the public conversation about the case.

"What's next? Discussing my menstrual cycle? Maybe an in-depth look at our sex life?"

Mick understood Mia's frustration. It must be very disconcerting to her to hear these very public disclosures about some very personal things.

"I understand, Mia. But this shifts the focus away from the shooting and that's a good thing. In a few days, the media will find something else to cover. I know it's not easy for you."

Mia thought about what Mick was saying and about the things Dr. Lusetti had been telling her in their sessions. She calmed down a bit.

"Okay. So what time will you be home tonight?"

"I'll be home by six, I promise. Can I take you out to dinner?"

"Actually a nice, quiet dinner at home sounds better. I can make something; it'll take my mind off things. And frankly, I'm not sure I want to be out in public right now."

"Okay, I'll see you at six."

By late afternoon Peggy had made the decision to stop answering the phone. The law office had been inundated with more than fifty phone calls and hundreds of emails blasting Leland Simpson for his comments about Mia's hormones. There wasn't a single call or email in support of his position. He had made a gross miscalculation and was paying a big price in the arena of public opinion for his inflammatory comments.

Simpson sat in his office, huddled with Alvie Rollins, trying to decide their next move. At first Peggy kept him apprised of the calls and emails, but after a while she didn't bother. He had turned down, for now, several invitations from the media to go back on camera and clarify his earlier remarks. He wanted to see how things played out before making any further comments to the media.

Rollins didn't know what to do—should he tell the family to cut their ties to Simpson immediately or ride out the storm? They had signed an agreement for services, but he thought they could get out of it given what Simpson had done. Hell, he thought, Simpson's actions might possibly be considered malpractice, although he thought that could be a tough thing to prove. Most importantly, Rollins knew his five percent of the eventual award granted to the family was definitely at risk.

"So, what are you going to do, Leland?"

"I think we wait until tomorrow and see if this story has legs. If it dies out, then we're good. If it doesn't then I'll do some TV time and clear the air."

"And how exactly are you going to 'clear the air'?"

"I'll find a doctor or two that can back up my comments. That's not a problem."

"Well, so far it seems like everyone thinks your viewpoint isn't valid. You think you can find a qualified medical professional who will publicly back your claims?"

"Sure—money talks, my friend. For the right price I can find someone who will say whatever I need them to."

Rollins shook his head. It was a dirty business, he thought.

Simpson continued, "In the meantime, you need to pray another big story comes along and bumps us off the front page. A nice tornado, a bridge collapse, or a nasty sex scandal at city hall."

Rollins nodded at Simpson. "We can only hope . . . "

CHAPTER 31

A fter leaving Mick's office, Mark returned to his own and checked his voicemail and email. He had been out of the office since before lunch—a long time for him to be out of touch with his media contacts. He had more than two dozen messages waiting for him, every one of them from a reporter asking for an official response from the RCSO on the Simpson comments. No problem there, he thought. The RCSO would have no official comment at this time. He would let the Leland Simpson story stew a bit.

Mark took a few minutes to reflect on his day. What had started out as routine had turned into anything but. It was one of the things he loved about his job—he never knew where things would take him. Then his thoughts turned to Rachel, his conscience bothered on several levels. Not only had he cheated on Angela, he had also entered into a sexual relationship with a married woman. She was clearly unhappy in her marriage, but that was no excuse to sleep with her. He had succumbed in a moment of weakness, brought on in part by his confusion about Angela and what she had done with the firebomb story. Could he be with someone like Angela? He had a reputation to uphold and knew a relationship with a reporter was pushing the border of ethical behavior. But really, who was he kidding? He had certainly been anything but ethical during his lunchtime encounter with Rachel. He was such a fraud, he thought.

So, what should be do next? What were Rachel's expectations now? It could just be a one-time thing, he thought, but he knew better than that. Rachel wasn't interested in a casual fling; she would expect more from him. What would he do now about Angela? What if Tom discovered the affair?

I am such an idiot, he thought to himself.

Mick, as promised, arrived home at six and found Chuck in the kitchen putting together a dinner of pork chops, mashed potatoes, and salad.

"Boy, that looks great, Chuck. Do we have time for a drink?" Mick asked.

"Sure, dinner is about thirty minutes out."

Chuck reached into the kitchen cabinet and grabbed a bottle of high-end vodka.

"Will this work?"

"Yeah, that'll do the trick."

Chuck poured an inch or so of vodka into each glass and filled them with ice.

"Where's Mia?"

"She's in the back bedroom. Why don't you go say hello?" Chuck replied, handing Mick his drink.

Mick tipped his glass toward Chuck, headed upstairs, and walked to the back bedroom. He poked his head in and was surprised by what he saw.

"Oh my God, Mia. It's beautiful!"

"Do you really like it, Mick? I wasn't sure about the color scheme but I think it's turning out pretty well."

"It looks fabulous, Mia. I can't believe you got all this done today."

"Well, I have time and this takes my mind off everything that's been going on."

Mick looked around at what would be the baby's room. Not knowing the sex of the child, Mia had chosen muted yellows and pale greens for the walls and bedding. The crib, matching dresser, and changing table were dark walnut and complimented the colors of the room.

"Its perfect, Mia. I really mean it, it looks like a professional decorator came in and did this."

Mia smiled. "Thanks, Mick." It was the first smile Mick had seen from his wife in several days. Decorating the baby's room was the perfect distraction.

Mick and Mia looked toward the open door as Sasha came running in the room. Chuck was not far behind.

"What do you think, Mick? She's been at it for hours. Didn't she do a great job?"

"I was just telling her that. It's like how they do it on those home decorating TV shows. Only better."

"Yeah, right," Mia replied, a bit embarrassed by the praise.

"Dinner will be ready in about fifteen minutes. Why don't you two go into the living room and relax and I'll call you when dinner is on the table?"

Mick and Mia agreed and headed back down the hall to the living room.

"So, how was your day, Mick?" asked Mia as they sat down on the sofa.

"Pretty interesting, actually. I can't believe the misstep by that attorney today."

"Yeah, it sounds like a pretty big stumble on his part."

"I'd say so. We'll see how things play out over the next day or so, but at the very least it took the focus off Alex's funeral today. The media likes to play up human tragedy stories, so the funeral would normally have received a lot of attention. But that idiot and his comments about your pregnancy got their attention on something else."

Mia knew the events of the day were advantageous for them, but she still felt angry that she was back in the news, especially with something so personal.

"So, what's next, discussing which days of the month I feel bloated?"

Mick wasn't sure if it was time for humor, but he took the chance.

"Yep, and the reporters will want video."

"Ha ha. Look, I'm trying not to get too upset by all this, but it's not easy. I can't believe they're talking about this stuff."

"I'm sorry, Mia. I didn't mean to make fun."

"That's okay, I just can't believe I'm at the center of all this crap."

Mick heard his cell phone chirp. He slipped it out of his pocket to check the message.

Your boy Jaquon is on the move, call me for details

"Anything important? asked Mia.

"Not really. When is your next session with Dr. Lusetti?" he asked, changing the subject.

"Tomorrow morning at nine. She's been the one bright spot in this whole mess. She's really helped me."

"That's great, Mia. I'm glad we brought her on board. You never know what you're getting when you retain someone like that."

"Well, she's fabulous, in my opinion. Any deputy that goes to her will be well served."

Chuck appeared in the doorway of the living room, "Dinner is ready."

"Go ahead, Mia. I'll be with you in a minute."

Mia left the room and Mick dialed Tim Dekker.

CHAPTER 32

A slow news day nationally resulted in the story about Mia's hormone levels getting picked up by NBC News. It ran in more than one hundred and fifty television stations around the nation, including KNBC in Los Angeles, the second-largest media market in the country.

Rose Cochran, a civil-rights lawyer known primarily for taking high-profile cases, watched the story on one of the six television screens mounted on the walls of her luxury penthouse office in Century City. She was stunned by what was being reported. A Colorado attorney claiming a pregnant female sheriff's deputy shot and killed a seventeen year old due, in part, to her hormones. Cochran had become famous and quite wealthy largely by taking on cases involving the protection of women's rights. She scribbled down the name of the deputy and called on one of her administrative assistants.

"David, get me the contact information for Mia Serrano-McCallister. She's a deputy with the Rocklin County Sheriff's Department in Colorado. Looks like somewhere near Denver."

"Will do, boss."

Cochran checked the other LA-area newscasts but didn't see the story getting covered by anyone but NBC. That was a good thing, she thought. It could give her time to wedge herself into the case before her competitors had a chance to do the same.

David came back into the office and handed Cochran a note with the phone number to the RCSO. It was just past six in California, making it just past seven in Colorado. She took a chance and dialed the number. It was answered by what sounded like an after-hours switchboard.

"Rocklin County Sheriff's Department, how may I direct your call?"

"I'm trying to reach Mia Serrano-McCallister."

"She's currently on administrative leave. Would you like her voicemail?"

"Do you know if she's checking her voicemails?"

The operator sounded a little put out.

"Ma'am, I have no way of knowing that. Would you like me to transfer your call to her line?"

"Does your department have a media liaison?"

"Yes, that would be Lieutenant Archer. Would you like me to transfer your call to him?"

"Yes, thank you."

A few seconds later, the call rang to Archer's office. Cochran was surprised when a live human voice answered.

"Mark Archer, can I help you?"

"Lieutenant Archer, this is Rose Cochran calling from Los Angeles."

Mark swallowed hard. He was instantly reminded of the old joke about knowing you're having a bad day when you learn Mike Wallace from *60 Minutes* is waiting for you in your office.

"Yes, how can I help you?"

"I'm an attorney in Los Angeles and I represent clients who are victims of discrimination. I specialize in women's issues, mostly, and I just learned about comments made by an attorney out there about one of your deputies."

Cochran didn't need any introduction, but he let her say her piece.

"Yes, go on."

"I was hoping to talk directly to Deputy Serrano-McCallister but was told she's on administrative leave. I was wondering if you might be able to put me in touch with her."

Mark quickly ran various scenarios through his head. He needed time to consider what it would mean for Mia and the RCSO if Cochran became involved in the case.

"I might be able to make that happen. Give me your contact information, but it'll probably tomorrow morning before she or I can get back to you."

"That'll be fine. I appreciate the help. I'll give you the number to my private cell."

Mark took down the info and contemplated his next move.

"What've you got, Tim?'

"A couple hours ago Jaquon attended a Black Lives Matter meeting at the Sonrise Community Church in Denver, the same place they had the Washington funeral. My surveillance team tailing Jaquon saw him go into the meeting so I had one of my guys slip in and record the meeting."

"And?"

"There's going to be a march on the RCSO headquarters tonight. They're meeting near the station at 9:30 then marching over. They're timing it to coincide with the ten o'clock Denver newscasts. The leader, a guy named Darius Curry, is putting it all together. They'll send out a press release later this evening."

"And Jaquon is part of it?"

"Well, it appears so, but there's a rub to it. Jaquon didn't agree with the 'peaceful march' on the RCSO idea. He thinks violence is a better approach. He as much said that to the group. The leader, Curry, shut him down and got everyone on board with the march but I wouldn't be surprised if Jaquon acted out in some way."

Mick replied, "Well, who knows what the little prick is capable of doing. And if he knows news media will be at the RCSO tonight covering this march, that could give him the audience he wants to do something really stupid."

"We have a close eye on him, boss. If he tries something we'll be on him like white on rice."

"Okay, I'll let the watch commander know what they're planning tonight so we can prepare our troops. I appreciate the heads up Tim, and thank your guys for me for the great work."

Mick placed the call to the RCSO and let the watch commander on duty know what to expect at the station.

"Everything okay, Mick?" asked Mia, as he took a seat at the dining room table.

"Yeah, just some work stuff. It never ends."

Mia looked at her husband and suspected there was more than what he was telling her, but decided to let it go. Time to relax and enjoy dinner.

Mick turned the conversation back to the baby's room and what they needed to do before the big day arrived in two short months.

Mark Archer wasn't sure what to make of the phone call from Rose Cochran. He kept going over various scenarios in his head about how her involvement could play out. It would certainly undermine Leland Simpson's credibility if Cochran went after him for his comments. But Cochran's involvement would also bring the RCSO shooting of Alex Washington into the national spotlight. Love her or hate her, there was no disputing the fact that everything Cochran touched became national news. She had made a career of showboating for the media. But Mark wondered if there were any possible outcomes where such attention could benefit the RCSO's case. He doubted it.

But the reality was that the RCSO couldn't stop Cochran from inserting herself into the case if she was determined to do so. But she would need to represent someone's interests and the only logical person was Mia. She was the one Simpson attacked, so she was the one Cochran would want to defend. But Mark couldn't see Mia wanting this kind of attention; she just wanted the case to go away as quickly and as quietly as possible.

The best way to shut Cochran out of the case would be to have Mia tell her in no uncertain terms that she did not want her help. Without a client, Cochran would be left with nothing except possibly offering her opinion on the talking head news programs popular on CNN and FOX.

He picked up the phone and dialed Mia's cell.

Jaquon Jackson was riled up as he left the BLM gathering at the Sonrise Community church. Darius Curry was nothing but an Uncle Tom, kowtowing to the almighty white man. This peaceful march bullshit wasn't going to get it done, that much he was sure about. His cousin was dead and not a damn thing was being done about it. He jumped on the train near Union Station and headed south, back toward Castle Springs, determined to do something to avenge his little cousin's murder. He pulled out his cell phone, a disposable, and began texting.

Six rows back on the train sat Bob Dawson, RCSO undercover detective, watching and wondering what exactly Jaquon might be up to.

Mia saw Mark Archer's name pop up on her caller ID and debated whether she should take the call during dinner. She didn't at first, thinking she'd let it kick to voicemail.

"Who's calling you?" Mick asked, seeing Mia's attention had been diverted.

"It's Mark."

"Go ahead and answer it; he doesn't usually call unless it's something important."

She grabbed the phone.

"Hi, Mark."

"Hey, Mia, I hope I'm not calling during dinner."

"Well, actually. . . that's okay. What's up?"

"Is Mick there?"

"Yeah, he and my dad are both here with me. Did you want to talk to Mick?"

"Actually, I'd like to talk to both of you. Can you put me on speaker?"

"Sure, hold on."

Mia hit the speaker button and put the phone in the middle of the table.

Realizing the conversation would likely be RCSO business, Chuck excused himself and started clearing the table.

"Hey, Mark. Whatcha got?"

"Hi Mick, I got an interesting phone call tonight. It was from Rose Cochran."

Mia looked at Mick. She didn't like where this was going.

"Yeah, I know who she is. What did she want?" asked Mick with some hesitation in his voice.

"She saw the coverage of Leland Simpson's comments today, and—"

"Wait a minute, she's in LA and she saw the story out there?" Mick asked.

"Yeah, the story has gone national. She saw it on the NBC affiliate out there and so she called. She actually called you, Mia, but when she found out you were on leave she reached out to me as the media contact."

Mia started to feel sick to her stomach.

Mick jumped in. "That didn't take long. I was really hoping the story would stay local and just die down after the funeral today."

"I was hoping for that, too, but it's looking like this story has legs so we need to gear up and get prepared."

"Okay, so what do we do?"

"I've given this some thought and I think the best way to shut her down is for Mia to tell her right up front that she's not interested in her representing her in any kind of legal action against Simpson. I think if Mia does that, Cochran'll be relegated to the political talk show circuit and not much else."

Mia glanced across the table at Mick, looking like she had something to say. He nodded at her.

"Mark, let me ask you this. If I file suit against Leland Simpson, what possible repercussions could there be for the RCSO?"

Mick was a bit stunned. "Mia, are you serious? You want to sue the guy?"

"I don't know, but I'm not going to close that door until I think about it a little bit."

Mark weighed in, "Okay, if you did pursue it, then the fallout for the department . . . well, let's think this one through. You'd absolutely generate a new level of interest in the story, Cochran would see to that. You'd be doing a lot of national news interviews, with her at your side, of course, and you'd either be applauded or vilified by the public, depending on one's viewpoint. I don't know, Mia . . . I mean, it's obviously up to you, but it could totally create a huge shitstorm."

"Would it affect the OIS investigation?"

The question was more for Mick than Mark.

He jumped in, "I don't think so. The facts are the facts in the case and I believe it'll all come out fine once the investigation is complete. You saved that girl's life, Mia—there's just no disputing that fact. So, while I agree with Mark about all the noise a lawsuit would bring, I don't think it would affect the investigation any."

Mia's voice grew stronger. "It's been five days since the incident and I have felt totally powerless about everything that's happened. I'm being judged in the media, I'm sure I'll be personally sued by Alex Washington's family, and who knows what this'll ultimately do to my career. My hormones are being discussed publicly and there's been violence at the high school and at Channel Eight. Maybe it's time I stand up and say enough is enough and actually do something about it. Maybe pave the way for other officers and deputies that are subjected to all this bullshit that comes after an OIS. People think these things don't affect the officer involved, like we all just high-five each other afterwards. That is such utter bullshit; nothing could be further from the truth. I mean, I'm sorry Alex is dead, and I'd give anything to change what happened. But I can't bring him back, so maybe I just need to do this—for me, the RCSO and every other officer who gets crucified for doing his or her job. Maybe stop all the armchair quarterbacks from asking why I didn't just shoot the gun out of his hand, or saying I should've shot him in the leg. Those people watch way too many cop shows and couldn't get through day one of the police academy, much less do the actual job."

Mia stopped talking and both men let her words sink in. Mick broke the silence after a few seconds.

"Is that what you want to do, Mia? I mean, you can't put the genie back in the bottle once you let it out."

"You think it's a bad idea?"

"No, I didn't say that. I just want to make sure you fully understand what the ramifications could be for you if you do this. And take the RCSO out of it, we'll be fine. Just think about yourself."

"I want to do it."

"Okay, then you need to call Cochran back and have that conversation with her."

"I'll text you her number, Mia."

Mick continued, "There's one more thing we need to discuss."

"What's that?" asked Mark.

"A few minutes ago I was told by our undercover guys that Jaquon attended a Black Lives Matter meeting today at the church where the funeral took place."

Mark groaned at the news while Mia rolled her eyes. So that was the business he was taking care of when dinner was being served, Mia thought. He should have told her what was happening.

Mark responded, "I wondered if they might involve themselves in this case. They've been pretty vocal about some of the OISes in Denver. I guess we shouldn't be too surprised."

"One of our undercover officers attended the meeting and found out that the group is planning a march on the RCSO tonight. It's set for ten, just in time for all the live newscasts. I'm not sure how large the protest will be, but I'm sure they'll be vocal and you can be damned sure they'll alert the media about their plans. I've let the watch commander know so we're putting plans into place to gear up for any and all possible scenarios."

"Okay, and I'll put out some feelers to see if the media knows anything about it at this point."

Mark's thoughts went to Angela. He hadn't spoken to her since their big blowup on Friday night and the text he had sent earlier in the day had received a rather terse reply. His mind flashed on his afternoon with Rachel and he quickly pushed those images away.

"That sounds good, and let me know what you find out from your media contacts. If it's going to be a big media thing then we need to be ready for a crowd that could start small but grow really fast with the live news coverage. You know how people like to show up when they see something going down live on TV," answered Mick.

"Oh yeah, they all gotta join in on the fun."

"Thanks, Mark. Talk to you soon."

Angela saw Mark's number pop up on her phone and her first instinct was to let it go to voicemail. But with the press release from the Denver BLM in her hand she thought better of it.

"Angela Bell."

The fact that she answered that way despite seeing his name and number on the screen was not a good sign, he thought.

"Hi Angela, it's Mark."

She didn't waste any time with pleasantries.

"I'm guessing you're calling about the BLM march tonight."

"Yeah, I just found out about it. I'm guessing they put out a news release?"

"I'm holding it in my hand as we speak."

"Any possibility you could send it to me?"

"I'm really busy right now. I'm anchoring and producing tonight. Erin called in sick."

It was clear that Angela wasn't going to do him any favors.

"Well, if you find some time, send it over to me. I'd appreciate it."

"I gotta go."

The line went dead.

CHAPTER 33

"Should I call her back tonight?"

Mia and Mick were still sitting at the dining room table going over the Rose Cochran issue.

"LA is an hour behind us so it's only about seven back there. If you're going to do this, you might as well make the call now. Unless you want some more time to think about it."

"I think I'll call her tomorrow. I'm really tired, and besides, I have an appointment with Dr. Lusetti first thing in the morning. It'll give me a chance to talk with her about this before I make the call."

"That makes sense. Look, I think I'm going to head into the station. I want to see how all the contingency plans are coming for handling the march."

"Yeah, that's fine. I've got a few more things I want to do in the baby's room and I'm sure Dad'll find something to watch on TV."

Mick stood up and kissed the top of Mia's head.

"Don't wait up for me. Not sure how long this will take. Get some sleep."

"I'll try."

"Oh, and the baby's room really is beautiful, Mia."

The RCSO briefing room was a hub of activity when Mick arrived. He found Jim Bailey, the watch commander on duty, and asked for a briefing.

"It's coming together nicely. I've called in a dozen deputies on overtime and we've got a total complement of twenty-six assigned to regular patrol duties tonight. Mondays tend to be a little slow, so I think I can cover the county with eighteen so that frees up another eight for our little show here tonight. So twenty in total are available. I've told them to have their riot gear ready but not to put it on unless I call for it. I don't want a peaceful march turning violent because they see us dressed out for a riot. I've also called for mutual aid and have six agencies on notice. They won't come unless we call for them. You know, the usual arrangement."

"Sounds like you've got it covered, Jim."

"I hope so, but as you know—always expect the unexpected."

"Did you call the fire department and let them know?"

"I did, and they have station seven ready to go. They're just two blocks away so their response time would be a minute or less. Hopefully we don't need them."

"Yeah, hopefully. But we've had firebombs thrown at both Wilson High School and Channel Eight, so you never know what could happen. These folks might lean towards Molotov cocktails."

"True, but I think we've got it covered."

"Okay, I'm going to head to my office and catch up on some paperwork. I'll come back down as we get closer to the ten o'clock hour. If anything new develops you have my cell."

"Yes sir."

～

By nine forty-five there were more than fifty people gathered at the Bean Crazy coffee house two blocks from the RCSO station. They were clad in t-shirts that referenced police brutality and injustice and many carried homemade signs touting the same. The crowd was energetic but offered nothing that would suggest pending violence. At the front of the group stood Darius Curry, offering words of encouragement as he outlined the plans for the march. He stressed again the peaceful nature of MLK and reminded the group to obey all traffic laws. He didn't want to give the RCSO or any other law enforcement agency any viable reasons to cite them or shut them down.

Jaquon Jackson, standing near the back, carried no sign but was dressed in a black, sleeveless *No Justice, No Peace* t-shirt. Off to the side stood Bob Dawson, keeping a close eye on things as he listened to Curry's instructions. Bob's *Fuck the Cops* t-shirt was a nice touch.

Curry raised his voice and got the group's attention. "Okay, listen up everybody. It's almost ten, so we need to get started. I'm expecting several reporters to be at the sheriff's station so be on your best behavior. We don't want this to turn into a story about BLM not behaving. We get enough bad press already. Once we're all there I will issue a statement and then we can be ready for interviews on camera. You all know what to say—don't forget your talking points."

As the group started up the street, Curry held back. He waited for most of the group to pass him and then greeted Jaquon.

"Glad you could make it."

Jaquon gave him a quick nod but didn't respond. Curry had seen him and that was the important thing. Jaquon had accomplished what he needed to do—establish an alibi.

CHAPTER 34

Damian "Shorty" Blackwell and Tracy "Iceman" Thompson parked their car a couple blocks away from their intended target. It was a rural, out-of-the-way part of Castle Springs and, if seen, they knew they'd stick out like a sore thumb. People would likely remember two young, heavily-tattooed, African-American males walking through their neighborhood. So they parked off the street and started hiking through terrain that was densely covered with pine and aspen trees. Neither of the gang members had ever been in this area of Castle Springs, preferring the far south side of Rocklin County where people such as themselves didn't really stand out.

"Damn, look at all these fucking trees. Don't have many of these down in the hood."

Iceman looked at his friend Shorty and just nodded at his comment. He wanted to get the job done as quickly as possible and get the hell out of there. The whole forest thing kinda creeped him out. Pavement was more his thing; it just seemed more natural to him. He checked his phone for the time—10:08. Good, he thought. Jaquon wanted it done at 10:10. They were right on time.

Mia's curiosity got the better of her and she decided to turn on the ten o'clock news. Tuned to Angela's station, she watched the protest at RCSO in full bloom. Typical bullshit, she thought, as she watched the fifty or so protesters walk around with their signs. I'll bet half of them don't even know about the shooting, they're just little lambs being led around by some shot callers. There were plenty of online videos of people interviewed at various protests around the country and when asked what or why they were protesting, many didn't have a clue. "I just hate the cops" was a common refrain. Pathetic, she thought.

She flipped the channel to see if other stations were covering the action. Sure enough, all the Denver stations were covering it live. She tuned to Channel Two and saw Denise Elliott interviewing someone on camera. Blah, blah, blah, she thought, as she watched a few seconds of the clip. Having had enough, she turned off the TV and headed back to the baby's room. She had a few more things to finish before going to bed.

❧

"Come on—hurry up and light the damn thing."

Shorty was fumbling with a lighter while Iceman held the device.

"I'm trying, man. It ain't easy. The lighter won't light, damn piece of shit."

"Forget the lighter, I've got some matches."

Clearly, Iceman was the brains behind the operation. He'd had the forethought to bring a book of matches, which he had scooped up at his stepdad's bar. He grabbed the matches from his jeans pocket and handed them to Shorty who was finally able to light the fuse on the bomb.

"Throw it, throw it!" Shorty yelled.

Iceman aimed and threw the bomb as hard as he could. He hit his target. The bomb smashed through the window of the house and exploded a second or two later.

"Run!"

∽

Chuck came bounding up the stairs as soon as he heard the explosion. He could see flames coming from the baby's room and smoke billowing into the hallway. He couldn't see Mia and started screaming her name.

A few seconds later Mia staggered from the baby's room into the hallway. She was coughing and had glass shards in her hair. One side of her face was bleeding. She was dazed.

Chuck grabbed his daughter and ushered her down the hallway, away from the flames. He told Mia to stay put and ran to another bedroom with a landline to call 9-1-1. Then he rushed back to Mia who was sitting safely in the hallway out of harm's way.

"Are you okay, Mia?"

He was trying to keep the panic from his voice, but the question came out high pitched and very fast.

"I don't know . . . what happened?"

"There was an explosion. I've called the fire department and they're on the way. Come on, let's get out of here."

Chuck helped Mia to her feet and, holding her arm, carefully walked her down the stairs and out the front door.

When they reached the street, he and Mia looked back at the house. They couldn't see any flames, only some black smoke coming from the back. Within minutes three large firetrucks and an ambulance came roaring up the street, their sirens blaring. By then several neighbors had gathered in the street in front of the house. Chuck waved at the ambulance and pointed at Mia. He wasn't worried about the house; he was solely concerned about his daughter, who seemed to be in shock.

The ambulance pulled up to where they were standing and two paramedics hustled over to Mia.

Chuck grabbed the arm of one of them, "She's seven months pregnant. She was in the room where the explosion happened. I have no idea what caused it. It doesn't make any sense!"

Tears filled his eyes and his knees buckled as he explained things. Paramedics grabbed him before he hit the ground and called for a stretcher. Immediately, they began working on Chuck, checking his vital signs. Next to him firefighters were attending to Mia, who had been placed on her own stretcher. She was holding her stomach, which concerned the firefighters.

Around the back of the house they made short work of the fire. It was contained to just the one room, although the room was a total loss.

Mick learned about the explosion at his house quite by accident. Standing inside the RCSO Operations Center monitoring the BLM protest, he heard the call dispatched by the fire department over the radio of a fire battalion chief he was standing with while keeping an eye on things.

At first he thought he had heard wrong—it couldn't be his address being given as the location of an explosion. He asked the battalion chief to double check the address and a few seconds later Mick was sprinting for his car. He called Mia's cell but it went to voicemail. He tried Chuck's cell with the same result. He dialed up the watch commander and got Jim Bailey on the phone.

Bailey had heard the call dispatched for fire and sent a couple deputies to the scene as a precaution. He was unaware it was the sheriff's home address. He assured Mick that he would send more deputies and call in the RCSO bomb squad to investigate. Mick thanked him and made another call.

"Tim, this is Sheriff McCallister. Who do you have on Jaquon Jackson right now?"

"Bob Dawson. Why, what's up?"

"There was an explosion at my house a few minutes ago. I'm heading there now. I need to know where the hell that asshole is right now!"

"Hold on, sheriff. I'll be back with you in a second."

Mick steered through all the emergency vehicles parked along his street as he waited for Dekker to come back on the line. He parked between two fire trucks and jumped from the car.

"Sheriff, Jaquon is at the RCSO; he's part of the protest. He's in plain sight and he's been there for at least twenty minutes."

"Then the motherfucker has friends!"

Mick ran to the ambulances and saw Chuck and Mia both laid out on stretchers. Each was conscious and talking with paramedics. Chuck had an oxygen tank next to his stretcher but appeared to be breathing on his own. Mia had some bandages on the side of her face and she was holding her stomach. Paramedics recognized the sheriff and let him approach.

"My God, Mia—are you alright?"

She looked up at him and managed a nod. He reached over and hugged her, kissing her forehead.

"Is Dad okay?" she asked in a whispered, hoarse tone.

Mick looked over at Chuck and saw paramedics were still administering aid to him.

"I think so; he's conscious. Paramedics are helping him. What the hell happened, Mia? Did you see anything?"

"No, I didn't. I was working in the baby's room and something came through the glass. The window shattered and a second later there was an explosion. Glass went everywhere and I got burned, I think. Mick—what if the baby had been in there?!"

Mia reached up and touched the bandages paramedics had applied to her face.

"It'll be fine, Mia. I just thank God you and the baby are okay."

"I'm worried about Dad."

"Let me see what I can find out."

Mick walked over to Chuck's stretcher and asked the paramedic how he was doing.

The paramedic motioned for Mick to follow him and the two walked to an area where Chuck couldn't overhear them. "It doesn't appear he has any injuries resulting from the explosion; his issues are likely heart related. We've got him hooked up to a monitor so we can see what's going on. His heartbeat is all over the map. Has he had any heart issues in the past?"

"None that I know of. He's a pretty healthy seventy-five year old. He does a lot of hiking and he doesn't smoke."

"Sometimes heart issues can be brought on by traumatic events. That could be what's going on. We'll stabilize him here and then transport him to the hospital."

"Okay, thanks. Now, I spoke with my wife and she seems to be doing okay, but obviously I'm concerned about the baby."

"The baby should be fine. We checked on that right away and the baby's heartbeat is good and strong. There's no evidence she fell or took any kind of direct trauma from the explosion, so I think aside from the burns on her face and some glass in her scalp, she should be just fine. But just to be safe I'd suggest she spend a night at the hospital for observation."

"Thank you so much. I can't tell you how much I appreciate all your help."

"No problem, sheriff."

Mick returned to his wife's side and let her know what he had learned from the paramedic. As they were discussing the possibility of Chuck having a heart issue, their attention was drawn to the street. Two satellite news vans had parked among the fire trucks. Denise Elliott and another reporter from Channel Eight raced from their vans toward the house. Right behind them was Mark Archer, who had learned about the explosion from Jim Bailey and rushed to the house. Before the reporters could approach the house, several of the deputies on scene put their arms up to block the way.

"We have a right to shoot from the street. It's public property and you can't stop us," the reporters each said, almost in unison. Their videographers each angled for the best shot of the house. The cascading lights coming from the tops of the emergency vehicles gave the scene a very dramatic look, perfect for TV news.

"Not if we designate this as a crime scene," countered Mark Archer, who had caught up with them.

Denise Elliott looked at Archer. "Good luck with that, lieutenant. We both know that extending your crime scene this far away from the explosion is nothing but a way to keep us out."

"Hi, Denise. Nice to see you this evening."

"Come on, Mark, just let us get our shot and we'll get out of your way. It'll take longer for us to argue about it than it will for us to get our footage."

Mark thought about what Elliott was asking. Technically, Elliott was right—the RCSO couldn't keep a reporter from videotaping something from a public place, and a street certainly qualified. The exception to that rule was that if the street was considered a crime scene then law enforcement could, by law, keep people out. At times, police were rather liberal with their crime scenes, drawing large perimeters around an area to keep reporters at bay. Mark didn't like doing that and he wasn't going to start now.

"Okay, I'll tell you what. Get your footage but there will be no zoom shots of the sheriff or his wife over by the paramedics' vehicles. They're off limits. Deal?"

Denise Elliott and the Channel Eight reporter, a young man whom Mark had never met, reluctantly nodded their agreement.

Mark kept an eye on the videographers as they moved around on the street getting their shots. After a couple of minutes they wrapped.

"Any chance we can get some time on camera with the sheriff?"

Elliott was nothing if not pushy, but Mark realized she was just doing her job.

"I think the sheriff has enough to worry about right now. Let's give him some space."

An hour after the explosion, most first responder emergency personnel had cleared the scene. The RCSO bomb squad had arrived and was carefully looking through what remained of the baby's room. The room and everything in it was a total loss, but fortunately the damage had been isolated to just that area. The bomb squad found the explosive device; it was relatively small and almost certainly homemade. It was clear that it wasn't dynamite or anything sophisticated. By all appearances this looked to be another Molotov cocktail, the third one the RCSO had investigated in five days.

Investigators broadened the investigation to outside the house. The cocktail had most likely been thrown by someone outside the bedroom, so a careful search was done of that area. Two bomb techs and two deputies combed every inch of ground, their flashlights making small trails of light in the pine needles. The distance between the McCallister home and their nearest neighbor was more than a hundred feet so the search took some time. But it paid off.

"Hey, I think I've got something."

An investigator kneeling in the pine needles stared down at an object on the ground. The other three men came quickly to see what he had discovered. One of the bomb techs shined his flashlight on the object.

"It's a book of matches. Looks like whoever tossed the cocktail used these matches to light the damn thing. What an idiot. The moron left the matchbook behind."

The tech fished some latex gloves from his pocket, put them on, and carefully picked up the matchbook. He held it up for the others to see. *Chookie's Pub* was printed on the outside cover.

"I know that place. It's a dive bar in south county . . . 120th Street territory."

CHAPTER 35

Both Mia and Chuck were admitted to Castle Springs Memorial Hospital. Chuck was the bigger concern; his heart rhythm was still out of sync and doctors were monitoring it closely. A cardiologist had been summoned but hadn't arrived yet. Mia was feeling much better and her concerns about the baby were lessening. She could feel it kicking up a storm as usual. The burns on the left side of her face were determined to be first and second degree. Doctors didn't think there would be any permanent scarring but told her it would likely be weeks before the wounds healed completely. A plastic surgeon could be called upon if necessary, but the doctors really didn't think that would be necessary.

Mick was angry as he paced around the emergency room. Mia kept telling him to relax, that she and her dad would be fine. It wasn't enough to calm him; he was determined to hunt down whoever did this. His mind kept jumping to Jaquon and the smug look on his face five days earlier at Wilson High School. He remembered him miming a gun with his hand, acting like the gangbanging thug that he was.

He was deep in these thoughts when he felt his cell vibrate in his pocket. He glanced at the screen. Mark Archer was calling.

"Hey, Mark."

"How you doing, Mick? How are Mia and Chuck?'

"I'm pissed, that's how I'm doing! Heaven help whoever did this. Thank God Mia and the baby are fine; right now the bigger concern is Chuck; they've got him hooked to all kinds of monitors, keeping an eye on his heart. They've got a cardiologist coming in to look at him."

"Well, it could have been a lot worse."

"Yeah, I know. I keep reminding myself of that."

"I just spoke to the bomb squad guys and they said they've found something. About twenty feet from the house, on the side with the window the bomb went through, they found a book of matches. There's no proof at this point these were the matches used to light the bomb but they're going to check for prints. The matchbook was from some bar in south county, so that fits as well, given that's 120th Street gang territory."

"That sounds promising. I know Jaquon was at the protest tonight so he has an alibi for when the bomb got tossed, but as a 120th Street asshole he certainly has friends. It would be easy to recruit a buddy to do this."

"Also, I took the liberty of calling in Jack Keller. He was on a day off but I was able to reach him and he'll be here first thing in the morning. I think having him lead the investigation is a good idea. I didn't mean to overstep my bounds, but you were focused on Chuck and Mia, and I thought you'd be okay with it. His work on the OIS is mostly over now so he'll have the time."

Mick thought about Keller and the very tumultuous relationship the two had. Just eighteen months earlier Mick had fired Keller, only to give him back his job a few weeks later. It was a move that few people understood, but Mick had his reasons. But Mick knew the guy could work miracles with difficult investigations so he decided to put aside his personal feelings about Keller. Mark was right.

"Yeah, I'm fine with it."

"Okay, good. He's already spoken by telephone with the bomb squad guys. They told him about the matchbook and so that'll be checked first thing in the morning. He knows this investigation is top priority."

"Any news coverage of the bombing yet? I know the ten o'clock news-casts were already over by the time the news vans arrived at the house."

"Quite a bit, actually. But all website stuff. The morning shows will jump all over it but that's still several hours away."

"Keep me apprised, will you? And I'm available for news interviews if anyone asks. I want to make some things very clear."

"Everyone will want a piece of you, Mick. You sure you want to spend all day doing the interview circuit?'

Mick considered Mark's question. "I really want to get some things said."

"Here's another idea. How about we do our own webcast? Put you on camera saying all you want to say, then putting it out on the RCSO website. Media can draw on the video to get their quotes from you, and even use the video for the news stories. It's worked really well when we've done it in the past. Are you up for something like that? It would save you a ton of time and we can control exactly what's said."

"Yeah, let's do that. Can we have it set up for first thing in the morning?"

"Sure, I can have our video crew in your office at eight. Would that work?"

"Yeah, I'll be there."

"Okay, before I let you go there's one more issue . . . does Mia want to go ahead with the Rose Cochran thing?"

Jack took Peter up on his earlier offer of using the private jet, opting to leave Puerto Penasco well before daybreak Tuesday to get back to Colorado. After landing, Jack checked his messages, looking for additional info on the case. He thought it odd that Archer had called him late the night before; typically the detective commander assigned cases. But he knew that Archer and the sheriff were tight and that the sheriff was probably overwhelmed by what had occurred. No doubt this investigation would be a top priority for the RCSO. Jack's thoughts went to

Mia, and while he and Mia certainly had their rough spots in the past, he was glad to hear that she and her baby were going to be okay.

Archer had told him the bombing was likely retaliation for Alex Washington's death. Jack thought back to the week before when he was working the case with Denver PD and the DA's office. It was a controversial OIS for sure, but it was pretty clear to everyone that Mia had acted properly.

Once on the ground in Denver he headed for his car in the long-term parking lot then drove straight to the McCallister home.

Mark managed three hours of sleep before his alarm woke him a few minutes before five.

He rolled over in bed and grabbed the remote from the nightstand. He flipped on the Channel Eight news to see what kind of coverage they had of the bombing. They were in commercial so he flipped to Channel Two.

"Good morning, Denver. We have breaking news involving Rocklin County Sheriff Mick McCallister. Denise Elliott has the story."

"Thanks, Brenda. I'm standing outside the home of Sheriff McCallister in Castle Springs and as you can see there's a lot of activity going on here. A few minutes after ten last night an incendiary device of some kind was thrown through the window of the sheriff's home. The sheriff wasn't here at the time, but McCallister's wife and father-in-law were inside the house at the time of the bombing. Now, you may remember that just last week Mia Serrano-McCallister, the sheriff's wife, was involved in a shooting at Wilson High School. That incident ended when Serrano-McCallister shot and killed seventeen-year-old Alex Washington, a student at the high school. There has been an angry outcry by some in the community about the shooting and now the home of the sheriff and his wife has been firebombed. My sources tell me that both Serrano-McCallister and her father were injured in the blast and are both at Castle Springs Memorial. Their injuries are not believed to be life threatening. Here's footage we shot last night just minutes after the explosion."

Mark sat up in bed and watched the video he had allowed Channel Two and Channel Eight to shoot. A few seconds into the package there was a close up of Mick, Mia, and Chuck.

"God damn it!"

Elliott's voice added color commentary over the video. "As you can see, Mia Serrano-McCallister suffered burns to her face. Her father, Charles Serrano, is being administered to by paramedics. His injuries are unknown. And a very worried Sheriff McCallister is there comforting the two. I've been told that there have been no arrests in the case, but you can be sure plenty of attention will be paid to bringing to justice those responsible for the bombing. Denise Elliott, Channel Two, reporting from Castle Springs."

Mark Archer grabbed his cell phone and found Denise Elliott's phone number in his personal contacts. Elliott picked up after two rings.

"You're up kinda early, Mark."

"Just caught your live remote from Castle Springs. I thought we had an agreement—no close up shots."

"Ah, Mark. You knew we couldn't pass up that opportunity. As a journalist I have an obligation to bring people the news. And what happened last night was big news. Sorry if you don't understand that."

"You promised you wouldn't do closeups, and there you are with fucking closeups of all three."

"Mark, I have a job to do and I'm going to do it to the best of my ability. And, really, I think you're overblowing this whole thing. What's the big deal about showing them in a tight shot? If anything, it creates a greater level of sympathy for your department. A firebomb through a bedroom window is serious shit. You should be happy with my story."

"Not the point, Denise, and you know it. I gave you permission to shoot the video within certain parameters and you went back on your word. Not very professional, Denise"

"You wanna talk about professional? That's a good one, coming from you."

Mark tried his best to keep his voice calm.

"What the hell are you talking about?"

"I'm talking about the media guy for a sheriff's department carrying on a relationship with a certain anchor woman."

"Careful where you're heading with this, Denise."

"I could overlook that, really. I mean, I can understand the attraction. But what exactly does she get out of the relationship? Hmmmm, let me think. Oh, I know, maybe getting an exclusive interview with the family involved in a certain highly-publicized case the RCSO is handling?"

Mark's heart sank.

"You've got quite the imagination there, Denise. Maybe you should be working for the *National Enquirer* . . . it might be a better fit for you."

"I've got a nice job here at Channel Two, but thanks for looking out for me."

CHAPTER 36

Mick arrived at the station a little after eight to find Mark Archer and a video crew setting up in his office.

"Good morning, boss. We'll be ready to go in just a few minutes."

"Okay, let's go over some of the stuff I'll be talking about."

The two had done several webcasts in the past so they had a routine worked out. Mark would ask the questions and the sheriff would respond on camera. They would outline the topics they wanted to cover beforehand, but were careful to make sure Mick sounded natural and unscripted. Mick had a lot of experience being interviewed and was quick on his feet, a very important skill for someone who faced the media on a regular basis. Mark scribbled some notes as the two spoke, highlighting the key points Mick needed to make. After a few minutes they were ready to roll.

Between nurses constantly checking on her and constant flashbacks of the bomb going off, Mia had gotten very little sleep. She was worried about her father, who had been moved to the intensive care unit after being looked at by a cardiologist. She kept reminding herself that he was a very strong man and hadn't had any heart problems in the past.

At nine thirty Mick walked into her room and gave her a big hug and a kiss.

"How're you feeling today?"

"I'm exhausted and I'm worried about Dad."

"He's going to be fine, Mia. You need to rest and get better."

"I'm fine," she replied, touching the bandages on her cheek, "I just want to go home."

"You should be discharged before lunch. I'll take you home and get you settled in."

"That sounds good. But you don't need to stay with me, I'll be fine."

"I know you will, but we've got twenty four-hour coverage on the house, just as a precaution. Got a deputy stationed down the road monitoring traffic and another one right outside the door. We'll keep them there until we sort out who did this and make an arrest."

"Do you think it was that Jaquon kid you've been talking about?"

"He was at the protest last night so he has an alibi, but that doesn't mean he didn't have a friend do his dirty work. Nothing would surprise me with that prick."

"I guess it could be him, but remember I got confronted when I was walking to my appointment with Dr. Lusetti the other day? They were 120th Street and pretty threatening. Who knows—maybe they were involved?"

"Could be, we'll just have to see how things play out."

"I could definitely identify two of them, the ones who were most confrontational, but probably not the others."

"Okay. By the way, Keller is leading the investigation."

Mia looked at her husband. She, like Mick, had had her share of issues with Keller, but she knew he was the best investigator in the RCSO.

"Well, if there's anyone who can catch the asshole that did this, it's Keller."

"Yeah, and they already have a possible lead. We canvassed the area outside the house and came up with a matchbook. It was close to the baby's room window so it adds up. They're going to check it for prints this morning. In fact, that reminds me, I've got to call Keller and check on it."

"Could he really have been stupid enough to leave the matchbook behind?"

"I'm guessing they were in such a hurry to get away they panicked and ran off. It may turn out to be nothing, but it does seem odd that there would be matches in that exact spot. And God knows we've seen dumber criminals than this."

⁓

Mark was still angry about his early morning exchange with Denise Elliott. He and Angela had always been so careful about their relationship; he wondered how Elliott had learned about it. Did she know that Mark and Angela were now basically on the outs? He thought about Angela and how angry she was about him questioning her about the timestamp on the website story. She certainly didn't like having her integrity questioned, but there was little doubt in his mind that she had something to do with the firebomb through the Channel Eight window.

And now Denise Elliott was onto them, and, even worse, Elliott knew Mark had been behind the Gillespie interview for Angela and Channel Eight. What Mark had done was borderline unethical. Who am I to start questioning Angela's integrity? he wondered.

Thoughts about the Gillespie interview brought to mind images of Rachel. He wasn't very proud of what had happened with her; he had succumbed in a moment of weakness. But deep down he knew he was just trying to justify his behavior. In truth, he knew there was no excuse for what he had done, and he had to figure out a way to make things right.

CHAPTER 37

⤬

Keller pulled up in front of the McCallisters' home and found a place to park among the half dozen vehicles there. RCSO personnel were in their ninth hour investigating the bombing.

He recognized one of the bomb techs so he approached her first.

"Jack! Rumor had it you were going to catch this case. Good to see you, old man."

Keller nodded and shook Molly Sirody's hand.

"So, let me give you a quick walk through so you can get your bearings. We'll start where we think the perp was when he tossed the bomb."

The two walked around to the evidence markers placed on the ground behind the house.

"So, that's the window the bomb went through. It's twenty-two feet from here to the window," Sirody said, pointing at the house.

"So at twenty-two feet they weren't likely to miss the target when they tossed the thing."

"That's exactly right. In cases like these the asshole will typically get close enough so as not to miss, but far enough away so they won't get any blowback. It's kind of a safety zone. Not uncommon."

Made sense, Jack thought.

"This is where we found the matchbook. It's likely the idiot left it behind in his rush to get the hell out of here. Again, not uncommon, but it does tell us this was amateur-hour stuff. A pro wouldn't make these kinds of bonehead mistakes. Whoever did this didn't really know what they were doing."

Keller looked at Sirody and shook his head. "No doubt."

Sirody continued, "We've got the CSI team working right now on lifting prints off the matchbook. We'll see what they get. The surface of the matchbook is actually fairly good, so it'll be an issue of how many people touched it."

"If there are only a few sets of prints we could still run them all in the system," Jack replied.

Sirody nodded. "Let's head inside."

The two entered the home and walked upstairs. Sirody led them back to the baby's bedroom and Jack immediately saw the crib and and changing table. He hadn't realized that the bomb had been thrown into the room the McCallisters had prepared for the arrival of their child. The damage was extensive, and it pissed him off. Jack had his differences with both of the McCallisters, but this was total bullshit. A fucking coward did this, he thought to himself.

Sirody could see the resolve in Keller's demeanor. She said to Jack, "I've been told the baby is due in a couple months. I hate to think of what might have happened here if the baby had been born and was in this room when the bomb got tossed. There's no way a baby could have survived. Look at the crib—it's totally destroyed."

Jack didn't answer, but surveyed the damage. Not being an arson investigator he didn't fully understand all he was seeing. Sirody filled him in.

"So the bomb came in through that window. It was thrown with enough force to break the window, obviously, but the energy from the toss would have largely been absorbed by hitting the window. But it made it into the room and landed here, under the crib—you can see that spot is blacker and more burned than the rest of the carpet. That's our point of origin and with the bedding on the crib it went up in a matter of seconds. Thirty or forty seconds later the rest of the room was engulfed in flames. There's a lot of fuel in this room, that's why you see so many fire-related deaths in people's bedrooms."

Jack nodded.

Sirody led Jack back outside. "We've interviewed all the neighbors and nobody saw anything. Keep in mind it was after ten so it was dark and these homes are spaced well apart. The nearest neighbor is a hundred feet away or more. We're not going to find any footprints—the ground is covered with pine needles. And the streets are paved so tire tracks aren't a possibility."

Keller looked at Sirody. "Did you check for any skid marks? I mean, the prick would've taken off running and may have laid down a little rubber on his way out of here."

"Not yet. It was dark until an hour ago but we'll have that checked by the CSI team."

"Let's do that. It's a long shot but you never know. Our strongest lead is the matchbook—we need to get the prints off that thing ASAP."

"As I said, CSI is working on it."

Jack took out his phone and called the RCSO lab. "Jackie, this is Keller. Do we have anything on the matchbook from the sheriff's house?'

"I was just going to call you, Jack. We got lucky—there were only two sets of prints. Manscrusi is checking them now. Should have something for you shortly."

"Great news. I'm wrapping up at the scene. I'll be there in a bit."

Chuck was not a happy patient. It was nearly ten by the time the cardiologist came by to see him and Chuck started by explaining that he was just fine and should be discharged immediately. The doctor, a relatively young man from California who had just recently moved his practice to

Castle Springs, told him the battery of tests taken the night before had revealed some problems.

"That can't be right! I don't smoke, I eat right, I exercise, I don't have any heart issues. You must have grabbed the wrong test results."

"I'm afraid not, Mr. Serrano. The good news is that we caught things early when they're a relatively easy fix. The scare you had last night caused your heart to go into arrhythmia and fortunately paramedics were nearby to stabilize you. Now we just need to fix the underlying problem."

"Can you explain all this to my son-in-law? I'd call my daughter but she's in the hospital too, somewhere on the third floor, I think."

"Of course, how about if I come back in a little while. Will that work?"

"I think so."

Once he finished at the McCallisters' house, Keller drove to the station. He was hoping that Carla Manscrusi had some news about the fingerprints from the matchbook. He made his way to the lab where he found Carla looking at the computer screen on her desk.

"Hey, Carla."

"Good timing, Jack. I was just about to call you."

"With good news, I hope."

"I think you'll be pleased."

"Sounds promising. What do you have for me?'

"There were only two sets of prints on the matchbook so if either or both are in our database we should have an ID here shortly."

"That's what I like to hear. Let's do it."

"Working on it right now. Want to watch? Shouldn't take too long."

Jack looked at the young CSI tech. He had seen techs run prints more times than he could count, but he knew Carla would like it if he watched her perform her magic.

"Absolutely. It amazes me what you guys can do."

Carla beamed. "Have a seat."

Carla entered the prints into the database and watched the screen as it did the comparisons. She was running the prints through the county system, thinking if local perps tossed the bomb they would pop up right away, provided they had an arrest history with RCSO.

Within a minute they had a match.

"Well, looky here. One set of the prints matches one of our local 120th Street knuckleheads."

Jack took out his notebook and started scribbling the information displayed on the screen.

Damian Mychael Blackwell

AKA Shorty

DOB 5/16/97

21135 East 135th Street

Castle Springs, CO

"Get me a look at his history. Let's see what Shorty got popped for."

Carla minimized the screen and searched the database for Blackwell.

"Looks like he's been arrested twice by RCSO. Once for burglary and the second pop was a drug charge . . . looks like meth sales. He's also listed as a 120th Street banger."

Jack continuing scribbling.

"This is great, Carla. Can't tell you how much I appreciate it."

"No sweat, Jack. Happy to help."

"Let's see if we have any luck with the second set."

Carla returned to the search screen and a minute later she had a hit.

"Damn, Jack. Gotta love it when the fish jump into the boat."

"Makes up for all the dead ends we usually run into."

Jack studied the screen.

Tracy Dewayne Thompson
AKA Iceman
DOB 6/19/93
1485 East Guava, Apt 5B
Castle Springs, CA

"History?"

Carla tapped an inquiry into the database.

"He's another 120th Street chump . . . history includes small-time stuff. Drugs, auto burglary, vandalism."

"I wonder where he got the moniker Iceman?" wondered Jack.

"Who knows where they come up with these bullshit names. Probably puts lots of ice in his Coors Light."

Keller laughed. "The name on the matchbook cover is Chookie's Pub. Can you run it and see what kind of calls for service we've gotten there?"

Carla opened a new screen and ran the search.

More than two pages of data popped up.

"Oh yeah, this is a place that should be quite familiar to our deputies working the south end. All kinds of shit going on there."

"Like what?"

"Typical bar-type calls, but also a lot of gang-related stuff."

"That fits with our two perps if both are 120th Street bangers."

"So, they decide they want to blow up the sheriff's place, grab some matches from the little bowl sitting on the bar, and off they go?" asked Carla.

"Who knows, but with only two sets of prints, it's a definite possibility."

"Makes sense."

Keller finished writing everything down in his notebook, stood, and said, "You're the best, Carla."

"Ah, thanks Jack. Just doing my job. Hey, keep me posted, will you?"

"Will do. Now print me out a nice glossy of each of our knuckleheads."

CHAPTER 38

ose Cochran was growing impatient. She had seen the news coverage of Mia Serrano-McCallister being rushed to a Colorado
hospital following an explosion at her home. Things were clearly out
of control out there, she thought, and they certainly needed her legal
help. She had called the office number for Mark Archer several times
that morning but each call had gone to voicemail. This time she dialed
the switchboard for the RCSO.

"Rocklin County sheriff, how may I direct your call?"

"Yes, this is Rose Cochran calling from Los Angeles. I've been trying to reach Mark Archer all morning but have been unable to do so.
Is there a way you can get a message to him and ask him to call me
immediately?"

"Have you left him a message on his voicemail?"

"No, but I've called him several times this morning. Look, it's
urgent I get in touch with him."

"Usually the best way to reach Lieutenant Archer is to leave a voicemail. I know he checks them several times a day. Would you like me to
connect you to that number?"

Cochran, barely able to contain her exasperation, replied, "No, I'd
like you to tell him to call me. My number is 213-555-7777. As I said,
this is extremely important."

"Normally, we don't do things this way—"

"Can you please do me this favor?"

The caller was so pushy the switchboard operator decided it would be easiest just to take her information.

"I can make an exception just this once. Now what was your name again?"

"Rose Cochran, the attorney from Los Angeles."

"How do you spell your last name, ma'am?"

"Oh, for God's sake. It's C-O-C-H-R-A-N."

<hr />

As soon as the doctor left, Chuck called Mick and learned that he was already at the hospital, visiting Mia two floors below. After hearing Chuck describe, in cryptic terms, what the doctor had said, Mick told him that he'd speak to the doctor to clarify things. He hung up the phone and turned his attention to his wife.

"That was your dad. The doctor met with him and Chuck wants me to speak with him to get a clearer understanding of what his condition is and what his options are at this point."

Mia looked concerned. "Not sure I like the sound of that."

"I don't think he fully understood what the doctor told him, so he wants us to talk to the guy."

"Let's get me out of here so we can go up to his floor."

Mick summoned a nurse and asked about getting Mia discharged.

The nurse said, "She'll have to leave in a wheelchair. Hospital rules. Give me a minute and I'll grab one."

"Is that really necessary?" Mia asked.

"Yes, I'm afraid so. It's for your own safety."

Mick interceded, "That's fine. We'll wait here for the wheelchair."

As Mick was reassuring Mia, his cell phone rang. Seeing it was Mark Archer, Mick answered the call.

"What's up, Mark?"

"Sorry to bother you, but are you going to see Mia anytime soon?"

"I'm with her now; she's about to be released from the hospital. I'll put you on speaker."

"Hi, Mia. I just spoke to Rose Cochran and she's really hot on this case. She saw the news coverage of the explosion at the house and she wants to get on board immediately. I told her that you were considering all your options and that she'd get a call back soon."

"The story made the LA news again?" Mia asked.

"Yep, and it's only going to get bigger now, in part because of the bomb going off at the house and also because of Cochran. If you bring her on board, she'll make this a headline story in every paper in the country. Believe me, if there's one thing this woman knows, it's how to generate publicity for her clients."

Mia suddenly looked uneasy. She had decided the night before to proceed with Cochran but that was before the explosion.

Mick, picking up on his wife's hesitance, offered, "You don't have to do this, Mia. No one is expecting you to become the poster child for every officer involved in an OIS. You can do it if you want to, and I'll certainly support you all the way, but it's your decision."

Mia thought about the explosion in the baby's room and her resolve grew stronger.

"Yeah, I want to do it."

※

The doctor returned to Chuck's room shortly after Mick and Mia got there. He explained that the tests run on Chuck's heart had shown some blockage in a particular artery and that a stent was the proper course of action. The relatively simple procedure would open the blocked artery and restore normal blood flow to the heart muscle. He stressed that it wasn't major surgery, saying that he could do the procedure the next morning.

It was a bit overwhelming but they all knew it was the best course of action.

"Let's just get it done, Dad. Why put it off?"

"Yeah, I know you're right, Mia. But it's a lot to take in, you know?"

"Sure, I understand. But as the doctor said it's almost routine. And you can go home the day after the surgery. You just have to do it."

"What's the recovery time?" asked Chuck.

"You'll be back on your feet in a few days, and able to resume all normal activities a week or two later. It's really the best option, Mr. Serrano."

"Okay, let's do it."

❧

After talking with Mia about Rose Cochran, Mark headed out to grab a bite to eat. As he was walking across the street to Gino's, his favorite bagel shop, his phone chirped. Looking down he saw it was a text from Rachel.

> "How are you doing?? I saw the news about
> the Sheriff and his wife. Just awful!

Mark slid his phone back into his pocket and walked into Gino's. He placed his order and took a seat near the back. He took out his phone and reread the message. Should he respond right away? Should he wait a while, then respond? Should he ignore it?

❧

After Chuck's cardiologist left, Mia dialed the number for Rose Cochran and was surprised when Cochran answered the call herself.

"Ms. Cochran, this is Mia Serrano-McCallister calling from Colorado."

"It's wonderful to hear from you! Please, call me Rose. May I call you Mia?"

"Of course, that's fine."

"Terrific. So, first off, how are you doing? I'm so concerned for you."

"I'm holding up okay, but I'm worried about my dad. The stress of the bombing caused his heart to act up and the cardiologist just informed us that he needs a stent. So that's going to happen tomorrow."

More ammunition for the lawsuit, Cochran thought. "Oh my word, I am so sorry to hear that. And the doctor thinks this was all brought on by the stress of the bombing?"

"Yes, his heart went into an arrhythmia immediately after the explosion. I think he was terrified that something had happened to me. By the time we got out of the house he wasn't feeling right and he sort of collapsed while talking to the paramedics."

"Well, thank goodness the paramedics were right there!"

"That's very true; we owe them a lot."

"And everything is good with the baby?"

"Yep, kicking non-stop as usual."

"Is this your first?"

"Yes, I'm due in two months. We're really excited about it."

"Boy or girl?'

"We don't know—we want to be surprised."

"Good for you! I love it—doing it the old fashioned way."

"Yeah, it's been fun wondering about it."

"Any names picked out yet?"

"Nothing firm. We're still throwing around some options."

"Well, I have three children, all grown. My oldest is turning forty this month. Ugh! I can't be that old!"

"Well, I've seen you on television plenty of times and you don't look old enough to have a forty year old."

"Well, aren't you sweet, Mia. You've made my day!"

Cochran was pleased with the flow of the conversation. She was forging a personal relationship with Mia, something she excelled at doing with all her clients. But now it was time to land the deal. She lowered her voice a bit and struck a serious tone.

"Mia, I'd love to represent you in this case. I'm confident we can win, and at the same time send a message to all those Neanderthals like Leland Simpson that the comments he made were totally out of line and will not be tolerated. Kinda strike a blow for all women. I've been following your case through the news reports and I must say that I think what you have been going through over the past six days has been just awful. Simpson clearly overstepped the bounds of decency with his outrageous comments."

"Yeah, it hasn't exactly been fun. I can't believe all this has happened to me. It's like a nightmare, only I'm not waking up."

"I totally understand. Look, I think we should jump on this case as soon as possible. My thoughts were to fly out to Denver later today and do a press conference the day after tomorrow announcing we're going to file a suit against Simpson. Ideally, you'd be with me during the press conference, but I would do most of the talking. You can participate as much or as little as you want—whatever you're comfortable with. But now that you've told me the news about your dad's procedure being set for tomorrow . . . I mean, I don't want to be in the way. You've got more important things going on right now."

Cochran deliberately chose the word *procedure* rather than *surgery*. She wanted to proceed with the press conference on Thursday, but wanted it to be Mia's idea. The term *procedure* was a subtle way to downplay the urgency of Chuck's medical condition.

"I think Thursday should work. Like you said, the sooner the better."

Perfect, Cochran thought.

"I'll fly out today. I can't wait to meet you, Mia!"

CHAPTER 39

M ark took a couple of bites of his toasted bagel and cream cheese before he pushed it away. Staring at Rachel's text had made him lose his appetite. While contemplating the situation with her, his mind drifted to Denise Elliott and the conversation between the two earlier that morning. Elliott somehow knew that Mark had been present during the Channel Eight interview at the Gillespies' and had concluded the obvious—that Mark had set it up. Elliott also knew about Mark's relationship with Angela. He and Angela had been so careful to keep it a secret, but both he and Angela knew that someday word would likely get out, and that day had arrived. Elliott knew that Mark had overstepped his bounds by showing favoritism to a particular reporter by arranging the Gillespie interview. That could seriously hurt his credibility as the public information officer of the RCSO.

He knew he had two calls to make. One to Rachel and the other to the sheriff telling him about Denise Elliott. He wasn't sure which call he dreaded more.

Cochran was on her way to LAX thirty minutes after she ended her phone conversation with Mia. She kept a packed suitcase in her office for situations like this. It wasn't uncommon for her to learn about a case and be on a plane an hour later. Having a suitcase packed with a few days' worth of clothes was a lifesaver for her.

She landed in Denver a few minutes before three. She took a limo the thirty miles to the RCSO and met Mia and Mick at the station. Mia couldn't believe it was all happening so fast—she had just talked to Cochran five hours earlier.

"It's so nice to meet you in person, Mia," Cochran said, giving her a big hug.

Cochran turned her attention to Mick. "And you must be Sheriff McCallister."

"Welcome to Rocklin County," replied Mick, shaking Cochran's hand.

"I'm happy to be here, sheriff. I wish it were under different circumstances, but it is what it is and I'm here to help."

"Why don't we go to my office where we can talk?"

The three walked through the station. Cochran's presence didn't go unnoticed by those still working; she was a nationally-known figure. She didn't seem to notice all the gawking.

"Can I offer you some coffee?" Mick asked.

"No, I'm fine. Had plenty on the flight from LA."

The three took seats at the conference table in Mick's office. Cochran started right in.

"Thank you for seeing me. When I saw the footage of the Washingtons' attorney talking about Mia's hormones, I almost fell out of my chair. I knew I had to come to Denver to see if I could help."

"We couldn't believe it either," answered Mia. "This whole thing has been a complete nightmare. It hasn't even been a week and it seems like ten years."

"Well, my practice doesn't specialize in officer-involved shootings, but I've dealt with them peripherally. And this one looks clean to me. You saved that girl's life, Mia."

"I know, everybody tells me that. But still, I took a life and that'll be with me forever. I still see his face in my dreams."

"It'll take time, Mia. You took a life but you saved one as well. And while that's a very difficult thing to live with, the young man put himself in that position. Remember that."

"I know all that, at least I do in my mind. But my heart aches for Alex and his family. It really does. I was a high school teacher before becoming a deputy. That was seventeen years ago, but I still feel a real connection to kids. I mean, Alex could have been one of my students."

"I had no idea, Mia. That's got to make this extra hard for you. That hasn't been part of the media coverage, at least from what I've seen."

"No, they haven't figured that out . . . yet."

"It shouldn't be an issue. In fact, we could probably turn it into a positive—how you tried your best to talk to him using your teaching background, et cetera."

Mick stayed quiet. While he totally supported Mia throughout the ordeal, he felt it was important not to interject himself into the conversation.

Mia paused for a few moments, then responded. "Well, there's more to that story. I left teaching in 1999. I was at Columbine."

Cochran looked at Mia before responding, trying to get a read from her.

"Oh, Mia. I am so sorry. That must have been a horrible, life-changing experience."

"It was, and that's why I left teaching and came to the RCSO."

Cochran hesitated before continuing. Mia picked up on it.

"Yes, I was a witness to what happened. I was in the library and saw a lot of the carnage. I haven't set foot back on the campus since then. I just walked away." Tears rolled down Mia's cheeks.

Cochran stood up, walk to Mia, and embraced her. "I am so, so sorry, Mia."

Mia wiped away tears. "Thanks. It was a long time ago, but I still think about it often."

Cochran returned to her chair, looked at Mia, and said, "I need to give this some thought. Your Columbine experience could be a positive or a negative factor as we go forward."

"What do you mean?" asked Mick.

"May I be blunt?"

Mia shifted a bit in her chair.

"Please."

"The Columbine issue hasn't been brought up publicly, correct?"

"No, the only one speaking out officially against me is Leland Simpson. And he didn't mention anything about it yesterday after the funeral."

"Good. Which means he doesn't know because if he did that's what he would have gone after, not a pregnant woman's hormones."

"Lucky me."

"I know it was a painful thing to go through, Mia, but believe me, we can turn all of this into a positive."

"Really?'

"Yes, it's what I do."

"So, what's next?"

"Do the press conference Thursday and get things rolling. I'd like you at my side, Mia. Are you up for that?"

"I think so. I want to be at the hospital tomorrow for my dad's procedure, but Thursday should be fine, he'll be home by then."

"What time is the procedure?'

"The doctor wants to do it early, like seven."

"Then he should be in recovery by eight."

"Yeah, he said it wouldn't take very long."

"Let's do the press conference at noon on Thursday. That'll allow the noontime newscasts to cover it. You have three stations doing news then. It'll get us decent coverage."

Cochran had done her homework, thought Mick. She knew the Denver media game.

"So what do I need to do at the press conference?'

"You can just be present, or you can speak if you'd like. But understand, if you do speak we need to make sure you stick with our game plan. We'll go over your talking points in advance. We have a day and a half to get ready—you'll be fine."

Mia looked a little surprised. Cochran picked up on it.

"It's been my experience that when people go off script that's when they get in trouble. It's no reflection on you, Mia. When he was running for president Jimmy Carter went off script after he thought his interview with Playboy Magazine was over and he talked about 'lusting in his heart.' Next thing you know that's all that was ever talked about."

"Okay, you know what you're doing so I'll just follow your lead."

"Perfect. I'll get you those talking points tonight so you'll have some time to look them over. It won't be anything too major. The bigger issue is dealing with your Columbine history."

"You said you need to think about it, but what are the issues with Columbine?'

"There's an expression in my business—go ugly early."

"What does that mean?"

"It means that if you have something bad or controversial to deal with, it's always better to get it out early. First thing, really. The Columbine thing may not be bad per se, but Simpson will try to use it as ammunition. So we take that opportunity away from him by bringing it up first. Typically whoever is first in bringing up something negative, or something that could be twisted—they win the public opinion battle. It's human nature, really."

"And the Columbine angle they will try to twist is . . . ?"

Cochran looked at Mia, then leaned in and said, "That you suffered some kind of PTSD episode on the campus the other day. That what you witnessed that day at Columbine all came flooding back and you shot Alex Washington unnecessarily."

Mia covered her mouth and looked at Mick. He grabbed her hand.

"I'm just telling you what we could be facing. But if we get it out first, the fallout will be much more manageable. I'm sorry to upset you, Mia."

"No, no . . . I need to know this. I don't want to be surprised by anything," she responded, thinking about her session with Dr. Lusetti a few days earlier.

"It's my style, Mia. I like to be very upfront with my clients. It really works best, but it's hard sometimes."

Mia nodded. Mick jumped in, "So, exactly what legal action are we taking in the case?"

"We'll sue Leland Simpson for defamation."

"And damages?"

"Probably ten million. It's a nice big round number that'll get everyone's attention. Now, in reality we won't get anything close to that, and frankly, I'm not sure we'd ever collect anything from Simpson if we did win a judgment. But we'll get his attention and strike a victory for all women, especially those who are pregnant."

"I don't care about the money. I just want the guy to get the message."

"Oh, we'll get his attention. We'll yank his chain pretty good."

"Okay, that all sounds good. What about your fee?"

"It'll all be on contingency. I'll get one third of anything we collect from Simpson. That's the only way I'd get paid; there are no legal fees for you."

Mick looked at Cochran. She was obviously in it for the publicity and clearly knew exactly what she was doing.

CHAPTER 40

~

Floyd Liston didn't visit Jaquon's neighborhood very often, but he was determined to talk to him. Liston had called and texted numerous times since learning of the firebomb at the McCallisters' home. He planned to ask Jaquon face to face if he was involved. Liston feared he was, even though Jaquon was at the protest at the RCSO when the bombing happened. The most likely scenario was that Jaquon had put someone up to it. There were certainly enough gangsters in his neighborhood; he didn't think his nephew would have any trouble finding someone to put in the time, so to speak. It was how life in the ghetto worked—score points with the higher ups and good things happened for you. And, no doubt, Jaquon was a rising star in 120th Street.

Graffiti covered the walls of the mostly unoccupied, abandoned buildings in the neighborhood. Young African-American men congregated on street corners. Liston was filled with both anger and disgust as he drove through Jaquon's neighborhood. Such stupidity, he thought, and a waste of life. These men standing on the corners acting tough, clowning with their gang signs, with nothing better to do.

Liston was always amazed that the neighborhoods that were most run down and in need of repair were the same neighborhoods where people stood around wasting time. He had grown up on the streets of St. Louis, but had been fortunate to get away from the life, thanks in large part to a minister at a local church who took an interest in him.

A stint in the army hadn't hurt either. Let these tough guys experience how things were in Iraq or Afghanistan, he thought; they wouldn't last a day.

He turned up Jaquon's street and soon located the address. He tried to remember the last time he had visited his nephew. It had been long enough that he couldn't recall what the place looked liked. He parked his car in front and walked to the door of the small bungalow. He knocked loudly, but no one answered. He walked around the back, calling out Jaquon's name. Still nothing. As he reached the backyard a female voice rang out from the house.

"Can I help you?"

"I'm looking for Jaquon Jackson. I'm his uncle."

A pretty young woman appeared at the back door.

"Jaquon's got an uncle? He never mentioned you. Wait a minute, I know you—you were at the funeral yesterday."

"Yes, I was. Is Jaquon around?"

"No, he's out right now. He should be home soon. Wanna come in and wait for him?"

Liston considered the offer. He didn't want to have to come back to the neighborhood, so he accepted. The woman opened the door and extended her hand.

"I'm Alondra, Jaquon's girlfriend."

"Hi, I'm Floyd."

The woman had a firm, confident handshake. Liston couldn't help wonder what she was doing with someone like his nephew. They walked into the small living room and took a seat on the sofa. Liston looked around; the house was surprisingly well kept.

"Can I get you something to drink while you wait?"

"Coffee, if it's not too much trouble . . . or a soft drink, if that's easier."

"How about a Diet Coke?"

"Sure."

Alondra left and returned a minute later with a Diet Coke in a tall glass filled with ice.

He took the drink and asked, "So, how did you meet Jaquon?"

"We were friends from school. Elementary school to be exact. We lost contact for a long time but we reconnected about a year ago. Bumped into each other at the market and, well, here we are."

"You live here, then?"

"Yes, I moved in a few months ago. We started seeing each other after we ran into each other and it's gotten pretty serious."

"Do you go to school? Work?"

Alondra looked at Liston and knew what he was really asking. Was she some dumb hanger-on?

"I'm a manager at a bank in Highlands Ranch. Been there almost four years. It's a good job. I'll have my bachelor's degree in finance in June. Been going at night . . . Colorado State, extension classes."

"Wow, impressive," he replied, trying to hide his surprise.

"Thanks," Alondra answered, smiling.

"Did I say something amusing?"

"No—I just know what you're thinking."

"Really?" Liston replied, trying to figure out this young woman.

"What is someone like me doing with someone like Jaquon."

Liston didn't respond, embarrassed that he was that transparent. The woman was sharp.

Alondra continued, "Well, am I close?"

"Yeah, okay. So, what's the answer?"

"The simple answer is that I love him."

"Okay, so what's the answer to the more complicated part of the question?"

"At the risk of seeming like a total stereotype, I think I can save him."

"Save him from what, exactly?"

"I think we both know the answer to that question, Floyd."

Liston nodded. The woman didn't mince words. He liked that.

"So, you're a woman on a mission?"

"I guess so, but I gotta be honest—it's been a challenge."

"I can imagine."

"Things were going pretty well until his cousin got killed last week. That really set him back and he's slid into some of his old ways. But I'll get him back on track."

Floyd thought about the questions he wanted to ask Jaquon about the bombing at the sheriff's home, but was interrupted by the sound of someone coming through the front door.

"Uncle Floyd, what you doin' here, man?"

Mark Archer texted the sheriff saying he needed to talk with him and to call when he could. A minute later his phone was ringing. Before answering he got up and closed his office door.

"Hey, sheriff, thanks for the call back."

"Sheriff? Uh oh, this must not be good. You never call me that."

"It's not good. Listen, I spoke with Denise Elliott at Channel Two this morning and she knows about me and Angela. She brought it up and suggested that it was a conflict of interest . . . "

"How'd she figure that out? You guys have been together for a while and no one else has brought it up."

"I don't know. But there's more."

Mick took a breath, "What is it, Mark?"

"She also knows I orchestrated the Gillespies' interview with Channel Eight."

"Ah, shit. How the hell did she figure that out?"

"I don't know. But she definitely knows and is being a bit of a bitch about it."

"Damn it! We don't need this right now. We're going to need the media to give us a fair shake with this OIS and this sure as hell doesn't help any."

"I know, and I'm sorry."

Mick paused, "It's not your fault, Mark. I agreed with your idea to get the Gillespie interview on Channel Eight. How well do you know Denise?"

"Fairly well, I've dealt with her a lot over the years. She's always been very aggressive but the RCSO has never been the target of that aggression before."

"Is she fair?"

"Yeah, I think so. But she's a veteran and so she can play the game pretty well. I have no doubt she'll use the info as a chit . . . get something from us down the road at some point."

"I guess we'll find out what that is when the time comes."

"Yeah. And there's something else I need to tell you about."

"Am I going to like this any more than the Elliott thing?"

"Nope. I have a suspicion that the firebomb that went through the window at Channel Eight the other night may not have been Jaquon or anyone else from the Washington family. Or 120th Street, either."

"Really? I thought they were good for it."

"I did, too. But things don't add up and I think Angela may have had something to do with it."

"What the hell are you talking about? She was live on the air when that thing came through the window."

"Yeah, I know. I'm not saying she threw the bomb herself, but she may have arranged for it to get tossed."

"And her motive would be . . . ?"

"To get attention for her interview with the Gillespies. And remember, it's sweeps week."

"Oh, for God's sake. Would she really do that?"

"I wouldn't have thought so, but the circumstantial evidence certainly points to her."

"Jesus, that's criminal!"

"Yeah, I know. But let's give it a little more time before we lower the boom. It's only been a few days and no one is talking about it since the bombing at your place."

"But we can't just let her get away with that shit."

"Look, there were no injuries, a minimal amount of damage, and it's off the front page now. I'm not saying we let her walk, I'm just saying we give it a little time and see how things play out."

"Does she know that you suspect she was involved?"

"Yeah, and it hasn't been pretty. She's pretty pissed off at me for suggesting that she was behind it. We haven't really spoken for a few days."

"Okay, I'll give it some time but eventually I'm going to have to have investigators take a look at her."

"I really think it's a back burner thing. And keep in mind that Angela did us a huge favor with the Scott Lennox trial. When she found out about the relationship between Keller and Lisa Sullivan she could have blown the whistle on it and let Lennox walk on a murder charge. She chose to keep that secret and Lennox went down for the 187. We owe her for that."

Mick considered what Archer was saying. He didn't like all these secrets, but saw no choice but to go along.

"You got any more good news for me?"

"Nope, that'll do it for now."

"Hello, Jaquon. I've been having a nice talk with Alondra here."

"I can see that. So what brings you to this part of town?"

"To see you. We need to talk."

"'Bout what, man?"

"Is there somewhere we can go? No offense, Alondra, but this is a private family matter."

"That's fine. I gotta run to the library anyway."

"You don't have to leave, Alondra. There's no need to hide anything from you."

Floyd looked at Alondra and then back to his nephew. "It's up to you. I don't care either way."

"Stay."

Alondra gave Jaquon a look of concern. She sat back down on the sofa. Jaquon plopped down next to her.

"What you gotta say, old man?"

Alondra glared at Jaquon. "That's your uncle, Jaquon. Show some respect."

Liston didn't waste any time.

"Someone bombed the sheriff's home last night. It happened a little after ten. I want to know if you were involved."

Jaquon put both his hands on his chest as though he was personally hurt by the accusation.

"Uncle Floyd, I can't believe you'd think I'd do something like that!"

Alondra shot Jaquon a look. "Answer the question. Did you have anything to do with it?"

"Nah, I got me a alibi. And it's solid, man."

Liston responded, "Yeah, I know you were at the protest at the sheriff's station last night. But I need to know if you had anything to do with it. Maybe you set it up? Anything like that?"

Shaking his head, Jaquon replied. "Can't believe you'd think that about me. Here I try to do the right thing last night and exercise my constitutional rights. Do things all peaceful like. And I still get blamed for something I had nothin' to do with. It ain't right, man."

Alondra looked back and forth at both men. She wanted to believe her boyfriend but she was leery.

"Jaquon, are you telling the truth?"

"Now you? Ain't nobody believe me." He folded his arms across his chest.

"I want to believe you. You know that. But I need to know . . . did you have *anything* to do with that bombing last night?'

"No, man. Not a goddamn thing."

Just then Jaquon's cell rang. He looked down at the number, angrily excused himself, and walked outside, leaving Floyd and Alondra alone in the living room.

CHAPTER 41

Once he finished the call to his boss, Mark sent a text to Rachel.

Can we meet today for a few minutes?

Her response was immediate.

Sure, when and where?

Bean Crazy Coffee in Parker… 5:30 pm

See you then

Mark was a few minutes late arriving at Bean Crazy in Parker. He saw Rachel's car in the lot as he pulled in and his stomach seized in knots. This wasn't going to be easy.

He walked in and found her sitting in the same booth they'd been in a few days earlier. He slid in across from her without a kiss or any kind of physical contact. It didn't go unnoticed.

"Thanks for meeting me. It's been a crazy few days."

"I've been following things in the news."

Mark got right down to business. "Look, I've been thinking a lot about what happened the other day and I think it was a mistake."

"Why?"

"Because you're a married woman. And I'm in a serious relationship as well."

"Are those the only reasons?"

"Those are pretty big reasons."

Rachel looked at Mark with a sense of resolve. "Tom and I are splitting up."

Shit, he thought. Now he was breaking up a marriage. Rachel could sense what he was feeling.

"Look, Mark, it's not because of what happened with us the other day. The marriage has been dead a long time. Kendra is going off to college soon and frankly she was the only reason we didn't split up sooner. You saw what he was like. I can't take it any longer and I'm going to file for divorce as soon as Kendra leaves for school next fall. I've wasted enough of my life with Tom."

"I'm sorry, Rachel. Sorry that you're having to go through this."

"Thanks. So you don't need to worry about breaking up my marriage. It wasn't you; like I said, it's been dead for years. So I hope we can have some kind of relationship—whether it be romantic or just as friends. I like you and I'd like you to be part of my life."

Not what he had expected from this meeting, Mark thought.

"Okay, fair enough."

"So, tell me about Angela."

Mark had told Rachel a little bit about his relationship with Angela at their rendezvous days earlier. She had picked up on the vibe between the two of them the day of the interview at her home and had asked him about her. He was surprised by her perceptiveness; he didn't think the relationship he had with Angela was obvious to the casual observer but Rachel was hardly a casual observer.

"We've been together, off and on, for about three years. We met at a victims' rights rally in Denver and just kind of clicked."

"You say 'off and on' . . . tell me about that."

Mark looked at Rachel and hesitated before responding. She was obviously interested in learning about the competition, he thought.

"Oh, you don't have to tell me if you don't want to, Mark. It's okay."

"There's not that much to tell. A couple years ago I wanted to marry her and she didn't want to commit. Her job is very important to her. So we split up but then we got back together and things have been really good. But now we've hit a bit of a snag and I'm not sure where things are going from here."

"She's very pretty, Mark, and very smart, very successful. I can see why you're attracted to her."

"Those things aren't the issue."

Rachel looked at Mark, nodding knowingly. She was doing her best to forge common ground, trying to get Mark to see that his relationship with Angela was as troubled as hers with Tom.

⁂

Mick and Mia went by the hospital after the meeting with Cochran to check on Chuck. They found him sitting up in his bed, reading the sports page.

"How you doing, Dad?

"Hey, Mia, it's good to see you guys. I'm hanging in there. Just ready to get this thing over with so I can go home. These beds are awful and the noise levels in this place are unbelievable."

"Yeah, I know," responded Mia, thinking back to her less-than-restful night's sleep the night before.

"So, we're set to go at seven tomorrow. Will you guys be here for it?"

Before Mia could answer, Mick jumped in. "Actually, we have a tee time in the morning so if you could just grab a cab home afterwards, that would probably work best."

Before Chuck could offer a comeback, Mia elbowed her husband in the ribs.

"Maybe you should take a cab home now!"

"That's my girl, putting the sheriff in his place!" Chuck replied with a little fist pump.

"We'll be here tomorrow by six. Now try to get some sleep."

By dinnertime Jack had obtained arrest warrants for the two 120th Street gang members whose prints were on the matchbook cover. He was working alone on the case at this point; the bomb and arson guys rarely did the follow up on their cases. Their expertise was on the technical side, essentially the bomb aspects of the investigation.

Jack didn't mind working alone, but knew he'd need some help carrying out the arrests. He briefed his boss, Commander Bob Elder, who said he could have the SWAT team carry out the warrants first thing the next morning. Once he confirmed the details with Elder, Jack headed home. He was exhausted from a day that had begun in Mexico some eighteen hours earlier. He needed a good night's sleep. It would be an early morning the next day helping execute the arrest warrants.

CHAPTER 42

～

The eight on-call SWAT deputies gathered at exactly 6:00 a.m. in the RCSO downstairs squad room. Elder asked Jack to do the briefing.

"Good morning, all. Through fingerprints found at the scene of the bombing we've identified two persons of interest. Both are members of the 120th Street gang and live in the south end of the county. Our intel indicates that neither is employed so I'm hopeful that hitting their residences early this morning will yield some results. Let's split into two teams and hit the houses simultaneously, so neither can alert the other as to what's happening."

Elder took the floor. "Keep in mind that this case has attracted a good amount of publicity and media attention the past couple days. The victim is our own sheriff and his wife, Mia. Obviously, this needs to go down well."

Fifteen minutes later both teams were headed south on the I-25. Jack had decided he'd drive his own vehicle rather than riding in one of the two RCSO armored Bearcat vehicles. There wasn't really room for him inside and he preferred traveling unencumbered.

Jack watched the two Bearcats rumble down the interstate, surprised at the seventy-miles-per-hour pace they kept. The RCSO had acquired the two vehicles after 9/11 and had found them quite useful. They had impressive off-road capabilities and with more than three quarters of Rocklin County being rugged forestland the Bearcats had been used hundreds of times. But the use of such vehicles by law enforcement agencies had been criticized by some politicians in Washington as being "intimidating to some residents." The vehicles, which were surplus military equipment donated to police agencies to handle dangerous situations, were now being recalled by presidential order. Fortunately, the RCSO had not yet been asked to forfeit their two Bearcats.

The vehicles exited at MLK Boulevard and found the fire station where they would do their final preparations for the raid. Within a few minutes the two vehicles went their separate ways, each headed to its assigned task. Jack followed one Bearcat to Tracy Thompson's residence. Jack believed that Thompson was most likely the ring leader on the bombing. He was four years older than Damian Blackwell and had the more extensive arrest record.

The Bearcat stopped a few houses around the corner from Thompson's house. Jack listened on his police radio as the two teams coordinated the hit. Time was of the essence as neighbors in the area would likely see the vehicles moving into place. A phone call or two made by neighbors warning others in the area could easily blow the operation. Less than a minute later both teams were in position and, once given the go ahead, proceeded quickly to their targets.

Jack parked his car and walked up the driveway of Thompson's home, taking cover behind the Bearcat. He wasn't equipped like the SWAT officers so he took a position out of harm's way. The four SWAT team members approached the door. One held a small but powerful battering ram and the other held a large bulletproof shield for protection. A third stood behind the group, keeping his eye on what was happening in the surrounding area. The final member of the team stationed himself around the back to watch for anyone who might try to escape.

"Open up—police!"

There was no immediate answer. One of the deputies put his ear to the door and listened for any activity inside the home.

He shook his head at the others. Nothing.

"Open up, we have a warrant! This is the Rocklin County Sheriff!"

Still nothing. The sergeant nodded at the deputy with the battering ram, giving him the go-ahead to make entry.

One quick blow to the front door and it swung wide open.

The deputies ran through the door yelling, "Police! Come out with your hands up!" They went from room to room, yelling "Clear!" each time they determined that no one was in the room being searched. Nothing—no one was home.

The sergeant came out, shaking his head. "We got nothing, Jack. Nobody home."

"Shit."

The sergeant grabbed his radio and checked in with the second team hitting the Blackwell's house.

"Same. Not a damn thing."

Chuck Serrano was convinced the stuff being put into his veins wasn't working. He was in the OR and the anesthesiologist had just loaded him up for his procedure.

Chuck looked at the doctor. "This stuff isn't doing anything. Maybe I need stronger meds."

"Oh yeah? I wish I had a nickel for every time I had a patient tell me that," he responded smiling. "See you in recovery, Mr. Serrano."

Chuck looked at the doctor and mouthed the words "It's not working" to him, and a few seconds later, he drifted off.

Mia had a look of concern on her face.

"He's going to be fine, Mia," said Mick.

"I know, but I'm still worried about him."

"I know. Come on, let's go get some coffee." Mick asked.

"Okay."

Mick wrapped his arm around her shoulder as they made their way to the cafeteria

After coming up empty with the warrants, the SWAT team was soon headed back to the RCSO. Jack called into dispatch requesting that APBs be put out on both Blackwell and Thompson. For the time being he would have to depend on patrol to scoop up the pair. As he considered his next move, he took out his phone. He googled *Chookie's Pub* and found he was less than a mile from the place.

He headed back down MLK Boulevard. Two minutes later he pulled into the parking lot of Chookie's Pub and did a quick look around. The place was a dump—rundown, in need of paint, with weeds growing up through the cracks in the pavement of the parking lot. There were no cars in the lot, which wasn't surprising given that it was barely 8:00 a.m. He thought about heading back to the station, but that was a good twenty-minute drive back up I-25. On the door of the pub hung a sign that said "Open everyday - 9:00 am to 2:00 am." With an hour to kill, he pulled back onto MLK Boulevard and soon located a coffee shop. He went inside and found himself a quiet booth near the back. A waitress soon came with a menu but Jack waved it off.

"Bacon and eggs over easy, hash browns, wheat toast, and a cup of coffee."

"Coming right up."

Jack looked around and his thoughts wandered to the southern part of Rocklin County. During his dozen years at RCSO, nearly half of all the homicides he'd investigated had occurred within a five-square-mile area just west of the I-25, not far from where he was sitting. And most of those 187s involved the 120th Street gang. The vast majority of the killings were gang on gang, fueled largely by warring factions competing in the meth trade.

By Denver standards the 120th Street gang was small, with only a few hundred members. Of those, about fifty were known to be violent. The rest were just wannabes and hangers-on. But those fifty gangsters were particularly vile and did not look kindly on anyone coming into south county to peddle meth. If someone was brave (or stupid) enough to do so, they didn't usually last very long; 120th Street made sure of that.

Jack made short work of his breakfast, finished up a second cup of coffee, and paid the bill. He pulled onto MLK and was back at Chookie's Pub a few minutes after nine. There were just a few cars in the lot, not surprising for a Tuesday and given the early hour. Keller had been in plenty of bars in his time, but not since he had given up drinking. He pulled off his tie, undid the top buttons of his shirt, climbed from his unmarked unit, and headed for the entrance.

As he pushed on the small glass door he could immediately detect fresh cigarette smoke. A clear violation of Colorado law, he thought. Not exactly a felony, but possibly something he could use, if needed. He walked in and took a seat at the bar, allowing his eyes a few moments to adjust to the dark, dank environment.

He did a quick look around, getting his bearings. The place was small, with no more than a dozen tables and a pair of pool tables toward the back. Outdated, tattered, and graffitied liquor advertisements were tacked to the walls. A couple, both puffing on cigarettes, sat at one of the tables and another customer sat at the bar. Jack took a seat at the opposite end of the bar.

"What can I get you?"

Jack looked at the woman behind the bar asking the question. She was in her late thirties, tattooed, and forty pounds overweight. She wore a very revealing low-cut blouse. Her name tag read *Chookie*.

"Vodka on the rocks."

"Coming right up."

Jack looked around and his eyes locked on a glass bowl at the end of the bar. He walked over, reached in and grabbed a Chookie's Pub matchbook.

He slid them in his pocket and returned to his seat just as Chookie was putting his drink on the bar in front of him.

"Want me to run a tab?"

"No, I'll just have the one. What do I owe you?"

"Six fifty."

Keller grabbed a ten from his wallet and laid it on the bar. She grabbed it and looked at him.

"Keep the change."

"Thanks, mister."

"Where's the men's room?"

"In the back over by the pool table."

Jack grabbed his drink and headed for the back. Inside the restroom he emptied his glass of the vodka, careful to keep the ice from coming out of the glass. He filled it with water from the tap and returned to his seat.

Chookie was behind the bar, washing some glasses. She caught his eye.

"I don't think I've seen you in here before."

"No, first time. Just passing through and needed a little break."

"Where you from?"

"Cheyenne, but I'm on my way to Santa Fe."

"Business?'

"Yep."

"What do you do?"

"Sales. Latex products mostly."

"Latex products? I've heard of latex, but what the hell is it?"

"Something found in many household products, from clothing to a surprising number of manufactured items. Couldn't live our lives without it," Jack answered, smiling and raising his glass. He sounded like a PBS ad.

Chookie chuckled. "I didn't know that."

"Not many people do. So tell me—Chookie's Pub. I gotta assume that the place is named for you?"

"Yep, my husband bought it a few years ago and named it in my honor."

"Where'd the name Chookie come from? I'm guessing it's not your real name."

"It's a nickname—had it since I was little."

"Nice."

Jack heard the front door swing open and glanced back over his shoulder. Two young African-American men walked in, ignored Chookie, and went directly to the pool table. White t-shirts, Dickies sagging well below their hips, three hundred dollar sneakers on their feet. Jack watched the two out of the corner of his eye as they grabbed pool cues from the rack on the wall. The taller of the two walked to the table and jimmied the coin mechanism, freeing up the balls.

Jack looked at Chookie to see her reaction to these gangbangers playing a game of pool without paying. She looked away, ignoring what was happening.

"Regular customers?"

"Yeah, and they have a lot of friends. Been a real problem for us."

"How so?"

"They've scared away a lot of our regulars. People don't want to see that crap so they find another place to drink. Our business is down more than forty percent since we bought the place."

"That's a bummer. Is there anything you can do about it?"

"Not really. These aren't the kinds of people you can reason with and if you ask them to leave, well, there's a price you pay for that."

"What about the cops? They can't do something?"

"We tried early on, but they can't be here all the time, so we don't even bother to call anymore. And the vermin have kinda taken over."

"Geez, that just doesn't seem right."

"Tell me about it."

"The whole damn world is going to hell, y'know?"

"Yep."

Keller looked at Chookie and felt bad for her. She struck him as a decent, hard-working person trying to make a living. The fact that the gangsters had taken over her bar bothered him, but the fact that she felt the cops were no help bothered him even more. He decided to take a chance.

"Look, Chookie—what if the cops were to come in here more often, maybe do bar checks a few times a day. Do you think that would help?"

The woman looked at Keller, not understanding why he was saying these things. He was a latex salesman from Cheyenne.

"It couldn't hurt, that's for sure. But they don't seem to care. I've called a bunch of times asking for help, but it doesn't do much."

"I've got some friends in law enforcement and I'm thinking they might be of some help to you."

"Really? That'd be great. Thanks so much. Hey, I don't even know your name . . ."

"Danny," lied Jack.

"Well, thanks, Danny. Can I get you another drink? On the house."

Jack stood, "No, thanks. I need to hit the road."

"Okay, have a safe trip to Santa Fe."

"I will, and I think you'll see some police presence in here soon."

Chookie watched as Keller left the bar. Who the hell was that guy? she wondered.

CHAPTER 43

~~~

Back in Los Angeles, Rose Cochran's team sent out the media alert regarding the press conference scheduled at the Denver Marriott the next day at noon. Her people sent it out to more than three hundred newspapers and TV stations across the nation, with special attention given to getting the release into the hands of every Denver-area news agency. Associated Press was tipped off in advance, ensuring the best coverage possible. As a conduit for hundreds of newspapers, television, and radio stations, AP was an important resource for getting news distributed worldwide.

Angela Bell was in the middle of her morning workout when she received a text from her assignment editor.

> Just got a release saying Rose Cochran is representing the sheriff's wife in a lawsuit against Leland Simpson....wtf?

Angela climbed off the elliptical machine and stared at the text. She texted back her editor:

> Send the release to my cell

She headed for the shower, trying to process this news. Leland Simpson had made derogatory remarks about Mia's pregnancy and hormones. Not really sure how that would amount to a lawsuit, she thought; but then she knew that Rose Cochran took a lot of cases for the publicity. Her thoughts went to Mark. No doubt he knew about this, yet he hadn't tipped her off.

That spoke volumes about the status of their relationship.

"The cops just hit our fucking house, man."

Jaquon closed his eyes. "Whaaaaat?"

"Me and Shorty. The cops came looking for us."

"When?"

"This morning. My neighbor called and tipped me off, man."

"Shit, how the fuck did they know it was you guys?"

"I don't know, but what the hell do we do now? You said this was foolproof, man."

"Calm the shit down. They got nothin'. The fucking bomb blew everything all to hell. They're just fishing. That's gotta be it."

"Fishing, my ass. They know it was us, homes."

"Where you at now?"

"I'm with Shorty at his cousin's place, picking up the shipment. We got a delivery to make tonight."

"Okay, sit tight for now. Let me think about things and I'll call you back. Don't sweat it, Ice."

Jaquon sat on the edge of his bed, thinking through the events of the morning. The fact that the cops had hit the homes of both Iceman and Shorty worried him—it sure as hell wasn't a coincidence. But he knew that the only way the bombing at the sheriff's place could be tied to him was if Shorty or Iceman ran his mouth. He didn't think they would be inclined to do so, since going against a higher-up member of the gang meant big trouble. People had died for lesser offenses.

By nine thirty Chuck was out of surgery and the doctor met with Mia and Mick.

"The procedure went well and your dad can go home tomorrow. I'd like to keep him here until then just to make sure there are no complications. I don't expect any, but I like to play it safe."

"That'll be fine. Thank you so much, doctor."

"No problem. He should be up for some company in a couple of hours. He may be a little groggy but I'm sure he'll be happy to see you both."

As the doctor walked away, Mia turned to Mick. "Rose wanted to meet with me this morning to go over the plans for the press conference. I'm thinking now might be a good time since we have to wait a couple hours before Dad can have visitors. Maybe she'd be willing to come to the hospital and we could meet in the cafeteria."

"Good idea. I need to get into the office for a little bit. Just text me when you're ready to go in and visit your dad and I'll come over and we can see him together."

"Sounds good."

Mick left the waiting room and Mia made the call to Rose Cochran. She was quick to agree to the meeting and said she'd be at the hospital within thirty minutes.

∾

Once Jack hit the interstate he made a quick call on his cell.

"Hey, Trevor. It's Keller."

"Jack, it's been a while. What's going on?"

Trevor Carpenter was a beat coordinator for the southern end of Rocklin County. As such, he had responsibility for overseeing things in the beat. From attending neighborhood meetings to directing patrol activities, he was the go-to person for anything related to the area.

"Are you familiar with Chookie's Pub down off MLK?"

"Sure, I know the place."

"I was wondering if you could give me a little assistance."

"What do you need?"

"I'm working on the bombing at the sheriff's place and we've ID'd a couple of asshats we think did the bombing. We hit their residences a few hours ago but came up empty."

"Yeah, I saw the APB."

"Anyway, I was at the pub just now doing a little snooping and I met the owner. She was telling me about how the gangsters have taken over the place."

"Yeah, they have their share of problems in there, but the whole damn beat has bangers crawling everywhere. I've asked for more resources, but you know how that goes."

"Yeah, I know. I didn't identify myself to her or tell her why I was there. She really seems like a decent person, she just doesn't know what to do about the problem. Any chance your guys might do some bar checks to create a presence in there?"

"Sure, I can do that. What's the goal here, Jack?'

"I want her to see the cops in there doing proactive stuff and develop a positive relationship with her, because I'm guessing if we show her the photos of the knuckleheads we're looking for she'd drop a dime next time they're in and we can scoop them up."

"I'm working the beat now; I can drop by in a few minutes. And I can ask my guys to drop in four or five times a day. How's that?"

"Thanks, Trevor. I owe you."

"No sweat, Jack. Are you going to show her the mugshots or do you want me to do that once we gain her confidence?"

"Best if you do it. She thinks my name is Danny and I'm a latex salesman from Cheyenne."

Trevor burst out laughing. "Really? How are sales, Jack?"

"Kinda slow right now, but let me know if you need any. It's on the house."

CHAPTER 44

⁓

Mia was surprised at how well her dad looked. Less than four hours after the procedure and he was looking like his old self. She was there with Mick and Rose Cochran. Mia and Rose had had a productive meeting in the hospital cafeteria.

"Hey Dad, how are you doing?" Mia asked, grabbing her father's hand.

"Pretty good, Mia. The doctor says I can go home tomorrow."

"Wow, that's great news. You look good! Oh, Dad—I want you to meet Rose Cochran."

Cochran extended her hand. "Mr. Serrano, it's great to meet you. And I am so happy your procedure went well."

"Thanks, it's nice to meet you. I recognized you as soon as you walked in. Sorry you're not seeing me at my best."

"You look great, Mr. Serrano. And by the way, I had a stent put in two years ago."

"Really? Looks like you came through it just fine."

"I did, and I was back in my office the next day. Don't tell my doctor. He wanted me to take it easy for a week or so but I felt so good I ignored him. Of course, I'm not suggesting that for you."

Chuck laughed. "I'll take it easy for a few days, but then I want to get back into the swing of things. I'm an avid hiker. We've got some great trails here and I can't wait to get back to it."

"I've never done any hiking. LA's not really a great hiking town, y'know?" she said, with a chuckle.

"I'll have to take you hiking at Red Rocks. There are some beautiful trails up there. You'll love it."

"That's a deal. I'm going to hold you to it."

Mia looked at the two chatting. My God, my dad's flirting, she thought. With Rose Cochran, no less. She couldn't help but smile.

"So, did you guys get some prep work in for the press conference?" asked Mick, interrupting the conversation.

Cochran turned her attention to Mick.

"Yep, it went really well. Mia is terrific—an old pro, really. She'll do great tomorrow."

"Ms. Cochran's right. Mia is going to be wonderful tomorrow," added Chuck.

Cochran looked at Chuck. "Please, call me Rose."

"Okay, Rose. And you can call me Chuck. *Anytime*."

Mia looked at her dad, rolling her eyes.

⁂

"Can I get you guys something to drink? It's on the house."

It was the third time in six hours Trevor Carpenter and his partner, Gustavo Vasquez, had stopped in to Chookie's Pub for a bar check. Chookie was bewildered—these visits had started almost immediately after the mysterious man from Cheyenne had left the bar hours earlier. He really does have friends in law enforcement, she thought.

"No, we're fine."

"Okay, just let me know. I really appreciate you guys being here."

"No problem at all."

Vasquez and Carpenter looked around the bar. The gang presence was in full swing, which was surprising since typically gangbangers came out later in the evening, closing down bars. Vasquez and Carpenters' shift ended at six, but Carpenter had put the word out with a group text to all his fellow beat officers. He had directed his team to "frequent patrol, check for gang activity" every chance they could until the place closed at two the next morning. Several gangsters were congregating around the pool tables near the back. The two deputies kept a close eye on them, which didn't go unnoticed by the group.

"Maybe I will have something. Can I get a Diet Coke?" asked Carpenter, turning his attention back to Chookie..

"Of course. Are you sure you don't want anything?" Chookie asked, looking at Vasquez.

"Yeah, okay. I'll have a Diet Coke, too."

Both deputies slid onto stools at the bar, keeping their bodies turned at an angle so they could continue to monitor activity around the pool tables.

"Here you go."

Both took long sips on their drinks.

Trevor decided the time was right. He took the photos of Iceman and Shorty from his uniform pocket and laid them on the bar.

"Maybe you could help us with something. Do these two individuals ever come in here?"

Chookie turned her attention to the photos. Immediately, Trevor detected a little hitch in Chookie's expression. A sign she recognized the two.

"Why do you ask? Are they in trouble?"

"We want to talk to them about a case our investigators are working. Do you know either of them?"

Chookie looked long and hard at Deputy Carpenter before responding.

"Yeah, I know them. In fact, that one's my stepson, Tracy Thompson," she replied, putting her finger on one of the photos. "The other kid is his buddy. Damian something, I think."

Carpenter looked at Chookie, understanding that it probably wasn't easy IDing a family member.

"He's your stepson?"

"Yeah, it's a long story. So what did he do now?"

"As I said, our investigators just want to talk to him about a case."

"Don't sugarcoat it. He's a dirtbag and we all know it."

Vasquez spoke up. "Any idea where we might find him and his buddy?"

"No, but I can text him. Tell him to get his ass down here."

"Will he come?"

"Yeah, he'll come if I make up a story."

Carpenter and Vasquez both looked at the woman, surprised at her willingness to help.

Chookie leaned in and said, "Look—my husband and I have hit rock bottom with him. We tried to get him to go into the military, thinking that might straighten him up. But hell, they didn't want him. He's got a criminal record and he's just not right in the head sometimes. I hate to sound like a mother that doesn't care, but we've pretty much reached that point with him. I can have him here in ten minutes. Should I text him?"

CHAPTER 45

Iceman and Shorty finished packing the shipment underneath the spare tire in the trunk of Iceman's car. It was twelve kilos of meth with a street value of nearly $200,000. With the legalization of marijuana in Colorado, demand for meth had fallen way off. The stuff was to be shipped somewhere back east where meth prices were much higher. Shorty and Iceman didn't know much more than that; they were small players in the distribution business. The two would split the $2,500 they would be paid for their role—getting the stuff to Aurora, an hour or so north. It was easy money and business was good. It would be their fourth delivery in the past two weeks. The stuff was to be delivered to some trailer park to a guy named Jed in space #83. That's all they knew and all they wanted to know.

"Ah shit, my stepmom just texted me."

Shorty looked at Iceman. "What does she want now?"

"She wants me to come to the bar."

"We don't got no time for that, Ice. We gotta get to the trailer park. We're supposed to meet the guy in an hour."

"Yeah, yeah, I know."

"So, come on—let's go."

"We can stop on the way. It'll only take a minute."

"What the hell is so important?"

"I don't know but she put 'important' at the end of the text."

"Alright, then let's get the hell outta here. We got a delivery to make."

∽

"He's on the way. Should be here in a few minutes."

Carpenter and Vasquez quickly excused themselves from the bar and went to the parking lot. They drove their patrol car to the other side of MLK, parking in an area not readily noticeable from the bar. They hustled back across the street and took cover behind a large moving van parked nearby. A minute later an older model Honda Civic pulled into the lot and parked near the entrance.

"It's our lucky day—looks like both our subjects are in the car," whispered Carpenter.

Vasquez nodded and whispered back, "Ol' Chookie really came through. We should nominate her for RCSO's Citizen of the Month."

"Yeah, no kidding. She must really have it in for her stepson."

"Whatever. Works to our advantage in this case, huh?'

Carpenter nodded, not wanting to make any more noise.

Shorty and Iceman climbed from the Honda and started toward the front door of the bar.

The deputies moved quickly from their hiding place behind the van, cutting off the pathway to Chookie's.

"Gentlemen, stop right there. Hands in the air!"

Shorty and Iceman both froze, stunned by what was happening, and quickly put their hands in the air.

"Your fucking stepmom," said Shorty, looking at Iceman. "We've been set up!"

Vasquez cuffed both men while Carpenter kept his gun pointed at the two.

"You have the right to remain silent—"

"Yeah, yeah, I know the routine," said Iceman.

Vasquez continued reading both men their rights. Carpenter called the station and let dispatch know the two wanted suspects were in custody. Additional patrol units were dispatched to assist. Once the other units had arrived, Iceman and Shorty were separated, each placed in the back of a patrol car. It was important to keep them apart so they couldn't cook up a story. Vasquez and Carpenter walked to the Honda the two had arrived in.

By this time a small crowd had gathered to watch the proceedings. Several of the men who had been playing pool inside were now standing on the sidewalk, offering idle commentary about how the search was illegal and the cops were just there to harass these two young black men. The deputies ignored it and continued on.

"The car is fair game—let's toss it," Vasquez said.

The deputies started with the inside of the car, checking the glove box and underneath each seat. They felt along the roof liner to see if anything was stashed there, then checked under the hood. Nothing. They popped the trunk and started searching through an assortment of junk, carefully looking at each item before placing it on the ground. Vasquez unscrewed the bolts holding the spare in place and lifted up the tire. Carpenter reached in and felt around.

"Well, look what we have here!" he said, holding up a carefully wrapped brick-sized item.

"Aw, shucks, don't tell me these altar boys are involved in the transportation of an illegal substance."

"It would appear that way. And by the looks of it, there's more where that came from," Carpenter replied, holding up another brick.

"I'll call in the narc team. Looks like we hit paydirt—got our suspects in custody for the sheriff's bombing and we've got them peddling this shit as a bonus."

"I'll contact Keller," replied Carpenter.

⚬

Keller was just leaving the station for the day when he got the text from Deputy Carpenter telling him about the arrests.

He immediately texted back, When can you transport?

Carpenter responded, We're searching the car and have found what appears to be a considerable amount of meth. We may be here awhile

Keller: Okay, I'll come down there. Be there in 30

Keller arrived at Chookie's and got a quick rundown from Deputy Carpenter, then walked over to the patrol car with Iceman in the back. A deputy was standing guard outside the vehicle.

"I'd like a couple minutes with this guy. Can you crack the window?"

"Sure."

The deputy climbed into the car and lowered the window about six inches, giving Keller enough room to chat with Iceman.

Keller leaned over and asked, "So, how's your evening going?"

"Fuck you."

"Snappy comeback, Iceman. My name's Keller and you and I are going to have a little talk."

Iceman, his hands handcuffed from behind, tried to squirm away from the window but he was buckled in.

Keller continued, "So, look—we've got you dead to rights on the dope in the trunk of your car, and that's good for fifteen to twenty in the pen."

"That's not my shit. That's Shorty's business. I didn't even know he put that stuff in the trunk. You're talking to the wrong guy."

"You're telling me that you didn't know about the stuff in the trunk of *your* car? That's rich. The Honda's registered to you. What did your buddy do, hide that shit in the trunk while you were in taking a whiz?"

"I don't know how he did it, man. But it's the fuckin' truth. I didn't know about it!"

"You know, the two of you should have gone into the weed business with it being legal and all in Colorado. But no, you guys peddle meth. A really, really poor business decision."

"I didn't do nothin'!"

"Okay, sure. Let's change topics for a moment. While I'm very concerned about the major felony you're under arrest for here, I'm also interested in another crime committed up in Castle Springs a couple nights ago."

Iceman looked at Keller, shook his head, and then looked away.

"I don't know what the hell you're talking about," he muttered.

"I think you do. I think you know exactly what I'm about to say."

"You're one crazy cop, man. I don't know what you've been smokin'."

"Two nights ago someone threw a homemade bomb through the window of the sheriff's place. Nearly killed his wife. What can you tell me about that?"

"I got nothing to do with that. You're shitting on the wrong toilet, man."

Keller leaned in closer to the window opening. "To tell you the truth, I'm really more interested in the bombing the other night than your meth trafficking."

"I got nothin' for you, man."

"Look, Mr. Iceman, I've been a cop for more than forty years. I know a lot of people—folks in the DA's office. There's a lot of interest in this bombing case, it being the sheriff, and all. I'm just saying . . . "

"So, what are we talking about?"

"If I could get a little cooperation from you on the bombing, then maybe the DA will look at these dope charges a little more favorably."

"You wanna cut a deal? Who the fuck are you to do that?"

"I can have a DA here in an hour. I'm just giving you a little bit of advice. Tell me about the bombing and the DA will take that into consideration when he files the drug charges."

"But I don't know about this bombing. I ain't ever been up there in tree land."

Keller looked at Iceman. Referencing "tree land" was a slip up; he would see if he could exploit it.

"Interesting that you would say 'tree land' since the sheriff's place is in a very wooded area. It's almost like you've been there before."

"No man, I know there's fucking trees around here. That's all."

It was time to lower the boom.

"Tell me, Iceman, how is it we found a matchbook twenty feet from the sheriff's place, and that matchbook has your fingerprints on it?"

Iceman shifted in his seat. "That's impossible. You're lying—just another full of shit cop."

"So, it's just a coincidence that I drive all the way down here tonight from Castle Springs to ask some knucklehead who's been popped for trafficking about a bomb that was tossed two nights ago? What am I—a fucking psychic?"

"No, man. You're just a nutjob. That's all."

"Okay, if that's the way you want to play it. I think I'll go have a little chat with Shorty over there in the other patrol car. I'm really curious if your stories match up. I ran his history in the box; he's kind of a junior player in all this, the kind of person who will cave in about fifteen seconds. I'm guessing he'll turn on you before I can finish the question."

Keller looked at Iceman —it was the moment of truth.

"Wait a minute. What kind of deal are we talking about? I mean, hyperthetically . . . "

Keller smiled at the mispronunciation.

"It's simple, really. I just wanna know who gave the order to you and Shorty to toss the bomb. I mean, it sure as hell wasn't your idea. You tell me now and I think the DA will be willing to charge you with a lesser crime tonight."

Keller was going out on a limb speaking for the DA's office. But he was confident that getting to the person responsible for the bombing would be of greater interest to the DA than just another dope peddling case.

"No man, that ain't good enough. I gotta get me some immunity. No drug charges or no deal."

"Okay, let me go see what Shorty wants to do. The deal may be of more interest to him. Of course, that'll leave you kinda hanging. You'll go down for the whole thing and he'll be the one with the better arrangement. But that's your call." Keller turned and began walking away from the car.

"Wait."

Keller came back and peered through the window. "So, whatcha gonna do, Iceman?'"

"The order came from above. We just carried it out."

"From above? The guy have a name?"

"Jaquon Jackson. He ordered the bombing."

Bingo, thought Jack.

"Well done, Iceman. You made the right decision. I'll get the DA down here and you guys can talk."

Icemen stared straight ahead, pondering what kind of fallout would come from Jaquon and his buddies. It wouldn't be pretty.

Keller called Commander Elder and filled him in on what had happened. Elder said he'd put out an APB for Jaquon Jackson. As Jack walked back toward the bar, he looked up and saw Chookie standing outside on the sidewalk, her arms folded.

Keller nodded her way.

She gave him an icy glare. "So, how's the latex business, Danny?"

∽

It didn't take long for the gangbangers at the pool table to figure out what was going on. They had watched the proceedings, taking a special interest in watching Keller talking to Iceman. As they watched Keller walk from the patrol car, James "Dawg" Fullerton dropped a dime on Iceman, alerting Jaquon to what was happening.

CHAPTER 46

Jaquon was at home with Alondra when he got the text message about the arrests.

Alondra could tell by Jaquon's expression that something was wrong.

"What's going on, Jaquon? Who's texting you?"

"It ain't nothing."

"Jaquon, don't lie to me. What's going on?"

"I told you, it's nothin'."

Alondra stood there in the kitchen, arms folded, looking at her boyfriend.

"I gotta go out for a bit."

"Jaquon, I'm getting tired of all this nonsense. You promised me that you'd given up the life, that you were going to become an honest man. But ever since your cousin got killed you're back to your old ways. And I don't like it one bit."

"You don't get it, that's all."

"Oh, I get it all right. I get the fact that you're slipping back in your old ways. You still don't have a job, and as far as I can tell, you're making no effort to get one."

"Jesus, how many times do we have to talk about this? I'm trying. Get off my fucking back."

"Don't raise your voice to me, Jaquon. We have a deal and as far as I can see you're not living up to your end of things. Maybe this was a mistake."

"I don't need this shit right now. I'm outta here!"

"Well, maybe you shouldn't come back!"

Jaquon grabbed his keys and left without another word.

Jaquon wasn't sure where he was going to go but he knew he couldn't sit and listen to Alondra. His world was coming apart—his cousin was dead, Alondra was losing patience with his antics, and now Shorty and Iceman had been busted. The arrest of his two associates was the biggest worry; if they caved and admitted that he had sent them to do the bombing at the sheriff's house he'd be done. He could run, but where would he go? His funds were limited, so fleeing the country wasn't an option.

Or, he thought, he could go out with a bang . . .

Mick and Mia were having a quiet dinner at home when the call came in from Commander Elder.

"Good news, sheriff—we scooped up the two subjects wanted for doing the bombing at your place. And better yet, they fingered Jaquon as the guy who gave the order. We've just issued an APB for him."

"That's fantastic. Give me the particulars."

"Looks like Keller worked his magic. He pretty much ran them down with some help from a couple of southend deputies. The guy is good—less than thirty-six hours on the case and he's got the main players wrapped up. Now we just gotta nail Jaquon. And these two were transporting a significant amount of meth. We found it in the trunk of their car. Jack twisted him pretty good and got him to talk."

"So the two jackasses whose fingerprints were on the matchbook are in custody and they said Jaquon was the shotcaller?'

"Yep. Jack worked his charm on one of them and the guy gave it up. We need to talk with the DA about the drug charges that'll be filed against the one they call Iceman. He was cooperative and I think Jack sweetened the pot a bit to get him to talk."

"We can do that. I don't think Dave Baxter will have any problem with that."

"Well, I'll let you go. Just wanted to call you with the good news."

After driving around for an hour, Jaquon parked on the street in front of Reginald Gray's house. Reginald was a forty-year-old gangster, an old timer revered by the 120th Street gang. He was several levels above Jaquon in the gang's meth distribution network and Jaquon was not someone he would normally associate with, but the two had struck up a friendship a few years earlier when Jaquon went to bat for Gray. Jaquon had gotten him out of a difficult situation involving a woman and now Gray looked at Jaquon almost as a kid brother. Jaquon didn't know where else to go, but he knew he could hang with Gray, at least for a little while.

Gray's home was impressive, located in a very exclusive Castle Springs neighborhood. The place backed up to a golf course, and although Gray didn't play golf, he liked the privacy. When he had moved into the neighborhood years earlier he had told the neighbors he was a record producer, even going so far as to set up a dummy corporation. The neighbors bought the story and even bragged to their friends they lived next to a guy who ran some hip hop label. Reginald had never offered the kind of music his "label" produced; it was just assumed by his upper-crust white neighbors that would be the case. Either way, he fit quickly into the community, even hosting an annual Super Bowl party for all the neighborhood.

Jaquon walked up the long driveway toward the front door. Two dogs, fenced in the side yard, began barking. Motion sensor lights went off, illuminating the area around the front of the home. Jaquon had been through this routine before, and he waited patiently at the door until Reginald was able to check the camera monitors to see who was visiting. A minute later the door swung open.

"What the hell, Jaquon? What are you doing here?"

"Can I come in?" he asked nervously.

Reginald didn't respond, but motioned for Jaquon to come inside. He entered the large foyer and waited while Reginald closed and locked the door behind him.

"I've got a phone Jaquon—why didn't you call first?"

"I'm sorry, man. It's just that—"

Gray could see Jaquon was upset.

"That's okay, come in."

Gray led Jaquon through the foyer and into a massive great room. A woman whom Jacquon didn't recognize was sitting on the large sectional sofa.

"Jaquon, this is Shalon Marangi."

She smiled at Jaquon and he nodded in return.

"Shalon, could you excuse us for a few minutes?"

The pretty woman stood and left the room without comment.

"Sit down, Jaquon, and tell me what's going on."

Jaquon took a seat on the sectional, stared out toward one of the large picture windows into the darkness, and began.

"I got trouble."

"What kind of trouble?"

"You know about my cousin, right? The cops killed him last week. Shot him in the back of the head."

"Yes, I heard about that. I'm sorry for your loss, Jaquon."

"It ain't right, man. They're gonna get away with it. The cop that did it is married to the fuckin' sheriff. Ain't no way she's going down for this."

"The system is stacked against us, Jaquon—you know that."

"Yeah, I know that, but this is personal. It's my cousin, man. He was just seventeen."

"So is that what brings you here tonight?"

Jaquon looked away from the window and locked eyes with Reginald. "No, there's more."

"Tell me, Jaquon."

"I was pissed about Alex. I did some shit—"

"Like what?" asked Reginald, growing concerned.

"The day he was killed a bunch of us went to the school and started some stuff. Torched some cars and a couple of classrooms. I know they're looking at me for it."

Reginald looked at his young friend. What a stupid move, he thought. Letting his emotions get the better of him.

Jaquon continued, "Then a couple days ago I had some of my guys toss a bomb into the sheriff's house. I just wanted to scare them—get their attention, y'know? But his fucking wife was there, the one who killed Alex, and she got hurt. And her old man was there too and he's in the hospital."

"Jaquon, I'm disappointed with you. You know better than this."

Jaquon hung his head. Neither spoke for several seconds.

"There's more."

Reginald looked at him.

"The two guys I got to do the bombing got popped tonight. I'm worried they'll give me up."

"Why do you think that? I mean, you trust these two enough to do your work. Would they turn on you?"

"Normally, no. But when they were arrested tonight they had a shipment with them and the cops found it. They questioned them and I don't know what the fuck was discussed, y'know?"

Reginald closed his eyes and sat quietly before speaking.

"How much stuff were your boys moving?'

"Twelve Ks"

Reginald calculated the loss in his head. Street value was near two hundred grand. Wholesale was closer to fifty thousand. In the grand scheme of his operation it didn't amount to much, but still it was stupid and he was out fifty large.

"Well, you've got yourself into a mess, Jaquon. First, you're right about the cops coming after you. You went after the sheriff's family and that was a big mistake. You're probably at the top of their list right now so they'll have every cop in Colorado looking for you. Second, there's the issue of the 12 Ks. Fortunately, you have me to answer to for that. We'll deal with it later, but make no mistake, Jaquon; we will revisit the issue."

"I know, boss. I'm sorry."

"What's done is done. You'll stay here tonight. The cops aren't likely to show up here looking for you. Is your car on the street?"

"Yeah."

"First thing we need to do is get it out of sight. Go out and move it to the back; I've got room in the garage. In the morning we'll discuss a strategy for what you do next."

Jaquon went outside and moved the car. He returned to find Reginald in the media room, watching a big screen TV the size of a pool table. He was tuned to the Channel 2 ten o'clock news.

"Sit down, Jaquon. Let's see what they have to say about you tonight."

Jaquon took a seat and nervously turned his attention to the television.

"You think it'll be on the news?"

"No doubt. You're about to become a rather infamous young man."

"Good evening, everyone, I'm Karis Drake and here's what's happening at ten. The Rocklin County Sheriff's Department is asking for the public's help tonight. As you may recall, the sheriff of Rocklin County, Mick McCallister, had his home firebombed two nights ago. There's been a significant break in the case this evening; police have named a suspect in the bombing and that individual is on the loose."

Jaquon felt the bile rise in his throat. He looked at Reginald but could see no response from him. The anchorwoman continued.

"Here's a photo of the man police are seeking. He has been identified as Jaquon Jackson of Castle Springs. He's twenty-three years old, five foot ten, one hundred and sixty pounds."

Jaquon stared at an old booking photo on the screen. He felt like a caged animal. He knew he'd be safe at Reginald's place tonight but tomorrow was another day.

"Police would not say how they came to name Jackson as the person behind the bombing, but they do say they are very confident that he is the one responsible. The sheriff's wife, Mia Serrano-McCallister, who was the deputy involved in the shooting death of Alex Washington a week ago, was injured in the blast, and her father was also hurt."

A photo of Mia Serrano-McCallister filled the screen.

"That's the bitch that killed Alex. She fucking needs to pay!"

Reginald looked at his young friend, worried that he was going to do something stupid.

"Calm down, Jaquon. You need to gather your wits. You need to be thinking very carefully in the hours and days to come."

The anchorwoman continued, "In a related story, famed Los Angeles-based attorney Rose Cochran will be in Denver tomorrow. She has been retained by Mia Serrano-McCallister and the two plan to announce the filing of a lawsuit against Denver attorney Leland Simpson. Simpson made what many consider to be derogatory remarks about Serrano-McCallister, essentially citing hormones as the reason she shot and killed Alex Washington at Wilson High School last week. Serrano-McCallister, who is seventh months pregnant, will join Cochran at a press conference scheduled for tomorrow at noon. We will have live coverage of that press conference tomorrow at the top of our noon-time broadcast."

"Unfucking believeable."

"You're in a world of shit, Jaquon."

CHAPTER 47

～

Jaquon didn't sleep much. He kept going over and over his situation in his head. He climbed out of bed around seven, the earliest he'd been up in a long time. He went downstairs to the kitchen and grabbed some juice from the fridge. He looked around the kitchen and great room; the house was impressive. Given the mess he was in, he realized that any hope he had of having a lifestyle similar to Reginald's was quickly disappearing. He would be a man on the run, his relationship with Alondra was over, and he knew he needed to leave the area quickly. And all this because of that cop who shot Alex. And now she was going to be in the limelight, suing the attorney who had talked shit about her. It wasn't fair, and the more he thought about it the more enraged he became. Too bad the bomb didn't kill her, he thought.

He was deep in thought when Reginald came into the kitchen.

"Hey, Jaquon. You sleep okay?"

"Not really."

"Look, you need to beat it this morning, ASAP. I can't risk having you here."

"Yeah, I know."

"I've got an old Nissan pickup in the garage. The VIN has been washed, so there's no tracking it back to anyone. I want you to take it. You can't risk driving your car anymore. I'll have it dumped somewhere. But you need to clear out, like soon."

"I understand. Thanks for the car. I'll leave in a few minutes."

"Upstairs in the bathroom Shalon left you some hair dye. I'd suggest you use it. The whole state of Colorado is looking for you. Or there are some clippers if you want to shave your head. Your call. Shalon worked in the beauty industry so she can help you out with whatever you want to do. I think she just finished her workout."

"Okay, that sounds good," replied Jaquon, rubbing his head.

"So, what are your plans? Any idea where you'll go?"

Jaquon looked at Reginald and lied.

"No man, I got nothing. But I'll figure something out. And thanks for the help. I owe you big time."

"No sweat. Now get going so you can get the hell outta here."

Mia didn't sleep well, tossing and turning most of the night; she was unable to shake off thoughts of the press conference set to take place at noon. Her nervousness wasn't centered on whether or not she should pursue legal action against Leland Simpson, she was certain of that, it was just the unfamiliarity of doing a press conference that would put her center stage with a national audience.

She went downstairs and found Chuck in the kitchen making a pot of coffee.

"Good morning, sweetheart. I can have a cup of coffee in your hands in about two minutes. Interested?"

"Yeah, that would be great, Dad. I didn't sleep well and I need to wake up."

Chuck looked at his daughter and said, "That's understandable, Mia. Things are going to be fine. You'll see."

"I know, it's just unfamiliar territory to me, you know?"

"Of course. It's new to all of us. But you're doing the right thing."

Chuck paused, then added, "Your mother would be so proud of you."

Mia looked at her father, touched.

"Thanks, Dad. I hope so. I miss her. I've been thinking about her a lot during this pregnancy."

"God, she'd be so thrilled about the baby. And she would have been a wonderful grandma. But I know she's looking down from heaven at you, proud of the woman you've become."

Mia walked to her father and gave him a hug.

"Thanks, Dad."

Members of Rose Cochran's legal staff from Los Angeles made all the arrangements for the press conference. They set things up at the Marriott Hotel in Denver, a location chosen with care. Cochran didn't want it to look like someone with unlimited funds who had just swept into Denver to take the case. Mia had asked about having the press conference at the RCSO station, but Cochran quickly shot that down. She was representing Mia, not the RCSO. Further, Cochran didn't want Mick to be at the table with her and Mia as Mick could be a distraction, and this was clearly Mia's case. He understood the concern and agreed to wait in an adjoining room until the conference was over.

She and Mia had spent another two hours going over the plans for what would be said. Cochran would do the majority of the talking, but Mia would be called upon to talk about her experience at Columbine High School. It was part of Cochran's strategy. Go ugly early, she said.

Jaquon grabbed the keys Reginald had left for him and found his way to the garage. The small pickup was nothing if not inconspicuous. He drove away from the house, sporting newly-blonde hair cut very short. He had a few hours to kill so he headed toward the Rockies, taking I-70

west. He didn't want to get too far away from Denver; he had a noontime appointment to make.

Mick found Mia in the bathroom getting ready for the press conference.

"Rose had some ideas on what I should wear."

"Really?"

"She wants me to look very pregnant. In something professional, not frumpy. Hair up."

"You don't own anything frumpy."

"Thanks, Mick."

"She's certainly particular about things."

"She knows what she's doing, that's for sure. I understand what she wants. It makes sense."

"Hair up, huh? That's your sexiest look."

Mia poked Mick in the chest. "Well, aren't you being nice today."

"I speak the truth," he replied, smiling.

CHAPTER 48

By 11:45 more than two dozen reporters had gathered in one of the large meeting rooms at the Marriott. At the front of the room were a table and two chairs. A small podium sat on the table and reporters placed their microphones in positions to pick up sound. Three dozen chairs were lined up for the audience. A handful of newspaper reporters sat in the first row; the television and radio reporters all stood.

Rose and Mia waited in the adjoining room with Mick, making small talk. Cochran wanted to keep Mia as calm as possible; she knew how intimidating the situation could be for someone unaccustomed to all the cameras and attention.

Mia glanced at her watch. "It's noon, should we go in?" she asked, nervously.

"Not yet. Gotta keep 'em waiting a bit. We'll go in at ten after. It builds a bit of suspense and gives the latecomers a chance to get set up. Plus all the television news stations are talking breathlessly on air right now about this conference. It's good to let 'em stir up some anticipation."

"Wow, you've really done this before, huh?'

"Hundreds of times. But over the years I've learned that it's really more of an art than a science."

"I can imagine."

They went over the game plan one more time. Then, looking at her watch, Cochran said, "Okay, it's time. You ready to go?"

"Sure, let's do it."

Cochran led Mia to the entrance of the room, leaned over, and whispered, "We walk in together. Don't get ahead of me or fall behind. We're a team."

Mia nodded and the two walked in. Heads turned and cameras swung around to capture the two striding confidently to the table and taking their seats. Cochran grabbed Mia's hand and leaned into the microphone.

"Good afternoon and thank you for being here. My name is Rose Cochran. I'm going to make a short statement and then take any questions you might have. But first, let me introduce Rocklin County Sheriff's Deputy Mia Serrano-McCallister. Deputy Serrano-McCallister is a seventeen-year veteran of the RCSO, currently assigned to the investigative division as a homicide detective. She has previously served the people of Rocklin County as a patrol deputy and a traffic investigator. Her record at the RCSO is impeccable and above reproach."

Cochran continued, "And as many of you know, Mia is married to Mick McCallister, the current sheriff of Rocklin County. She is seven months pregnant and is currently on administrative leave following the officer-involved shooting last week at Wilson High School."

Mia noticed Cochran was now referring to her as *Mia*. She was trying to personalize her to the public, something Cochran had explained to her before the press conference.

"That incident resulted in the death of Alex Washington, a young man who made a series of tragic decisions that day. Mia's actions saved the life of Kendra Gillespie, an innocent seventeen-year-old student who had been taken hostage by Mr. Washington in front of hundreds of students in the quad of the school. For her heroic actions Mia has been subjected to physical threats, a bombing at her home, and very unfair and inaccurate commentary by a handful of those in the community wishing to exploit the situation."

Hands in the audience started to go up but Cochran shook her head and continued.

"And while we enjoy freedom of speech in this great nation, there are limits to that freedom, and Leland Simpson, the attorney for the Washington family, clearly went past the bounds of decency with comments he made about Mia a few days ago. To suggest that Mia's actions on that campus, actions that saved a young woman's life—to suggest that those actions were brought on by pregnancy hormones is an insult to not only Mia, but to women everywhere. Those comments are not only inflammatory, but they're grossly inaccurate as well. For these reasons we are bringing a defamation suit against Mr. Simpson and will be asking for damages of ten million dollars."

Virtually every hand shot up and reporters began shouting questions at Cochran. But she pressed on, again waving them off.

"Something that many of you may not be aware of is the fact that Mia was a high school English teacher before she became a deputy with the RCSO. She spent five years teaching and molding young lives. Her record as an educator was excellent, but ultimately she changed careers and went into law enforcement. Now, the reason I'm mentioning this is because Mia was a teacher at Columbine High School."

A silence fell over the room, but it only lasted a couple seconds. Denise Elliott, seated in the front row, jumped to her feet.

"Ms. Cochran, did Deputy Serrano witness what happened that day? And was that the reason she left a teaching career and went into law enforcement?'

Cochran had done her homework and knew who most of the reporters in the room were.

"Yes, Ms. Elliott, to both your questions. But let me elaborate a bit on this point. Mia was a witness to much of what happened that awful day. She was in the library where many students had fled to escape the shooters. But as many of you may remember, the shooters did in fact go into that library. Mia witnessed some horrible things there, but she also did everything she could to save the lives of many students seeking shelter there. Her actions that day were heroic, just like they were last week at Wilson High School."

A clear, confident voice came from the back of the room.

"Ms. Cochran, Angela Bell from Channel Eight."

Cochran recognized Angela and called on her.

"With what she saw that day at Columbine, is it possible that some of those images came back to her while things unfolded at Wilson High last week?"

Cochran looked at Mia.

"I'll let her respond to that question."

Mia cleared her throat and looked out at the phalanx of reporters that filled the room. There were cameras everywhere, all pointing at her. It was quite intimidating, but as she surveyed the scene before her she recognized a familiar face. In the very back of the room, looking somewhat out of place, stood Jack Keller. It was the first time she had seen him since the interviews the day of the shooting. She knew he was responsible for the arrests of the two men responsible for the bombing of her home. Somehow, seeing him there calmed her and gave her some comfort. She slowly reached over and slid the microphone in front of her.

"What happened on that campus more than seventeen years ago did have a huge impact on me. It essentially caused me to look at life from a totally different perspective. And while I enjoyed teaching, I just felt I could do more as a deputy than I could as a teacher. Witnessing what happened that day made me want to help people, especially if I could somehow protect the public from things like what happened at Columbine. I applied to the sheriff's department a few days later and was hired soon after that. It was the right move and the RCSO has been a wonderful career for me."

Angela followed up quickly, "Did any of what you witnessed at Columbine affect the way you handled the situation at Wilson High School?'

Mia paused. It was the million-dollar question.

She moved the mic closer to her mouth and spoke confidently.

"Not at all. My training at RCSO prepared me for handling all kinds of difficult situations. That training kicked in and the images of Columbine never came into my head. I did what I needed to do. I feel terrible for Alex Washington and my heart goes out to his family. I think about him constantly, but I did what I needed to do that day. A young, innocent girl was in grave danger and I knew I had to save her. I tried very hard to talk Alex down, even offering to lay down my weapon if he would do the same. We were making progress and I was hopeful that things could be resolved peacefully. But that wasn't to be."

Cochran took back the microphone.

"We need to be careful not to get too much into the specific events of the other day. That's what investigators are working on and I'm sure they'll do a very thorough and professional job."

"What exactly was said between Washington and the deputy?" asked another reporter from the Denver Post.

"As I said, we aren't going to elaborate any further on the particulars of the case. We'll leave that to the professionals."

Cochran moved the conversation to Leland Simpson and the $10 million lawsuit they would soon be filing.

⁂

Mark Archer watched the press conference in his office at RCSO. He did a quick check of the media websites in the Denver area and had noted mostly positive trends in the comments sections. The story had also been picked up by CNN, Fox, and MSNBC. None carried it live, but each ran some footage and it was always interesting to see what clip each chose to showcase. It was Mark's experience that Fox was the most conservative network (and the most pro-police) while MSNBC had definite left leanings. CNN was somewhere in the middle.

Looking at the coverage, Mark's expectations held true. Fox had portrayed Mia as a hero, while MSNBC had played up the angry BLM protests following the shooting. CNN had a little of both. Mark knew that people who watched cable network news tended to watch the same stations consistently. Viewers watched the network that best represented their personal outlooks and opinions, which resulted mostly in affirmation of those particular views.

CHAPTER 49

⚊⚊

Jaquon arrived at the Denver Marriott a little before noon. He listened to KDEN, Denver's all-news, all-the-time station, carefully monitoring their coverage prior to the start of the press conference. He parked in a public lot across the street from the hotel parking lot, out of sight of the news crews carrying their equipment into the hotel. He pulled his Rockies cap lower on his head and kept a constant watch in the rearview mirror. With the new cap and sunglasses he had purchased that morning, along with his short, blonde hair, he figured he was pretty much unrecognizable. He checked his phone and besides a dozen text messages from Alondra, there was nothing of importance. He noted the time—12:18 pm. He continued to listen to the press conference; that lawyer bitch just kept on talking. *Blah, blah, blah.* Rage started to build, growing even stronger when he heard Serrano speak.

He did a quick look around the lot where he was parked and, seeing no one, figured it was time. He reached into the glove box and grabbed his gun, a semi-automatic with a twelve-round capacity. He shoved the gun into his waistband and climbed from the car. He popped the trunk and grabbed the suitcase he had requested from Shalon. It was empty but would serve as a good prop. He walked confidently from the car toward the entrance to the Marriott, looking like someone ready to check into the hotel. He walked into the lobby and found an electronic board listing events taking place in the various meeting rooms that day.

Serrano Press Conference - Aspen Ballroom (Upstairs)

He headed for the elevator.

Rose Cochran did a masterful job wrapping the press conference. She cut off the questions while there were still hands in the air, creating the sense that she was the most important person in the room. It also allowed for some one-on-one interviews with reporters in the hallway outside the ballroom, letting them feel important getting some alone time with the famous attorney. News stations liked it when their reporters gave the impression that they were the primary source covering the event.

Cochran moved from the ballroom into a large foyer where she paused, pretending to say something privately to Mia, and giving the reporters a chance to approach.

"Ms. Cochran! Ms. Cochran!"

"I only have a few minutes but I can answer a few questions."

Mick met Mia and led her to the other side of the foyer, several yards away from where Cochran would be holding court.

Mick wrapped his arm around his wife. "You did great, Mia. It went really well. I'm so proud of you."

"Thanks."

Just then, Mia noticed a man approaching.

"Good job, Mia. I was impressed."

"I didn't know you were coming, Jack," replied Mia. "It's nice of you to be here."

"No problem."

In reality, Jack felt a bit uneasy being present, but was glad he had made the effort. Mia and the sheriff had been through a lot and maybe it was just the way for Jack to make amends for the past.

The trio looked over at Cochran who was talking animatedly to Denise Elliott.

Mick spoke, "The woman sure knows how to work the room, doesn't she?"

Just then Keller noticed a young black man walking toward them. He was pulling a suitcase behind him and Jack felt it odd that the man would be in the ballroom area and not in the main part of the hotel. He looked more closely at the man and instinctively started to take a step toward him just as the man grabbed something from his waistband.

"Get down! Gun!" yelled Jack.

Mick and Mia instinctively dropped to the ground as gunshots rang out in quick succession. *Tat, tat, tat, tat!*

Jack knew there was too much distance to get to the shooter so he moved to cover to Mia. He dropped to the ground, protecting her body. Mick, who was on the ground, grabbed his duty weapon from his holster and fired off a half dozen rounds. The people standing in the foyer screamed and ran for cover. It was all over in less than five seconds.

For a moment an eerie silence filled the room. Then utter chaos reigned.

Mick jumped to his feet, his weapon still drawn, and ran toward the man he had shot. He was sprawled on his back with several bullet wounds in his chest. He wasn't moving and Mick knew he was dead. He kicked the man's weapon a safe distance away, then bent over, looked at the man's face, and immediately recognized him. He ran back to Mia and Jack. He could see that Jack had been hit at least twice, with blood oozing from wounds in his back. Mick grabbed him by the shoulders, rolled him onto his back, and saw that he was unconscious. As he began working on Jack, he spoke to Mia. He was confident that she hadn't been hit; Jack had shielded her from harm.

"Mia, are you okay?" he pleaded, checking for a pulse in Jack's neck.

"I think so. Is he okay?" she asked, as she attempted to sit up.

"He's been hit at least twice. He has a pulse, but it's faint. We need to get him to the hospital, like right now!"

"What happened? Why did this guy start shooting?"

"It's Jaquon, Mia. And I think you were his target. Jack saved your life."

"Oh my God."

Mia grabbed her purse and found her cell. She dialed 9-1-1 and told the dispatcher what had happened. The dispatcher interrupted her and said they were aware of the situation and that help was already en route. Mia requested an ambulance, but again the dispatcher said there were several on the way. She relayed the info to Mick.

"We've gotta help Jack. We can't lose him. His pulse is very faint. I'm going to start CPR."

Mick loosened Jack's tie and spread open his coat. He started chest compressions while Mia went to check on the others still in the foyer. Most had fled once the shooting had begun but there were still a couple of diehard videographers getting footage of the scene. It didn't appear to Mia that anyone else had been injured. She looked around for Rose Cochran, but she was nowhere to be found.

Mia moved back to Mick and said, "It looks like Jaquon and Jack were the only two that were hit. There are still a few people around, but no one else is hurt."

Mick nodded, and continued working on Jack. Perspiration ran down the side of his face.

"He saved your life, Mia. I'm not going to let him die."

Mia, starting to feel the effects of what had occurred, lowered herself to the floor. Mick looked at his wife and grew concerned.

"Mia, are you okay?"

"I don't feel right."

Mia put her hand on her stomach and felt for the baby.

"Is the baby moving?" asked Mick, still working on Jack.

Mia didn't answer, and Mick watched as the color drained from his wife's face.

"Help, I need help in here!"

As he yelled for assistance, two paramedics burst through the door.

"Oh, thank God. The shooter is over there—he's dead. Check on my wife—she's seven months pregnant and I think she's in shock."

One paramedic knelt down next to Mia while the other took over performing CPR on Jack.

Mick went to his wife's side and took her hand.

"It'll be okay, sweetie. The paramedics are here and they're going to take good care of you."

As Mick was doing his best to calm Mia, two more paramedics arrived.

"We need to transport ASAP. Bring in two stretchers," said the paramedic doing the CPR on Jack.

"Ten-four," responded the other paramedic. He did a quick one-eighty and headed back out to get the stretchers.

⁂

Mark Archer was stunned at what he was witnessing on the TV in his office. A shooting had occurred outside the press conference and the media were reporting at least one person was dead. There were live pictures coming from the scene and it appeared that others were hurt. Denver PD officers were everywhere and a couple of paramedics busily worked on people on the ground. Mark couldn't tell who was being worked on because the people in the room obscured them from view. Mark could see that Mick was there but he couldn't see Mia and that greatly concerned him. He picked up his cell and sent a text to Mick but received no reply. He thought about Angela and decided to send her a text as well.

CHAPTER 50

The medical staff at Denver First Methodist Hospital had been alerted that two seriously injured people were en route from the Marriott. There was a heavy presence of Denver PD both inside and outside the hospital. Doctors were standing by in the emergency entrance breezeway as the two ambulances pulled up. Even before the ambulances had come to complete stops the staff was in motion. Within seconds physicians and nurses were evaluating Jack and Mia and soon each was being wheeled into the hospital on a stretcher. Mick followed Mia in, telling the medical personnel that she was seven months pregnant. The doctor nodded and told Mick that his wife was in good hands and that things would be okay. It was reassuring to hear, but Mick wasn't sure he believed him.

Mick looked over at Keller being wheeled in just ahead of Mia. He was getting a lot of attention but it didn't appear that CPR was still being administered. Mick took that as a good sign although he knew there was the possibility that it was too late for Jack. Mick wasn't a religious person but he found himself praying to God for both his wife and for Jack. Whatever differences he had had with Jack Keller were in the past now. Jack had undoubtedly saved Mia's life and now there was a chance those heroic actions would cost him his life.

Inside the hospital Mia was taken to a private bay in the emergency room where the doctor spoke with her.

"Mia, I'm Dr. Ed Paul. Can you feel the baby moving?" the doctor asked.

"Yes, a little bit, but not as much as usual."

"Okay, we're going to do an ultrasound and see how the baby's doing."

Mia nodded, and instinctively moved her hands to her belly. She was still having trouble processing all that had happened. It seemed like a dream—a very bad dream.

The nurse grabbed the transducer, and after putting gel on Mia's belly, began the ultrasound. Dr. Paul and the nurse looked carefully at the images on the screen and saw nothing out of the ordinary. The screen showed a healthy, active baby.

"The baby looks great, Mia. Do you know the sex?"

"What?"

Mia was still not functioning at a normal level.

"Do you know the sex of the baby?"

"No, we're going to wait."

"Okay, then I won't spoil it for you."

The nurse removed the transducer and wiped the gel from Mia's belly. The doctor walked out of the emergency bay and found Mick waiting nearby.

"Sheriff McCallister, I'm Dr. Ed Paul and I'm attending to your wife. We did an ultrasound and the baby looks great. My bigger concern now is Mia. It looks like she's having trouble processing what has happened, which is not uncommon for someone in shock. I'd like to keep her here overnight just to be safe. That way we can carefully monitor her and the baby and I think by tomorrow morning she'll be doing much better."

"Of course, whatever you think is best. Thank you so much for everything you've done."

"No problem."

Just then, a voice came from the emergency bay.

"Doctor, we need you in here. Her water just broke."

Mark Archer learned from the news coverage that those injured in the shooting had been taken to First Methodist Hospital in Denver. He hadn't received a return text from Mick or Angela so he decided to head to Denver.

Dr. Paul asked Mick to stay behind as he ran back into emergency. After examining Mia, it was determined that the baby should be delivered via C-section. Mick was allowed to accompany Mia while she was moved by gurney from the emergency room up to labor and delivery. Mick held her hand, offering comforting words as they made their way to the fourth floor of the hospital.

Mark arrived at the hospital in record time. He sprinted past a half dozen reporters standing outside the front entrance to the hospital, managing not to be recognized. He went immediately to the emergency room and asked the first nurse he saw about Mia.

"Are you a member of the family?"

"Yes, I'm her brother," he lied.

"She's been taken to labor and delivery on the fourth floor."

"Was she shot?"

The nurse looked puzzled. "Shot? No, she's going in for a C-section."

Now it was Mark's turn to look puzzled. "She's having the baby?"

"Yes, her water broke so they decided to do a C-section. You can probably learn more if you go up to the fourth floor."

Mark thanked the nurse and headed for the elevator.

~

Emergency room staff had wasted no time getting Jack up to surgery on the fourth floor. There were two bullets lodged in his back and a third in his left hip. The most troublesome was one in his lower back; it was dangerously close to his spine. He had not regained consciousness, so it was too early to know how much, if any, paralysis had occurred. The doctor would know more once they opened him up. His surgery was on hold while they brought in a top-notch surgeon specializing in gunshot wounds to the spine. It was his day off, but hospital staff had managed to reach him. The doctor was en route and expected at any moment.

~

Mia was being prepped for surgery when Mark found Mick pacing outside the surgery center.

"Mick! What happened?"

Mick looked at his friend and started to choke up.

"Mia's having the baby. She's in shock and her water broke. They're doing a C-section."

"Who else was hurt at the Marriott?'

"Jack. He was hit three times. He's alive, I think, but he didn't look good."

"Anyone else hurt?"

"Jaquon. He was the one who shot up the hotel. I got him—the prick is dead."

Mark moved toward his boss and placed his arm around Mick's shoulder.

"Let's sit down, Mick."

The two moved to a sofa in the waiting area. The place was vacant.

Mick continued, "I need to find out about Jack. He saved Mia's life. He threw himself across her and took all the bullets. Jaquon was there to kill Mia, but because of Keller she wasn't hit."

"My God."

"He's a hero, Mark. He saved Mia."

"Let me go see what I can find out. Wait here and I'll be back in a few minutes."

Mark stood and walked down the hallway to the nurses station. Two women were there, each entering information into a computer. Mark turned his attention to the one closest to him.

"Excuse me, I was wondering if you could tell me the condition of Jack Keller. He was brought here with gunshots wounds."

"Are you family?"

Mark paused for a moment realizing he'd already used that excuse to learn about Mia.

He badged her. "No, I'm Lieutenant Mark Archer with the Rocklin County Sheriff's Department. Investigator Keller is one of our people and I'm trying to get an update on his condition."

"Okay, hold on and let me check. He was just brought up a few minutes ago."

The nurse queried the computer and reported back to Mark.

"He's going into surgery soon. They're just waiting on the surgeon."

"What's his condition?"

"Let me see," she answered, scrolling down the page. "Here it is. He's listed as critical but stable."

"What are his injuries?"

"Three gunshot wounds—two to the back and one to the hip."

"Thank you for your time."

"Oh, before you go, would you happen to know who his next of kin are? We need to notify his family."

Mark thought about Jack's daughter Lisa Sullivan but didn't know how to reach her. Then he had another thought.

"No, I don't, but we would have that on file at the sheriff's station. If you'd like I'll make some calls and make sure you get the information."

"That would be great. I'll make a notation in his file. Thank you very much."

Mark walked back to Mick and gave him the news.

"At least he's alive, Mick."

"Yeah, but with bullets in his back—that concerns me."

"He's in good hands. We just have to wait and see. Let's focus on Mia. You're going to be a dad here shortly."

Mark was trying to put a positive spin on the situation, but Mick looked a million miles away.

Mick nodded. "They said I could be in with her when they do the surgery. I wonder what's taking so long?'

"It probably takes a little time to get set up. It doesn't seem like an emergency; they're doing this because her water broke. Mick, I'm sure they know what they're doing. It's going to be fine."

Mick stood. "I'm going to go find out what's taking so long."

CHAPTER 51

～

Chuck Serrano was growing impatient in his hospital bed. It was after two o'clock and he thought Mick and Mia would have arrived already to check him out of the place. He felt a little sore, but good. He'd had a decent night's sleep, probably because they doped him up pretty good. Valerie Tennesson, a nurse that had been taking care of him since his arrival, came into his room.

"How was lunch, Mr. Serrano? Looks like you finished everything."

"Hi, Valerie. Not bad for hospital food. Hey, have you seen my daughter or son-in-law around? They're supposed to be here to check me out and take me home."

"No, I haven't seen either one. But I'll tell you what—when they arrive I'll send them right in. How's that?"

"Can I call them? Check on their arrival time?"

"Sure, just dial nine on your phone there by the bed."

Chuck reached for the phone and lifted the receiver. He realized that he didn't know either of their phone numbers by heart. All the numbers he ever called were programmed in his cell phone and he just dialed by name.

"You know, I don't have their numbers memorized. But they're in my cell phone. Would you mind getting it for me?"

"Sure, where's your phone?"

"It's in my pants, hanging there in the closet."

"I'll get it for you."

Just as Mick reached the nurses station, one of the women said, "I was just going to come get you, Mr. McCallister. Your wife is ready for surgery. You'll need to change and scrub before you go in. Come on, I'll show you."

As the nurse led Mick to a changing area, he passed by Mark in the waiting room. "I'm on my way, but I have to scrub up. Keep tabs on Jack, will you?"

"You got it, boss. Good luck!"

Chuck tried calling Mia and Mick, but each call went to voicemail. Where the hell could they be, he wondered.

Mark tried to stay busy while waiting for Mick and Mia's new baby to arrive. He called into RCSO and got the contact information for Jack's daughter. It looked like she was living in Mexico. He passed it on to the nurse who had asked.

He checked his messages and, not surprisingly, his voicemail was full. The capacity was forty messages; no doubt everyone wanted the story of the shooting at the Marriott. He began listening to each one, jotting down names and phone numbers of those he'd need to call back. There were messages from reporters as far away as Australia and China wanting a phone interview. The power of the media—it always amazed him. As he continued listening, one message caught his attention.

"Mark, this is Angela. Look, I know you're going crazy right now with everything that happened at the hotel. No need to call me back. I just want to tell you how sorry I am about everything."

There was a pause, then Angela continued. "I hope Mia and Keller are okay. I wasn't in the foyer when it happened but I saw the footage of the shooting, and my God—we live in a crazy f'd up world. Anyway, I just called hoping to hear your voice, and see how you're holding up. Give me a call when you can . . . I mean, if you want to . . . "

Mark hit *save*.

Keller was wheeled into surgery fifteen minutes after Mia went in for her C-section. Mark saw the gurney go by with Keller hooked up to a bunch of tubes and monitors. He didn't make an effort to see him, assuming he was unconscious. He and Keller had certainly had their differences over the years, but Mark wished him nothing but the best as he fought for his life.

Mark continued working his cell phone. One of the last messages was a familiar voice.

"Lieutenant Archer, this is Chuck Serrano. Hey, listen, I'm sorry to bother you but I've been trying to reach Mick and Mia. I'm at the hospital and they're supposed to pick me and take me home. I know they were busy with the press conference today, so maybe they just haven't had time to pick me up. Anyway, I haven't been able to reach either one and I'm getting concerned. I didn't know who else to call, but I found your number in my phone and thought I'd give you a try. If you get this message and you can help me out, please give me a call. Thanks."

"Shit," said Mark, out loud. He stood and headed for the parking lot. He had to get to Castle Springs Hospital.

"It's time to check your vital signs, Mr. Serrano." Sandy Ruggiero, a young, pretty nurse working the afternoon shift was now assigned to Chuck's room.

Chuck looked at Sandy and replied, "I should be out of here by now. My daughter and son-in-law were supposed to pick me up by now."

"Maybe they got caught up with all the commotion today in Denver. They both work for the RCSO, don't they?"

"Yes, they do. In fact, my son-in-law is the sheriff. What do you mean, 'commotion'?"

"Oh, I didn't know he was the sheriff. There was a shooting today, but it was up in Denver. That's thirty miles from here. I'm sure it's nothing to worry about."

"In Denver? Where in Denver?"

"At some hotel. During a press conference."

"What?! There was a shooting at a press conference? In Denver?"

"Yes, around lunchtime, I believe. It's been on the news."

"Turn on the TV!"

Sandy was startled by Chuck's sudden change in demeanor and tried to calm him down. He was just a day into recovery from heart surgery.

"Okay, but you have to try to relax, Mr. Serrano. I'll turn on the news for you."

Chuck's eyes were glued to the TV as Sandy worked the remote.

"Hey . . . knock, knock."

Chuck looked up and saw Mark Archer standing in the doorway.

"Lieutenant, I just heard about a shooting in Denver. What's going on? Are Mia and Mick okay?"

"Yes, they're both fine. No worries, Mr. Serrano."

"Oh, thank God. For a split second I thought you were here to deliver bad news. You scared me!"

"Oh, I'm sorry Mr. Serrano. I'm actually here to deliver some good news."

"And what's the good news?"

"Mia is having the baby right now, up in Denver."

"What? She's having the baby today? I don't understand."

"She went into labor a couple hours ago and she's having a C-section. She and Mick are in there right now. Who knows, the baby might have arrived already. We've got to get you over there. You're going to be a grandpa!"

Mark had given serious thought on the drive down to the hospital to how much of the day's events he should share with Chuck. There was really no need to tell a man recovering from a heart procedure all the details about a shooting that involved the two most important people in his life. There would be time later to share all that, but right now he would play up the baby angle and get Chuck up to Denver to meet his new grandbaby.

"But she's only seven months along."

"Yeah, but the doctors are confident everything will be fine. The thing is, her water broke, so they really have no choice but to deliver the baby."

"Well, let's get the hell outta here. I've got a grandbaby to meet!"

Both Chuck and Mark looked at Sandy.

"All that's up to the admissions people downstairs. You need to be cleared by a doctor before you can go. I mean, that's protocol."

Mark was tempted to just leave with Chuck and bring him back later to do the official checkout, but he thought better of it.

"Okay, let's get it done. We've got to get to Denver!"

CHAPTER 52

An hour later Chuck and Mark arrived at Denver First Methodist and asked for directions to the maternity ward. Mark was assuming that's where they'd find everyone, given more than two hours had passed since Mia went in for the C-section. He was carefully monitoring Chuck, making sure he was physically handling all that was happening. He seemed fine, but just to be safe Mark held Chuck's arm as they traversed the hallways of the hospital. Finally, they arrived at their destination.

"I'm looking for my daughter and new grandbaby," Chuck said excitedly to the woman at the nurses station.

The woman smiled and asked, "What's your daughter's name?"

"Mia Serrano-McCallister."

"They just moved her from recovery into a regular room. Let me see . . . she's in room 407, down the hall and to the right."

Mark and Chuck walked down the hallway together. Both were beaming, and Mark considered it an honor to be part of this family's precious moment.

As they reached room 407, Mark hung back for a few seconds, allowing Chuck take center stage.

"Oh, my God, Dad." Mia said softly, still groggy from the surgery.

"Well, hello there! Is there someone here I should meet?"

Mick answered, "Come in, come in! Mia and I were just talking about you, trying to figure out a way to get you out of the hospital and up here to Denver to meet the newest member of the family. I see you found a way!"

Mark came into the room and gave Mick a hug. He walked over to Mia and kissed her on the forehead.

"I figured you guys were kind of busy today, so I scooped up your dad and brought him over."

"Yeah, I want to hear about all this later," responded Mick.

Chuck looked around the room but saw that there was no baby there.

Mia turned toward Chuck. "The baby is in the NICU, Dad. Your grandson was a little underweight given the premature delivery. So he'll have to be here for a few days until he puts on some weight. But otherwise, he's healthy!"

"*Grandson*?" Did you say *grandson*?"

"Congratulations, Chuck. You are officially a grandfather to a beautiful four-pound, one-ounce baby boy," Mick replied, offering a hug to his father-in-law.

"Oh my God. Can I go see him? Can I hold him?"

"You can't hold him quite yet, but we can go down and see him. He's in the neonatal unit until his lungs develop a little more. But he's going to be fine, Dad."

"Can we go now?'

"I think we can make that happen," answered Mick.

"You're okay, right Mia?" Chuck asked, looking at his daughter hooked up to several monitors.

"Yeah, just really tired. After a C-section they want you to take it easy for a little bit."

"Okay, once you come home, I'll take care of everything. I can help with the baby and do all the cooking and cleaning."

"That'll be great, Dad. Now you guys go see the baby, I'll be fine."

The three men made their way down the hallway.

When they arrived at the neonatal unit Chuck began peering through the glass.

"He's in the second row, over on the left," Mick said, wrapping his arm around his father-in-law's shoulder.

There, in a small clear crib, lay a tiny dark-haired baby boy.

The card on the crib read in large, bold blue letters:

Charles Jack McCallister

THE END

Made in the USA
Columbia, SC
24 September 2019